Some

She leaned forward, inviting him closer. He complied as if pulled by some magnetic force, until their lips met with tentative pressure. Wanting more, she nudged forward, but he eased back, keeping the contact light, elusive. She was forced to wait, accepting his restraint, even as her breath quickened with impatience. He kissed her slowly, teasing with soft strokes, until she writhed a little in the chair and tried to bring herself closer.

His hands gripped the upholstered chair arms so hard that she was vaguely surprised not to hear something splintering. But his mouth brushed softly back and forth over hers until he had coaxed her open and the tip of his tongue ventured into the silkiness. She held on to his shoulders, her fingers tightening against the heavy muscle like a cat kneading her paws.

He sealed their lips together and licked deep, and she yielded with a soft sound, her mind dissolving. The world was nothing but firelight and sensation, and the warm, erotic mouth of a man who kissed as if he were trying to steal the soul from her body.

He kissed her again, with deep, dizzying ardor, until her heart was pounding and every part of her thrummed with excitement. It no longer mattered whether this was foolish, wise, too soon, or too late. It was necessary. Inevitable.

By Lisa Kleypas

Standalone novels
STRANGER IN MY ARMS
WHERE DREAMS BEGIN
SUDDENLY YOU

Anthologies
WHERE'S MY HERO? (with Kinley
MacGregor and Julia Quinn)
THREE WEDDINGS AND A KISS (with
Kathleen E. Woodiwiss, Catherine
Anderson, and Loretta Chase)

LISA KLEYPAS

Someone to Watch Over Me

❧ Bow Street Runners ❧

A V O N

An Imprint of HarperCollins*Publishers*

This 2024 edition of *Someone to Watch Over Me* contains an altered version of the content that appeared in the original 1999 edition.

SOMEONE TO WATCH OVER ME. Copyright © 1999, 2024 by Lisa Kleypas. All rights reserved. Printed in the United States of America. No part of this book may be used or reproduced in any manner whatsoever without written permission except in the case of brief quotations embodied in critical articles and reviews. For information, address HarperCollins Publishers, 195 Broadway, New York, NY 10007.

First Avon Books mass market printing: May 1999

Print Edition ISBN: 978-0-06-333657-5
Digital Edition ISBN: 978-0-06-175247-6

Cover design by Amy Halperin
Cover art by Alan Ayers
Cover images © Depositphotos; © Shutterstock

Avon, Avon & logo, and Avon Books & logo are registered trademarks of HarperCollins Publishers in the United States of America and other countries.

HarperCollins is a registered trademark of HarperCollins Publishers in the United States of America and other countries.

24 25 26 27 28 BVGM 10 9 8 7 6 5 4 3 2 1

Foreword

When *Someone to Watch Over Me* was first published, it was an unusual story for the historical romance genre. The plot concerns a Regency-era police detective who's investigating the attempted murder of a young woman with amnesia. It's a love story between working-class characters, with action, mystery and intense emotion.

Since it's been twenty-five years since the novel was released, I knew I'd probably want to do a few tweaks before it was republished. Life is a process of learning and growing, and while many of my ideas about love, sex, and relationships have stayed the same, some have definitely changed. My readers deserve a romance novel to be more than an escape. It has to be uplifting. It has to celebrate a woman's strength and value, as well as her right to be loved unconditionally by a hero who treats her like a partner. The greatest romance novels aren't about perfect people, they're about the rest of us: imperfect, yearning, funny, frustrated, flawed, eccentric, lonely people who get to experience an epic love affair, even if they're not an aristocrat or billionaire or movie star.

But when I took a look at the original version of this novel, I realized it wasn't going to provide the kind of experience my readers have come to expect. A few tweaks weren't going to be enough. Even a rewrite wouldn't be enough—the book needed a complete reimagination.

I had the option of letting it be published "as is" with a note saying, "This is a product of its time." But I knew some people would buy it because my name was on the cover, and end up disappointed. I just couldn't let it go out there unchanged. And I couldn't stop thinking about what this particular book, with this particular title, so desperately needed. Kindness, for starters. Not to mention a healthy dose of humor. I thought the story deserved to be retold in a way that did it justice.

So I rewrote *Someone to Watch Over Me*, which has become, for all intents and purposes, a new novel. It's about strangers helping each other, and about maintaining hope and optimism even in difficult times. It's about forgiveness and acceptance, and the need to let go of past mistakes so we can move on toward the future. And it's about what being a hero really means.

I hope you'll enjoy this reimagined version of that long-ago story. It's been a labor of love, and a source of personal satisfaction that now, after all this time, the characters of Grant Morgan and Vivien Duvall have finally become who they're meant to be.

Love always,

Lisa

Someone to Watch Over Me

Chapter One

London
1830

"Where's the body?" Grant Morgan asked.
"This way, sir."

Grant followed the wiry, weather-beaten Thames boatman toward the river. He raised his bull's-eye lamp, casting an ochre glow through the gloom, but he still couldn't see farther than two yards in any direction. The evening chill slipped beneath his collar and cuffs as neatly as a knife blade.

Near Waterloo Bridge, the landscape was all shapeless menace, like something from a bad dream. Fog had mixed with coal smoke from thousands of chimneys, all of it pressing down in layers. It was a night when a man could walk straight into a lamppost.

"Don't know why they changed the rules," the boatman, whose name was Latch, commented, his voice drifting back over his shoulder. "We've always picked up the bloats and carted 'em off to the dead-box down the road. Never had to alert no police before, unless a corpse looked dodgy."

Grant found a certain grim amusement in the fact that finding human bodies in the Thames was so mundane—three to five per week on average—that only some occasions merited sending for law enforcement. "What makes a corpse look dodgy?" he asked.

"Oh, head bashed in . . . leg missing or the like . . ."

"But that's not the case with the one you found tonight?"

"No, it's just a regular bloat. Why do you want a look at it?"

"The Home Department has commissioned a report on Thames drownings. They want more done to identify corpses and causes of death."

Latch stopped and turned to face him with a befuddled expression. "Cause of death is, they're people! People drink gin, jump off bridges, fall off boats and embankments . . . You can't stop people from being people." His eyes narrowed in suspicion as he looked over Grant's simple black wool overcoat. "Say now . . . where's your pea jacket and glazed cap? Where's your metal badge?"

"I'm not River Police." Grant reached inside his coat and pulled out a short brass tipstaff with an oak handle. One had been issued to each of the eight Bow Street detective officers, to be used as either identification or a cudgel.

The boatman's eyebrows, bristly as coconut coir, lifted in surprised interest. "A Bow Street Runner, are you?" He leaned closer to inspect the engraved name and number. "Don't say you're Morgan? The one in the books?"

Grant responded with a single nod as he tucked the tipstaff back into his coat.

"Blimey," the boatman exclaimed in delight. "Detective Officer Grant Morgan! Why, you should be guarding royalty or hunting jewel thieves, not collecting bloats with the likes o' me."

Grant scowled, even though the man's admiration seemed sincere.

Two years ago, a London publisher had commissioned a series of adventure novels featuring the exploits of a fictional Bow Street Runner. The stories were based loosely—*very* loosely—on cases Grant had solved. Even worse, the main character had been named after him. He'd never been consulted or even approached about it. When he'd tried to read one out of curiosity, he discovered it was written in agonizingly overwrought prose that repeatedly described him as "lantern-jawed" with "penetrating eyes of veriest emerald."

To Grant's chagrin, the Morgan of Bow Street novels had become a runaway success. And the chief magistrate, Sir Ross Cannon, had refused to do anything about it, because the popular fiction helped to create a favorable public image for the entire Bow Street police office.

It was as embarrassing as hell. Grant hadn't asked for the attention, nor did he want it. His professional record hadn't needed embellishment, and God knew it wasn't fair to the other seven Bow Street officers, who deserved equal recognition.

"Ninety percent of those stories never happened," Grant said.

The boatman didn't appear to have heard. "Me favorite is *Murder in the Choir Loft*. The missus, though, she's partial to *The Puzzle of the Peculiar Pawnbroker*. The part where you fell through the trapdoor—she went on about that for days—"

"Latch," Grant interrupted curtly. "Where's the body?"

"This way, Mr. Morgan. Is this part of your next book?" He lowered his voice. "Are we being followed by your archenemy?"

"I don't have an archenemy."

"The nefarious Bartholomew Spade . . ." the boatman reminisced. "Keeps you on your toes, he does, with all his dirty tricks. But as you always say, 'Only a fool tries to fool Grant Morgan.'"

"I never say that."

They emerged from a narrow alley, passed through a water gate, and came to a set of stairs that led straight down into the river. It was one of many stone staircases built along the Thames for watermen to pick up and drop off passengers. Nearby, the looming bulk of Waterloo Bridge was almost obscured except for the row of tar oil lamps burning yolk-colored flames.

Low tide had exposed a causeway at the foot of the stairs, the wood-and-brick surface nearly flush with the surrounding water. The river moved with a slight rise and fall as if it were breathing.

Grant's gaze fell to the ragged length of canvas covering a small shape at the center of the causeway.

"Mind your step," Latch cautioned. "'Tis slick as soap-grease down there."

As Grant descended, he felt the familiar cold pang that happened whenever he had to view a human body in an unspeakable state. As if everything that made him vulnerable had withdrawn into some deeply protected place, leaving him numb enough to do his job. Later, when he was removed from the situation and having a drink, it would all unlock. The ability to feel sympathy, horror, sadness, would start to circulate through him again. But sometimes he worried that it might not, and he would be permanently walled off in his own head. A place no one would want to be.

He lowered to a crouch on the causeway, set down the lantern, and drew back the canvas with a gloved hand.

The corpse was—or had been—a woman, left in a jointless heap like an abandoned doll.

Grant began to turn it over. He recoiled in surprise as the still form began to cough and retch. "*Jesus.* She's still alive! And you left her down here?"

Latch, who had come to stand right behind him, let out a yelp. "She were dead meat, I swear it! When I pulled her out, she weren't moving nor breathing nor—"

"Shut your trap," Grant muttered.

The boatman fell obligingly silent.

Grant kept the woman on her side, letting the natural process clear her lungs. When the spasms had stopped, he pushed back a hank of her hair, slimy as kelp, and angled her face toward the light.

"Miss, can you hear me? Miss—" Grant broke off and looked at her more closely, astonished to realize he knew her. "My God."

To find Vivien Duvall here, in such a condition, was unfathomable.

She was a London courtesan, a creature of boudoirs and ballrooms, not at all someone who would venture near the Thames's crime-ridden wharves and shipyards. Grant had met her once at a ball attended by the *demimonde*—the French

word for half-world. It was a shadowy level of
society where so-called respectable men kept
their mistresses, using them to satisfy desires
they would never think of inflicting on a wife.

He and Vivien had taken an instant mutual
dislike to each other. But he'd never forgotten
how beautiful she'd been, the molten weight
of her red hair pinned up in a mass of coils and
twists. A stunning and self-assured woman who
didn't suffer fools gladly.

Was this woman really Vivien? At the moment,
he couldn't be absolutely sure. Regardless, it was
a miracle she'd survived the cold this long. And
the Thames was so polluted, every last fish had
vanished. He didn't want to think about whatever was now flourishing in those Stygian-dark
depths.

Moving fast, he stripped off his wool coat
and wrapped it around her. After shuttering
his lamp and hooking it to his belt, he lifted the
woman from the ground with a grunt of effort.
She was completely limp, which made her difficult to carry despite her small size. Icy fluid sank
through the coat, right down to his skin. He gri-
maced at the river-stench that a thousand laun-
derings wouldn't be able to remove.

The boatman stayed at his heels. "I'll lay she
tried to suicide 'erself."

"Could she have survived a fall from the
bridge?" Grant asked skeptically.

"Depends. Hit the water flat-on, you're done for. But go in head- or feetfirst . . . maybe land in the stream under an arch . . ." They reached the top of the stairs. "I'll leave you to your business, Morgan. Just tell me—where should I go for me reward?"

"What reward?"

"I done the lady a great service, didn't I, rescuing her as I done? And I helped with your case."

"Something of an overstatement, on both counts," Grant said acidly. "Listen to me, Latch. I want you to find Dr. Jacob Linley. At this time of night, he's usually at the tavern next to the timber yard."

"The Rag and Bucket?"

"Yes, that one. Tell him to come to my town house at Bedford Street right away—and tell him I said to give you a half-crown for your pains."

"Only a half-crown?"

"Good God, man, that will buy you fifteen pints of beer!"

"Cheap table beer, maybe. But I drink Newcastle."

"Just do it," Grant said. "And be quick about it—" He paused, having been about to say *or I'll have your license suspended*. But instead, he finished, "—before Bartholomew Spade catches up with you."

The boatman's face lit up. "You can count on me, Morgan!" He hurried off, his compact form immediately swallowed by the fog.

Clutching his unwieldy burden, Grant crossed a cobblestoned street and strode through a small court filled with stagnant water barrels, a cart with broken wheels, and an abandoned dog kennel. Any man in his right mind would be terrified to venture into this area of the city, but it was familiar territory to a Runner.

He reached Bedford Street, where decaying buildings abruptly turned into a row of tidy town houses and shop fronts. The Bow Street police station and its raucous surroundings were only a short distance away, but all that seemed far removed from this quiet location.

By the time Grant climbed the front steps of his town house, his arms were aching and every breath hissed with effort. Unable to knock or reach his key, he gave the door a hard kick. When there was no response from within, he drew back and kicked again.

The door opened and his housekeeper, Mrs. Buttons, appeared, spluttering with protests at his cavalier treatment of the painted paneling.

Ordinarily a man like Grant—working-class, with no expectations of inherited money—would never have had an opportunity to hire someone like Clara Buttons. She was an experienced housekeeper, who'd been born a butler's daughter and worked in service for her entire adult life. It was almost unheard-of for the highest-ranked servant of a grand country estate to leave the security and status of her position.

But the mistress of that great household had died in childbirth, and the master had soon remarried. His new bride, a young woman of volatile temperament, had abused the servants, accusing them of laziness and mendacity, claiming they had stolen items that she herself had misplaced. When the abuse had become physical, such as slapping the cookmaids or throwing a cup of scalding tea at a footman, Mrs. Buttons had gone to speak with the master of the house. He had immediately dismissed her without references.

Fortunately, Grant's employer, Sir Ross, the chief magistrate in charge of the Bow Street Runners, had learned of Mrs. Buttons's plight from his own housekeeper. He'd recommended her to Grant, who had hired her immediately.

It was a comedown for a housekeeper to work for a common-born bachelor instead of an aristocratic family. Now she was in charge of only two servants, as opposed to the large staff she'd once managed. However, Grant paid Mrs. Buttons far more than she'd earned in her previous position, and he treated her with respect. Not only did he defer to her when it came to household decisions, he listened closely to her advice. A gentleman, for example, wouldn't write his letters on cheap paper made of wood pulp—he would use heavy cream-colored rag paper.

Contrary to the stereotype of a housekeeper— stern and stately, mired in tradition—Mrs. Buttons was a warm and approachable woman. She actually seemed to enjoy the rough-and-tumble of a Bow Street Runner's household.

"Good heavens, sir, what's happened?"

"Near-drowning." Grant pushed past her, heading upstairs to his bedroom.

"Shouldn't you take her to hospital?"

"If my goal were to finish her off quickly, yes. But she's an acquaintance of mine."

"An acquaintance?"

"A lady of the evening, actually."

The housekeeper didn't bother to conceal her disapproval. "Sir, once again you have outdone yourself."

Grant wondered irritably why his servants seemed to have so many more opinions than other people's servants. "Help me with her, will you? Where the devil are the other two?"

"Peter's away visiting his family in Twickenham," she reminded him. "Miriam's in the kitchen. Shall I ask one of the neighbor lads to fetch Dr. Linley?"

"No, I've already sent someone for him."

While Mrs. Buttons called for the cookmaid to bring towels, scissors, and hot water, Grant continued up the stairs. Once in his bedroom, he deposited Vivien on the mahogany bed and paused to rub his aching arms with a sigh of relief.

Mrs. Buttons hurried to the bedside and made a revolted sound at the vile, smeary odor of the

Thames. "The bedding," she said in an aggrieved tone. "And your coat—"

"Never mind all that, help me remove her clothes." They both tugged at the woman's sodden gown and pelisse, but the garments had shrunk until the buttons and hooks were tightly entrenched in the wet wool.

"Miriam's coming with the scissors," the housekeeper said.

Unwilling to wait, Grant reached into his boot and pulled out a knife with a clip point steel blade.

Mrs. Buttons stepped back with a muffled exclamation as she watched him efficiently slit the long sleeves and separate the front of the gown from neck to hem.

No one could wield a knife with the skill of a former Billingsgate fishmonger. At the age of twelve, Grant had learned to open, skin, scale, gut, fillet, and pin anything sold at the London Fish Exchange. He spread the split fabric, revealing what had once been white linen undergarments, and he sliced through those too, down to chilled, tender flesh.

"Sir," Mrs. Buttons said, sounding perturbed, "Miriam and I will do the rest."

Grant understood her unease. The woman on the bed was utterly vulnerable. It seemed an unspeakable violation for him to strip her naked when she couldn't so much as lift a finger in her own defense.

"She doesn't have time to spare," he said,

methodically continuing to cut away the clothing. "Believe me, I have no lewd intentions."

The housekeeper seemed affronted by the very suggestion of impropriety. "I would never think so, sir." She let out a squawk as he dropped a handful of wet scraps on the carpet. "Wait!" Hastily she went to the coal bin from the hearthside, emptied the last of it onto the fire, and brought it to the bedside. "Put it all in here," she said. "Egad, it's not even fit for the ragman. That filthy river! And to think they used to sell Thames salmon at the market when I was a girl."

"Was it any good?" Grant asked, dropping more fabric into the bin. Hearing a *clank* against the metal, he reached in and fished out what appeared to be a house key. He tossed it onto a nearby table.

"Oh, the finest," the housekeeper replied. "Preferred even to Tweed salmon! But now everyone's forgotten there ever was such a thing as fish in the Thames." As Grant stripped away the last of Vivien's undergarments, Mrs. Buttons promptly weighted her with blankets.

Grant leaned over Vivien, staring intently at a tiny crescent-shaped abrasion at the front of her throat. He angled her jaw to view three parallel scratches high on the side of her neck, just below the ear. Gently he used his thumb to pull down her lower eyelids in turn, seeing a few tiny red blotches marring the whites of the eyes. His mouth tightened in a grim line.

Mrs. Buttons brought a thin folded towel from the washstand. "What are those marks on her neck?" she asked.

"It often happens with strangulation," Grant said quietly. He took the towel from her and wiped Vivien's face with great care. "She scratched herself while trying to pry him loose."

After a horrified silence, Mrs. Buttons ventured, "Wouldn't strangulation cause a great deal of bruising on her throat?"

"Not necessarily."

"Poor little thing," the housekeeper said, and glanced at the empty doorway. "Where is Miriam? I'll go hurry things along." She disappeared in a rustle of impatience.

After Mrs. Buttons had left, Grant sat on the edge of the bed and continued to clean the unconscious woman's face. Fine features, translucent skin, ruddy brows with arches like a bird's open wings. A drying tendril at her hairline glowed with the red of a paraffin flame. Even grimy and corpse-pale, she was recognizable as the woman he'd met two months ago at the Pantheon, a massive London concert hall with public assembly rooms.

Grant had wanted nothing to do with the event, a silly affair called "Pastimes with Neptune." At first he'd declined the invitation from the ball's hosts, Lord Sherbourne and his mistress, Harriette Porter, despite the exorbitant fee they'd offered for him to attend. However, the Bow Street chief magistrate, Sir Ross Cannon, informed Grant that he had no choice.

"Have one of the other men do it," Grant had told him.

"Sherbourne and Miss Porter believe your presence will provide the best security."

"They don't want me for security," Grant said scornfully. "They want me for amusement. All because of those damned books. I'll be expected to entertain the guests like some dancing bear."

"Having seen you attempt a waltz," Cannon said, "I concur with the analogy."

Grant had shot him a lethal glance.

"Morgan," the magistrate asked with a show of great patience, "is it really that heavy a cross to bear, being featured in a series of adventure novels? Think of it as a public service. For each of the past three years, the number of applicants for the horse and foot patrols has doubled, with a majority mentioning the Morgan of Bow Street novels as their inspiration. For the same reason, Parliament has just increased our funding in a rare show of goodwill. Moreover, you've been personally enriched by the publicity, to the extent that people are now willing to pay you a small fortune merely to attend a ball."

"Those novels are rubbish—" Grant had begun.

"Enough whinging, Morgan. Sherbourne has called in a favor. I've already accepted the invitation on your behalf."

"I don't owe him a blasted favor."

"I do, however. Go to the ball and try not to be a doorknob."

Grant's low expectations of the ball had been entirely justified. The event had been lavish and chaotic while somehow also managing to be dull. The ballroom had been decorated at astonishing expense, complete with indoor fountains and a replica of a sunken ship. More than four hundred guests had attended: politicians, aristocrats, actors, opera singers, and a great many women of "high keeping." It had been a jaded crowd, full of sophisticates who could no longer be dazzled or shocked by anything.

All around the ballroom, pavilions had displayed *tableaux vivants*, or living pictures, composed of volunteers who'd been painted and powdered to resemble marble statuary. One tableau depicted Venus emerging from a shell, while another showed Neptune frolicking with amorous nymphs. There had also been a trio of spread-legged sirens, and Melantho straddling the plaster figure of a dolphin, and a scene of the merman Triton seducing Hecate.

And every last one of the models had been as naked as a boiled egg.

Having seen the human body in every possible condition during the course of his work, Grant was hardly one to be shocked by nudity. But it had made him uneasy to mingle and converse in a ballroom with silent naked people posing nearby. He'd tried a little too hard *not* to look at any of them, which had ended up making his discomfort more conspicuous. And then he'd noticed that one of the other guests, a striking red-haired woman, had found him amusing.

She had been riveting, with hair that was the deepest shade of red he'd ever seen. A gown of translucent layers of green fabric, all seafoam and sparkles, had flowed over the beautiful curves of her body.

Grant had taken a glass of champagne from a tray carried by a passing footman, and brought it to her. After she'd accepted it, he'd bowed and introduced himself.

"I'm Vivien Duvall," she had murmured, her tip-tilted eyes smiling as she took a sip of champagne. "It seems you're real after all, Mr. Morgan. I thought you were merely a character in a book." Before he could reply, she'd asked in a lightly mocking tone, "How can a worldly man of action be so embarrassed by nudity?"

A quick grin had crossed Grant's face. "I'm not embarrassed," he'd said. "I just didn't expect to find it in a ballroom."

"It's no different from viewing Botticelli or Michelangelo at a museum," she'd said.

Grant had glanced at a nearby pavilion, where a pair of entwined naked people were posing as Triton seducing Hecate. "I'm not convinced this counts as art."

"Perhaps you're not aware that the living

statue has been an artistic tradition for hundreds of years."

"If you say so."

"What makes you qualified to judge artistic merit?"

"I'm not," Grant had said. "But outside of this ballroom, the only place you'll find a display of this many painted and powdered genitals is a brothel, not a museum."

Vivien's reply had been as frosty as the rim of an icing pot. "If you prefer prim and proper entertainment, Mr. Morgan, I suggest you don't attend a ball given by the *demimonde*."

"My apologies," he'd said instantly. "I was only being honest."

"No one wants you to be honest at a social event. You're supposed to be charming. That means saying things that are witty and complimentary and *pleasant*. Failing that, you should smile and keep your mouth shut."

"I didn't intend to—"

"Oh, do go away," she'd said impatiently. "My protector, Lord Gerard, is approaching, and he'll find you just as much of a boor as I do."

Later that evening, Grant had learned that Vivien had been on the ball's decorating committee, and she'd been the one to come up with the idea for the naked *tableaux vivants*.

That should have been the end of it, but after the ball, Vivien had insinuated to a host of wagging tongues that the arrogant Mr. Morgan had tried to proposition her, clumsily, and she'd rejected him. The story had spread, making him the target of laughter and mockery.

Grant's pride had smarted at the spread of deliberate lies. He had managed to hold his silence, however, knowing the rumor would fade more quickly if no fuel was added to the fire. Still, the thought of Vivien had never failed to annoy him.

No doubt she would have been appalled to learn that someday she would find herself so utterly at his mercy. If he were the kind of man who wanted revenge, fate couldn't have handed him a more perfect opportunity. But as he looked down at her, as helpless as a pinned butterfly, all he wanted was to take care of her.

A fine tremor ran through her, and another, and soon she began to shiver with bone-rattling force. Was that a good sign? It seemed better than deathlike stillness, but the violence of the shaking was alarming.

"Poor girl," he murmured, tucking the blankets more snugly around her. "You're safe now, Vivien. The doctor's on his way. Just hold on a little longer."

He had no idea what the hell to do for her, other than keep her warm. Filled with worry and frustration, he went to stoke the fire.

Mrs. Buttons came in with a tray of supplies,

accompanied by Miriam, who carried a heavy brass can of water in one hand, and a stack of folded toweling under the other arm.

"She started shivering," Grant said curtly, setting down the fireplace poker.

"That's hopeful," the housekeeper exclaimed, setting the tray on a small table beside the bed.

"Is it?"

"Indeed, sir, it's the body trying to warm itself."

"It is," Miriam agreed, busy pouring hot water into a basin. "Back home in York, my brother once brought in a barn cat that were near froze to death. We set it in the corner by the hearth, and it started shaking fit to come apart. But after it warmed up, it were back to rights. Went on to be a fine mouser."

Mrs. Buttons dipped a clean rag in the hot water, wrung it out, and paused to glance at him.

"Perhaps you might go downstairs and watch for Dr. Linley, sir," the housekeeper suggested. "Miriam and I will tend to her until he arrives."

Chapter Two

Grant stood at the window of the small entrance hall, staring grimly at the street. The woman upstairs was at the brink of death, and her survival mattered more than he would have expected.

Almost ten years of working on the Bow Street force had taught him to keep his emotions in check. Most of what he saw and experienced in the course of his work didn't affect him unduly. But now and then, something like this would break through and sink several layers below the surface. And if the outcome weren't good, there would be no liquor bottle deep enough to offer consolation.

Soon a hackney stopped in front of the town house. Relieved by the sight of Jacob Linley emerging from the vehicle, Grant went to welcome him inside.

The young doctor hefted his heavy leather medical case with ease and bounded up the front steps with his usual energy.

Linley had begun his career as the assistant of a well-connected old London physician whose practice catered to families of high rank. It was often joked that his golden good looks were the reason his services had become so sought after in London. To keep from being pigeonholed as a doctor for upper-class ladies, Linley had offered to provide medical treatment to the Bow Street police office and court at a cut rate. In no time at all, he'd become their preferred physician, doing everything from performing major surgery down to certifying the health of potential police recruits.

As Linley had gained experience at Bow Street, he'd developed an eye for detail that was particularly useful for investigative work. Whereas the coroner collected evidence by examining corpses, Linley excelled at analyzing the injuries of living patients. His natural skill in the developing area of what was called "juridical medicine" had been invaluable in solving and prosecuting cases.

Although Grant had known Linley for a relatively short time, it seemed as if they'd been friends for years. They had much in common, both of them professional men who routinely dealt with matters of life and death. They'd seen the way people, whether highborn or low, all had to contend with the same human experiences. As Linley had once put it, "If you break the human body down into its natural elements—oxygen, calcium, iron, sulfur, and the like—all totaled, it's worth approximately a shilling. By the time we end up on stone slabs, no duke or duchess has any more value than a beggar on the street."

"Morgan," Linley said amiably as he strode into the entrance hall. "This had better be worth abandoning a decent hand of cards and a bottle of porter. You owe me a half-crown, by the way."

"You still owe me for lunch at the Chop House," Grant reminded him.

"You're right," Linley admitted, shedding his overcoat. He paused, his nose wrinkling. "Good God. You smell like a compost heap. In a hog yard."

"I had to carry a woman who was pulled from the Thames about an hour ago." Grant watched impatiently as the doctor draped his coat over the staircase railing and set his hat on the newel post. "Quickly, Linley—she needs your attention."

Linley picked up his leather case and hurried after him. "Is she conscious?"

"Not that I can tell."

"External injuries?"

"No open wounds, but there's evidence of strangulation, including red splotches on the whites of the eyes—"

"Petechiae," Linley said. "Damn. There may not be much I can do for her, Morgan."

The words caused Grant's stomach to drop. "Would you at least have a look at the woman before making judgments?"

"I'm only warning you to lower your expectations."

"My expectations are for you to do your job. Which means saving her life."

"She may already have been so injured by exposure to cold, not to mention lack of oxygen, that recovery is unlikely."

"Why are you being so pessimistic?" Grant demanded.

"I'm being realistic," Linley said. "What's made you so irritable?"

"I've had a long day," Grant growled. "And I'd rather not end it with a woman dying in my bed."

"Why the devil did you put her in your bed?"

"She's an acquaintance," Grant said as they reached the bedroom door. After a cursory knock, he ushered Linley inside.

"Good evening, Mrs. Buttons," the doctor said pleasantly on his way to the bedside. "And to you—Miriam, isn't it?"

A flicker of surprised gratification crossed the cookmaid's face as she realized he'd remembered her name. "Good evening, sir."

"We'll need the windows opened and the fire banked," Linley said. "Right away, please. It won't do to rewarm the patient too rapidly, or there's a danger of—" He broke off as he reached Vivien. "Miss Duvall," he exclaimed softly.

"You know her?" Grant asked.

"We met on a previous occasion." Linley unlatched his case and pulled out various items, including a thermometer, a pocket watch, and a wooden cylinder with an attachment that resembled an ear trumpet. He leaned over Vivien and laid a gentle hand on her forehead. "Leave the room, Morgan, while I examine my patient."

"What if I stay in the corner with my back turned?"

"First, no. Second, as a mercy to the rest of us, go wash yourself head to toe with rosin soap. At least twice."

Mrs. Buttons murmured to Miriam, "We'll need more hot water carried up for Mr. Morgan's bath."

"Yes, ma'am."

The housekeeper turned to Linley. "Shall I leave as well, doctor?"

He had flipped open the pocket watch in preparation to take Vivien's pulse. "No, Mrs. Buttons, please stay. I expect I'll need your assistance."

Annoyed at having been banished from the room, Grant took some clothes from the wardrobe, and went to light a fire on the guest room hearth. By the time he'd pulled a copper hip tub out of a corner cabinet, Miriam had brought up the hot water.

After she left, Grant undressed by the fire, relishing the flickering warmth over his damp skin. He stepped into the shallow tub and proceeded to wash himself thoroughly with rosin soap that contained nearly enough alkali to take off a layer of skin.

Feeling restored after the bath, he went to pour himself a brandy from the dining room sideboard. He tossed it back in an efficient gulp, poured another, and took it upstairs.

To his disgruntlement, his bedroom door was still closed. No sound came from within. He rapped gently on the door with a single knuckle. In a moment, it opened a few inches and Mrs. Buttons's face appeared. She wore the resolute weariness of someone facing a night that was far from over.

"How is she?" Grant asked. "What can I do?"

"Dr. Linley has the situation in hand, sir. He asked that you remain outside the bedroom for now, and suggested you might try to rest."

Before the housekeeper closed the door, Grant asked gruffly, "Will she survive?"

"I don't know, sir." Worry had grooved her

forehead like the surface of a hob grate. "She had a seizure a few minutes ago."

As Mrs. Buttons retreated into the bedroom, Grant eased down to the carpeted floor and sat with his back against the wall. Slowly he drank the brandy.

Occasionally Miriam emerged with arms full of used rags and toweling, carried them downstairs, and returned with more supplies. The cookmaid was a hardworking young woman who was up every morning at dawn to light the grates and cook breakfast. She had to be exhausted, he thought.

"Go to bed, Miriam," he said brusquely, when she came upstairs with a pot of tea. "It's been a damned long day for you. If there's anything else they need, I'll fetch it."

She smiled at him gratefully. "You've had no more rest than me, sir."

"I'll manage. Go on."

After Miriam had retired for the night, the house settled into uneasy stillness. Between long intervals of silence, Grant would hear Linley's quiet voice, and Mrs. Buttons's muffled reply. He rested his head back against the wall, watching shadows thicken like cooling tar.

God, he was weary. But his mind was too full of sharp edges to sleep, and the liquor had done little to dull them. In the course of his work, he routinely saw the best and worst of people, but mostly the worst. He'd become more cynical than he wanted to be. Lately his opinion of human nature, never good to start with, had seemed to sink a little lower each day.

Perhaps he should have kept working for his old employers, Oswald and Fanny Keech, who had wanted him to take over the fishmonger's shop someday. It would have been a comfortable life. And there were some illusions it would have been nice to keep.

Moreover, Grant dearly loved the Keeches, a childless couple who'd hired him from a workhouse at the age of twelve. They had taught him their trade, starting with the proper care and use of knives. After that, Grant had learned where to make the cuts on different fish, how to remove scales, guts, and bones. How to wiggle a knife tip into the hinge of an oyster shell, twist and pry it open. How to slit a ring around an eel's neck and skin it.

At the beginning, Grant had been overwhelmed by blood, smells, slime, and viscera. God knew fishmongering wasn't for anyone with a weak constitution. Several times a day, Grant had run behind the shop to empty his roiling stomach. Even when there had been nothing left inside, he'd been shaken with dry heaves. "Flashing the hash again, eh?" the market costers and oystermen had asked, not without sympathy. He hadn't been able to eat. Nor could he sleep for dread of the morning, when he'd have to return to the long tables piled with fish, fish, and more fish.

One day Mr. Keech had found him behind the back of the shop, racked with nausea and despair.

"I'm going back inside," Grant had said defensively, dragging a sleeve across his wet eyes. "I just needed some air."

"Wait a moment, boy." Keech had towered over him, a big man with a broad face and a bulbous nose, and heavy gray brows corniced over a pair of spaniel-soft eyes. "I want a word with you."

"I have work to do," Grant had said, trying to avert his red tearstained face.

"It can wait." Keech had sat on a wooden crate and positioned another next to it. "Sit."

Grant had obeyed, terrified the man would send him back to the workhouse.

"You're turning into a rackabones," the fishmonger had said quietly. "Mrs. Keech says you wouldn't eat so much as a mouthful of bread this morning."

"It would only come up again," Grant had muttered.

"The work makes you boaky," the man had said rather than asked.

Deducing that *boaky* meant puking one's guts out, Grant had responded with a shamed nod.

"What's the worst part of it?" Keech had asked.

"All of it's the worst part," Grant had burst out. "I hate the smell, and the dead eyes and sharp gills and pointy bones. I hate skinning and gutting fish. It's disgusting, it's—" He hadn't been able to find any words to convey how utterly revolted he was. In the short silence that followed, he'd expected the older man to box his ears or knock him off the crate.

Instead, he'd felt Keech's hand, fleshy and scar-toughened, settle between his shoulder blades with the gentlest of pressure.

It had been the first time a man had touched Grant with kindness since his father had died.

Keech's voice had been calm and comforting. "Disgust is a natural feeling. It's meant to help us stay clear of trouble. But sometimes it's a hindrance to what must be done."

"I've tried to fight it," Grant had said hopelessly.

"Ah, well, there's the problem. We can't fight disgust. It visits when it wishes, always at great inconvenience, and must be tolerated until it goes. Like my mother-in-law." Keech had paused. "Take long, slow breaths, lad. You'll make yourself dizzy, huffing and puffing like that."

Grant had remained leaning over with his forearms braced on his knees. As he filled his lungs with a controlled breath, it provoked a squirmy pang of nausea. But it had eased, thank God, before the heaving could start again.

"You'll accustom yourself in time," Keech had

said. "The work becomes easier, the more you do it. Until then . . . a man can rule his feelings. He can say to himself, 'I'm strong enough to manage this. It won't get the better of me. Others have done it, and so can I.'" A gentle pat, and his hand had withdrawn. "Our work is important, young Morgan. It's a stewardship."

Which, in Grant's opinion, had sounded a bit high-flown for a Billingsgate fishmonger.

But Keech had gone on to explain, "Most people haven't the skills or stomach for what we do. They rely on us to do it for them. A mother needs us to pick out all the bones that might stick in her little ones' throats. A father buys a cut of salmon or a peck of oysters for his family's supper, trusting us not to sell him bad food that would make them ill. It's a privilege to look after others, even if they don't know what the job requires of us. Think on that when you start to feel squeamish and boaky. It helps."

The odd thing was, it *had* helped. After that, Grant had found the work slightly more tolerable. And eventually the lessons he'd learned from a Billingsgate fishmonger had guided him into a career as a Bow Street officer.

"Morgan. Wake up."

Grant opened his eyes with a start and found Linley squatting on his haunches in front of him. Groggily he realized he'd fallen asleep sitting up. "What time is it?" he asked.

"Four in the morning." Linley regarded him

with friendly exasperation. "What are you doing in the hallway, you pillock? You should be sleeping in the guest room."

Grant rubbed his eyes and struggled to his feet, his muscles and joints protesting.

"Just as well," the doctor continued without waiting for a reply. "I wanted to speak with you before I left." After stifling an eye-watering yawn, he reached up to rub the sore muscles at the back of his neck. He looked boyish in his exhaustion, his hair disheveled and his clothes rumpled.

"Why are you leaving?" Grant asked. "What about Vivien? Mrs. Buttons said she had a seizure—"

"She's resting now," Linley reassured him. "Her circulation and breathing have returned to normal. She was even able to swallow a few spoonfuls of sweetened tea."

"Will she recover fully?"

Linley hesitated before replying. "Too soon to tell."

"What's your assessment of her injuries?"

"Contusions and abrasions, but no broken bones, and no sign of sexual assault. But as you indicated, someone definitely strangled her. Most of the pressure was exerted on the arteries at both sides of her neck, which would have caused her to lose consciousness in a matter of seconds. My guess is, she was attacked from behind with a forearm."

"How long would it take to kill someone that way?" Grant asked.

"It would vary. But let's say at least three minutes of constant compression. Strangulation is a fast way to injure or render someone unconscious, but a slow way to murder someone, relatively speaking. It's a process."

"Then her attacker either misjudged the time it would take, or he was interrupted."

Linley nodded. "Ironically, if he meant to finish the job by disposing of her in the Thames, the shock of cold water may actually have revived her."

"I know Vivien has been through hell," Grant said. "But I need to ask her a few questions. When will she be ready?"

"Her condition is fragile. I expect for the next week or two, she'll sleep most of the time. There'll be throat and neck pain, headaches, possibly fever. If you try to bully her into talking before she's sufficiently recovered, you could do significant damage to her health."

"I would never bully her," Grant said, genuinely offended. "What do you take me for?"

"You're not exactly known for having a tender and sensitive side."

"Just because you haven't seen it doesn't mean it's not bloody there!"

"I'll take your word for it," Linley said dryly, and bent to pick up his medical case. "I have to go home and prepare for patient appointments.

I'll return later today. In the meantime, I've left instructions and medicine with Mrs. Buttons."

"Wait," Grant said. "When you met Vivien before . . . was the occasion social or professional?"

Linley hesitated for a long moment before saying reluctantly, "I paid a professional visit to her town house. Someone had recommended my services to her, and she sent for me."

"Where was it?"

The doctor searched his memory. "Trelawney Crescent. Not far from here, actually."

"How long ago did you visit her?"

"A month, perhaps."

"What was the consultation for?" Grant asked.

"You know I can't discuss that."

"Linley—"

"I'm leaving." The doctor started down the stairs. "Be gentle with my patient, Morgan."

"Of course," Grant said indignantly, and added for good measure, "I have a way with women."

Linley's only reply was a skeptical snort.

Admittedly, it was an overstatement. Ever since the first Morgan of Bow Street novel had been published, Grant had received a great deal of attention from women. He liked and respected them. But he didn't actually have a *way* with them.

In his defense, there was a limit to how much savoir faire one should expect of a man whose formative years had been spent in a London fish market.

If a woman was being harassed or attacked, or needed a bodyguard, or required him to solve a problem, he knew exactly what to do. But in a purely social setting—a drawing room or salon—he turned a bit awkward. Especially in the company of a woman he fancied. His mind would go blank, or the wrong words would come out. His usual physical agility would vanish. He might accidentally drop a teaspoon or overturn a vase.

It had been a while since he'd had that problem, however.

Brooding, Grant wandered into the master bedroom. Most of the rank smell was gone, the ruined counterpane and pillow replaced by fresh linen sheets and blankets. Vivien was clean and dry, dressed in one of his white cambric shirts.

Mrs. Buttons, who was straightening a few articles on the bedside table, turned to him with a questioning glance.

"Thank you," Grant said simply. "I can always rely on you in an emergency."

The housekeeper smiled. "I should hope so, sir."

Grant drew closer to the bed. Vivien's skin was ashen, her eyelids like bruised petals. Her hair had been washed and braided into a rope of fire that trailed over her shoulder. Cautiously he touched it with a single fingertip, almost surprised to feel that it was cool.

"How did you clean her hair?" he asked.

"Dr. Linley said it wouldn't do to wet her

head, but he let us rub in some hartshorn salts and brush them out. It will have to do until we can give it a proper washing."

Grant picked up a slip of paper from the small table at the bedside, and glanced over Linley's written instructions. *Keep her warm and dry . . . give sips of broth or sweetened tea . . . cherry-bark syrup for cough . . . salve for abrasions.*

In other words, there was damned little that could be done for Vivien, other than allow her time to heal.

How still she was. He touched her mouth and nose with his fingertips and was instantly reassured by a faint rush of air. After feeling how dry and cracked her lips were, he opened a little tin of salve and dabbed some on them. Gently he applied more to the scratch marks at her throat.

She seemed so lost and vulnerable, as if she were about to drift away or shrink to nothing. Carefully he reached for her lax fingers, so thin and cold, loose like a little bundle of rolled fireplace spills. He held her hand gently, wishing he could give her some of his strength.

"Mrs. Buttons," he murmured, "could I prevail on you to stay with her just a bit longer, while I pay a short visit to Bow Street? I need to speak with Sir Ross."

"Of course. But isn't it a bit early for him to be up and about?"

Grant smiled wryly. "I doubt it. The man keeps inhuman hours." He set down Vivien's hand carefully. "I'll return as soon as I can, to give you respite."

"No reason to hurry back, sir," the housekeeper said, casting a concerned glance at the sleeping woman. "I fear there are some long days ahead."

The icy winter air spun every breath into smoke as Grant walked past the outskirts of Covent Garden, which was already bustling as if the day were advanced. Greengrocers conducted business from their carts, selling potatoes, carrots, French beans, slender green stalks of asparagus grown in forcing-frames, and fat peaches and nectarines ripened in glasshouses. Porters carried hampers on their heads as they navigated the narrow spaces between stalls. Girls selling flowers or bunches of watercress threaded through the crowd with wooden trays slung from their shoulders on leather straps. At the pillars of the piazza, hawkers had set up their tables to sell tea, coffee, cakes, buns, and slices of buttered bread.

Grant was sorely tempted to stop at his favorite tea stall, Penny Crumpet's, where he often bought breakfast on the way to Bow Street. But he forced himself to continue past the stalls, wanting to meet with Sir Ross and return home as soon as possible.

Hearing a young voice calling out to him, he stopped and turned.

"Mr. Morgan! Sir!—" A skinny lad of perhaps

nine or ten came sprinting toward him. One of Penny Crumpet's brood, if Grant wasn't mistaken.

"Easy, lad," Grant said, catching the boy before he plowed into him. He steadied the child by the shoulders and straightened his small cap. "How can I help?"

Breathless and excited, the boy handed Grant a parchment sack. "Mum said to give this to you."

"For what?" Grant asked, perplexed.

The boy let out a guffaw, apparently thinking he was joking. "For saving all of England, o' course. Again."

"Oh, that," Grant said. "This is about one of the books."

"*Case of the Clockwork Soldier*," the boy said. "Mum and Auntie read it to us last week. If not for you, we'd all be ruled by Bartholomew Spade's clockwork army this very day!" He shook his head as Grant reached into his coat. "Mum says no charge."

Grant smiled and tucked a silver crown into the boy's hand. "Go buy your mum a basket of oranges, and give them to her with my compliments."

The boy looked up at him with a shy grin. "Is it true you was a market-boy? Like me?"

"I was."

"Someday when I'm big," the boy promised, "I'll join the police, and help you catch Bartholomew Spade." He dashed back to the tea stall, his voice floating over his shoulder. "You'll need me, cos you'll be an old codger by then."

"So will he," Grant called after him.

Touched by the gift, but feeling like a fraud, Grant headed to number 4 Bow Street. The world-famous address consisted of the police office, the chief magistrate's private residence, a court, and a strong room with prisoner cells.

It was there that, approximately seventy-five years earlier, the Bow Street Runners had started as a team of a half dozen well-trained detective officers. Their disciplined investigative methods and dogged pursuit of criminal suspects had met with remarkable success. In recent decades, the Bow Street force had expanded significantly with the addition of armed horse and foot patrols that policed the Metropolitan district day and night.

Few men would have been capable of serving as Bow Street's chief magistrate without cracking under the pressure. Sir Ross Cannon, however, thrived in the position. He was educated and wellborn, a natural leader with a cool and incisive nature and a Napoleonic ability to forgo sleep.

The job of chief magistrate was an uneasy combination of judge and police commissioner, and it came with enormous power. The position was also rife with potential conflicts of interest that would clear a pathway toward abuse and corruption. Fortunately, Cannon was a scrupulously honorable man with a reputation for sound dealing.

Although Grant admired Cannon more than any man he'd ever known, there had always been a certain distance between them. The magistrate was too guarded, too far above the ordinary human frailties that bonded a friendship.

Grant knocked at the door and was answered by Cannon's housekeeper, Mrs. Dobson, a lively and clever matron with a head of bobbing silver curls.

She welcomed him inside and helped him off with his coat, an old-fashioned caped garment he'd worn for years and had kept at the back of the wardrobe despite its shabby condition. Now he was glad he'd saved it, as he needed something to wear until he could have a new coat made.

Mrs. Dobson frowned at the mound of threadbare wool in her arms. "What happened to your good coat?" she asked.

"Ruined," Grant said.

"And what about your hat?"

"Lost."

"*Again?* How do you keep losing hats, Mr. Morgan?"

"Try pursuing a fleeing suspect in a top hat and see how long it stays on," he suggested.

"The other Bow Street officers manage to keep theirs on," she pointed out.

He leaned closer and lowered his voice, as if

sharing a secret. "But I'm so much faster than they are."

"If I were you," the housekeeper said, "I would try to outwit the criminals instead of simply outrunning them." She chuckled at Grant's mock-reproachful look. "Off with you, rascal. Sir Ross is in his office."

The chief magistrate sat at a massive oak pedestal desk, positioned beside a frost-rimed window overlooking the street. Shelves of ponderous law books lined the office, which was comfortably warm and well-lit. The air was fragrant with the acrid scent of black coffee, which the chief magistrate drank by the jug.

With black hair, wintry gray eyes, and a lean face, Cannon had a certain wolflike handsomeness. He was tall and almost rawboned, a man who allowed himself few indulgences. Having been born to a family of means, Cannon could have chosen a far easier life than this, but that wasn't his nature.

Countless women would have loved to capture the interest of the wealthy and well-connected widower, who was still in the vigor of his prime. But rumor had it that his young wife, on her deathbed, had made him promise never to remarry. That, along with Cannon's chaste and hardworking lifestyle, had led the public to refer to him as "the monk of Bow Street."

After closing the door, Grant sat at the other side of the desk. "Good morning," he said.

Cannon was focused on a stack of documents in front of him. "If you've come to deliver your report," he said without looking up, "leave it on the corner of the desk."

"My God, you're a master of small talk," Grant said. "Was it something you had to learn, or is it a natural skill?"

The magistrate reached for a pen on a brass stand and dipped the quill into the inkwell. A faint smile tugged at a corner of his mouth. "Are you here at six o'clock in the morning to make small talk, Morgan?"

"No, sir, it's about—"

"Wait." The chief magistrate proceeded to sign the documents, methodically rolling a blotter over the wet ink.

While Grant waited for Cannon to finish, he looked inside the parchment sack from Penny Crumpet. He was pleased to discover it was filled with his favorite honey cakes. He took one out, set the sack on the desk, and bit into the honey cake. The outside had been sprinkled with sugar before baking, which had formed a crisp roof over a tender interior spiced with cinnamon and nutmeg. He finished it in two more bites and reached for another, trying to minimize the rustling and crinkling of paper.

He felt the chill of the chief magistrate's gaze on him.

"You're eating on a desk that bears documents

pertaining to national security," Cannon informed him.

Seeing a few crumbs on the polished wood surface, Grant gingerly brushed them to the floor. He saw from Cannon's expression that it hadn't helped the situation.

"I had no dinner last night," Grant said defensively, "nor breakfast this morning."

Cannon picked up the sack and viewed its contents suspiciously. "What are these?"

"Honey cakes, bestowed on me as a reward for defeating a clockwork army."

Cannon pondered that for a few seconds. "Ah. Another of your books has been published."

"They're not my books. They're made-up stories about a character who has my name. Now I can't even go to market without feeling like an impersonation of myself."

The magistrate took one of the cakes and tasted it. With a sound of appreciation, he settled back in his chair to consume it. "Why are you here, Morgan?"

"It concerns the 'found drowned' I went to investigate near Waterloo Bridge last night. The victim was Miss Vivien Duvall."

Cannon looked at him alertly. "The one who gave you the shove-along at the Pantheon ball," he said rather than asked.

Grant felt a sting of annoyance, reflecting that everyone remembered Vivien's version of the story and not his. "Yes," he said. "As it turns out, she's still alive."

That seized Cannon's attention. He leaned forward, listening closely as Grant gave him a detailed account of the night's events.

"Her family should be notified," was the chief magistrate's first comment. "If she succumbs to her injuries, it's her right to have a loved one with her at the end."

"If they can even be located," Grant said. "Duvall could be an assumed name."

"You may be able to find out from her protector. Naturally you'll want to interview him."

"Why is *protector* the word for a man who keeps a mistress?" Grant asked. "As far as I can tell, all he's protecting her from is other men exactly like himself."

"These arrangements are consensual and legal, Morgan. It's not for us to pass judgment on them." The magistrate paused, looking thoughtful. "If Miss Duvall was attacked and cast into the river near Waterloo Bridge, there must be a witness who saw or heard something. There are many evening activities in the area . . . theaters, public houses, street sellers . . . and the foot patrol would have been nearby. I'll look through the reports as soon as they're delivered this morning, to see if any disturbances were noted."

"I'd prefer to keep Miss Duvall's survival, and her presence at my house, a secret."

"Naturally." Cannon's gaze turned sharp

and assessing. "It's generous of you to harbor Miss Duvall under your own roof despite your resentment."

"I never said I resented her," Grant countered.

"Come now," came the gently chiding reply. "You were run through the rumor mill because of her. You've never had any thought of retaliation?"

"*No.* I'd never stoop to petty revenge because of a few spiteful words. A man's pride shouldn't stop him from helping someone when it's needed."

The chief magistrate's expression gentled, and he gave Grant a look of warm approval. "Well said, Morgan."

Grant hated it that the praise filled him with so much satisfaction.

"As usual," Cannon continued, "I'll leave you to conduct the investigation as you see fit. If you require any counsel or assistance, I'm at your service." Deftly he filched another cake before Grant snatched the parchment sack from the desk.

Chapter Three

She felt so heavy, as if she were lying beneath the weight of fathoms. Sometimes a slow current would roll her from side to side, or lift and lower her. When quiet voices broke the silence, she couldn't assemble words into meaning. Her head was full of broken, useless things, like a bits-and-bobs drawer.

She couldn't think how she'd come to be in this situation.

Gradually she came to understand she'd been damaged somehow, that she was in a bed while the world kept rolling on without her. But she didn't know what she should be doing, or what she wanted to do if she could.

She could only lie there puzzled and worried, in a place where time had vanished.

Gradually she became aware of people taking care of her. An older woman with gentle hands, and a younger one who brushed her hair. And a man who was with her often, his dark shape looming over her in a way that felt comforting. Somehow he could always tell when she needed an extra blanket, or if she was thirsty or her throat hurt. His arms were hard and sturdy as he held her up to give her sips of broth or cherry-bark syrup. Sometimes he read aloud, the low timbre of his voice pleasant and soothing, and she would doze off knowing he would guard her sleep.

One night she awakened to a terrible heat scorching her from the inside out. She twisted and pushed frantically at the stifling layers of blankets over her. The man came into the room and pulled the covers away, and laid his hand over her forehead. She heard him calling for someone in an urgent tone.

There was a flurry of activity around her, and then he was lifting her with an arm beneath her shoulders. A moan broke from her throat. She didn't want to move, didn't want to be touched. Her bones ached and all her skin felt scalded. But he pressed the edge of a cup to her lips and wouldn't relent until she took a swallow of cold water.

He lowered her to the bed on her front, and

pulled her nightgown down to her waist. Too wretched to care about anything, she lay there with her face turned to the side. She felt him lean over her and begin to stroke something cool and soft along her naked back. The relief was so acute, she felt a tear sliding down her cheek, salty drops disappearing into the sheet beneath her. He was patient and tireless, dipping a sponge into a basin of water, wringing it out, bathing her fiery skin over and over. When she was finally relaxed and still, he pulled up her gown, drew a sheet and blanket over her, and sat at the bedside.

She closed her eyes and slept, and awakened later to find him still there. The window curtains had been drawn back, letting weak gray light filter through the glass panes. It was dawn, she thought.

And that was when she realized the jumble in her head was beginning to sort itself out. Time had started again, pulling her back into the rhythms of day and night.

The man stood and reached up to rub the sore muscles of his neck. She looked at him and truly *saw* him for the first time.

He was unshaven and rumpled, a big-framed man with shoulders that blocked out the light as he stretched. Deftly he opened a small tinder box, used a flint to strike sparks to a charred wick, and lit a lantern on the bedside table. After he'd fitted the lantern's glass globe back into place, it cast a golden glow over the hard angles of his face. A handsome man, with wisps of laugh lines at the outer corners of his eyes, and heavy dark hair that tumbled over his forehead as he leaned over her.

As he saw that she was awake, the hint of a smile touched his lips. Gently he laid a hand over her forehead, assessing her temperature.

"Better now," he murmured, seeming relieved. "I think we're through the worst of it."

"Thank you," she whispered.

From his blink of surprise, she realized he hadn't expected a reply. His hand lifted from her forehead and he stared down at her with intent green eyes.

"You're welcome?" he said tentatively, as if hoping she might speak again.

Her bewildered gaze drifted over their surroundings and returned to his face. "Who are you?"

He drew in a sharp breath. "I'm Grant Morgan. A Bow Street officer. We've met before. Not that you should remember. But you're among friends. You're safe. You're at my house in London. My servants and I have been taking care of you for the past five days, ever since—"

He broke off as he saw her blank expression, seeming to realize that had been too much for her to digest. "I'm Grant," he said simply.

Her lips shaped the name. She was in an unfamiliar room with someone named Grant.

This was all so very odd.

He propped some pillows behind her back and brought a cup of water to her lips, coaxing her to take a few sips. As he leaned close to help her, she couldn't help drawing in the scent of him, soap and the salty hint of sweat, and the herbal sweetness of winter cherry.

"Why am I here?" she asked.

"You were found in the Thames, near Waterloo Bridge. A boatman pulled you out."

"The river?" she asked in confusion.

"Yes."

"I was . . . *in* the river?" That didn't make sense.

"Never mind. Just rest for now, Vivien."

"Why are you calling me that?"

His expression turned carefully blank. "It's your name."

"No." It didn't sound right. It didn't seem right at all.

After a long moment, Grant asked gently, "Can you tell me your name?"

She licked at her lips, which had gone very dry, and searched through the chaos of her mind. No answer. Nothing. Her heart was racing. Her lungs couldn't pull in enough air.

"No, no," Grant said urgently, "all is well, don't be afraid. You don't have to remember anything right now, it's too soon." He stood at the bedside, watching anxiously as she struggled to calm herself. "You're still recovering from fever," he said. "People forget things when they have fever."

"Not their own *names*." She took the hand-kerchief he gave her and blotted her watering eyes. Her hands were trembling. Her temples throbbed painfully.

"You need more time, that's all. You're safe here, and you can stay for as long as you like. There's nothing to worry about."

Which she didn't believe at all. Obviously there was quite a lot to worry about.

"What happened to me?" she asked. "Why don't I know? Why can't I remember?"

"We'll find out. We'll find the answers together. I promise." Grant paused, then added in a pleasant tone that didn't quite mask the hard edge beneath, "I think we'll start with a visit from our friend Dr. Linley."

"I told you not to upset her," Jacob Linley said.

Grant had sent for him as soon as possible, having worded the message with such urgency that Linley had canceled a morning of patient appointments.

After spending at least an hour with Vivien, the doctor had emerged from the bedroom with a carefully bland expression. Grant had led the way to the library room, where they could talk without being overheard.

Linley half sat on the long oak table with one foot still on the floor, while Grant paced back and forth beside a row of floor-to-ceiling bookshelves.

"What you *didn't* tell me," Grant said, "was the possibility that Vivien wouldn't remember her name, her entire past, and every person she's ever known."

"No one could have predicted this," Linley protested. "Memory impairment sometimes occurs in cases of head injury or traumatic events, but it's usually limited to a particular period of time. As for *total* memory loss . . . that's not something I've ever encountered before."

"She's not shamming," Grant said.

Linley's mouth twisted impatiently. "I wasn't implying that. My God, you're as testy as a figged horse."

Grant stopped pacing and set his back against a bookcase. "What caused this? Lack of oxygen?"

Frowning, Linley tapped his fingers on the leather surface of his medical case as if on a row of invisible piano keys. "Possibly the seizure. I'm going to consult with a colleague who's written a paper on the connection between seizures and memory loss."

"When will her memory come back?"

"Any time between tomorrow and never. I have no damn idea. Memory is a delicate ability, Morgan. You'll have to wait for her to recover it. And in the meantime, Miss Duvall needs to be sheltered from distress and excitement."

Grant folded his arms and sent his friend a baleful glance. "Vivien knows *something* happened to her. She knows she had a life before she woke up in my house. She's going to ask questions, and God knows the answers aren't sunshine and rainbows." He leaned his head back and closed his tired eyes. "What am I supposed to say when she asks how she ended up in the Thames? Because the explanation rings a bit hollow if I leave out the 'attempted murder' part."

"Can't you delay that conversation?"

Grant opened his eyes and let out a taut sigh. "I can try. But the least *you* can do is let me read her medical file."

"Not a chance."

"Someone tried to kill her, Linley, in a very intentional and almost competent way. And once they find out she's still alive, they'll probably want another go at it. Accordingly, you're allowed to breach doctor-patient confidentiality if Vivien gives her consent."

"She's in no condition for that," Linley said. "When she recovers to the point of what I consider legal competency, I'll ask for her consent to share her medical records. In the meantime, kindly *shove off*."

"I'm trying to protect her," Grant growled.

"So am I. Which means for now, all I'm willing to give you is advice on her health."

Grant scowled. "As far as I know, Linley, being murdered is usually quite bad for the health."

After Linley had departed, Grant went upstairs to the main bedroom. He knocked on the closed door, and heard Vivien's muffled voice.

"Come in."

Grant's frustration was overridden by a rush of concern as he found her sitting on the edge of the mattress, her bare legs dangling over the side. "What is it?" he asked, reaching her in a few strides. "Do you feel ill? Or do you need the chamber pot?"

Vivien blushed, color racing over every inch of exposed skin with startling swiftness. "No. Thank you, I . . . no." She retreated back against the headboard and drew the covers over her legs.

The show of modesty surprised Grant. He realized the intimacy and familiarity of the past few days, when he could reach out to help her without even thinking, was over now. That was good news: it meant she was recovering. But he wanted to continue being close to her, and knowing it was impossible caused a perplexing new pain in his chest, as if he'd just been stabbed with an oyster knife.

"I'm sorry for having turned you out of your own bedroom," she said. "Perhaps I could move to a guest room as soon as—"

"No need. It's better for you to stay right here while you recuperate. The location makes it easier for us to take care of you."

"Thank you. I'll try not to impose on you any longer than necessary."

"No imposition." Assuming what he hoped was a friendly but impersonal expression, he asked, "Where is Mrs. Buttons?"

"She's gone downstairs to make tea and toast."

"Were you trying to climb out of bed just now?"

"I wanted to test my legs."

"I'd rather you didn't try that without me or one of the servants nearby, in case you have a dizzy spell and lose your balance."

"You're right," she said. "I didn't think of that."

She was so endearing that Grant felt all his defenses collapse like overloaded scaffolding. "Is there something you'd like me to bring to you?" he asked.

"A looking glass, if it wouldn't be too much trouble . . . ?"

For answer, Grant went to the gentleman's cabinet in the corner of the room. He rummaged through the narrow drawers until he found a leather-covered *nécessaire* case, designed to hold scissors, files, and grooming items. A rectangle of mirror-glass had been fitted inside the lid. He returned to the bedside and gave it to her.

"Thank you." Vivien opened the *nécessaire* and viewed her reflection gravely. A slender hand crept up to her cheek to touch a few broken capillaries, as gossamer-thin as spider silk.

"Linley said those will heal," Grant told her.

She angled her jaw upward and to the side, exposing the abrasions on her throat. Her delicate fingertips moved to the three parallel scratches . . . and rested precisely on the scabs where her nails had gouged in. Her gaze went to his.

"Those will heal as well," he said quietly. "Do you remember how they happened?"

Vivien shook her head and continued to inspect the rest of her face and throat. Eventually she set the case in her lap and met his gaze. "I would appreciate it if you could tell me whatever you know about me. It's very unnerving not to be able to remember anything. It's frightening, actually."

Grant began to sit on the bedside chair, and hesitated. "May I?"

Vivien caught him off guard with a sweet dazzle of a smile. "It's your bedroom," she pointed out. "And your chair. You needn't ask permission."

"This room is yours for as long as you're in it," Grant said. "You can tell me to leave whenever you like."

"Stay," she said, gesturing toward the chair. "Please."

Grant adored the graceful little movement of her hand, like the dart of a hummingbird. His brain took an indecent pleasure in the sight of her in his bed, wearing his shirt. Which, in the circumstances, made him feel like an absolute swine. But God help him, she was pretty.

"I feel like a ghost," Vivien said somberly.

At that, every hint of amorous interest vanished abruptly.

"If I can't remember anything about who I am," Vivien continued, "or what I've done, or the people I love . . . it feels as if I don't exist. As if my old self has died." She stopped and shook her head, and swallowed hard. Her blue eyes glittered as if they contained constellations.

Grant reached out to touch one of her lax hands . . . carefully, in case the overture wasn't wanted. But she surprised him by turning her palm up and gripping his hand tightly. The mantel clock measured out a full minute while he tried to figure out how to comfort her.

"Your old self is still there," he said. "Even when people try to run away from themselves, they always turn up." He angled their clasped hands so he could look more closely at her fingers, and he touched the faint, silvery vestige of a scar near the base of her thumb. "Burn mark," he said. "From cooking, maybe, or curling tongs." He found a small callus on the side of her middle finger. "This is from holding a pen or pencil. Not long ago, you did a considerable amount of writing." His gaze lifted to hers. "You've led a real life that's left plenty of evidence in its wake. Including a town house of your own, not far from here."

"I have a house?"

Grant smiled at the flare of interest in her face. "I'll try to go there later today and collect some of your clothing. Seeing a few of your own possessions might make you feel better. Or even help you remember something. Although . . ." He paused. "We'll have to proceed with caution. Linley made it clear that any distress might cause a setback to your health."

"I'm already distressed. The only thing that will help is information." She eased to her side on the bed, still clinging to his hand. "Grant . . . do you know anything about my family, or where I came from?"

"Not yet."

"You said we'd met before. Will you tell me about it?"

Grant took his time before replying. At some point, he would have to reveal how she had been earning her keep. Maybe it wouldn't bother her. But it seemed more likely that it would.

He thought back to how Vivien had appeared at the Neptune ball, a woman who hadn't given a damn about society's rules. Even after she'd rejected him summarily, he hadn't been able to stop himself from stealing glances at her from across the room. But then, everyone had been staring at her, men and women alike. Her beauty had been too radiant and provocative to ignore. Her smiles had burned the air.

Nearby, a prosperous-looking older man had followed the direction of Grant's gaze and said, "I saw her once in Paris, at an imperial banquet. It was rumored she'd been sent from London as a gift for the emperor's birthday. I asked a courtier about arranging an introduction, but he said her price was ten thousand francs a night. It would have caused considerable financial difficulty for me at the time, so I abandoned the idea."

"You made the right decision," Grant had said.

"Did I?" The older man had stared at Vivien pensively. "I think it might have been worth it."

Now as Grant sat in his own bedroom with Vivien, he was faced with the task of doling out the unpalatable truth in small, digestible increments.

"First," he told her, "I want to point out that no one likes everything about their past."

Vivien frowned. "Why? What's wrong with my past?"

"Nothing," Grant said hastily, seeing her flush with anxiety. *Damn it.* This was exactly what Jacob Linley had warned him about. "I met you at a ball at the Pantheon, approximately two months ago. I thought you were very beautiful. I introduced myself to you, and we chatted briefly."

"And then we danced?"

"No."

"Why not?"

"To begin with, I don't dance well. At least, not formal ballroom dances: too much toe-pointing and hopping."

Vivien regarded him sympathetically. "Have you ever considered taking lessons?"

"I did. But after three months, the dancing master said my footwork resembled a woodsman stamping out a brush fire." Grant paused as Vivien laughed. An irresistible laugh, sweet and throaty, but it led to a cough. She covered her mouth, chuckling and sputtering.

He poured some water from the jug on the bedside table, and gave it to her. "The other reason I didn't invite you to dance," he continued, "was because you wouldn't have accepted. I'm sorry to say I was rude to you."

Her eyes widened. "I find that hard to believe. You seem so very nice."

"I was an ass," Grant assured her.

"What did you say?"

"I criticized the, er . . . decorations. I said they made the ballroom look like a brothel."

Amusement danced in her eyes. "Were you right?"

"Yes. But I shouldn't have said so, as you pointed out at the time. And later I found out you'd been on the decorating committee."

"Oh, dear." She looked rueful. "That doesn't speak well of my taste."

"My opinion was in the minority," Grant said. "Everyone else seemed to enjoy the effect."

Vivien regarded him with a faint frown. "Was I there with a chaperone?"

Grant shook his head. "It wasn't that kind of ball."

"What do you mean?"

"It wasn't part of the Season. It wasn't for matchmaking, or to benefit a charity."

She stared at him anxiously. "Then . . . why was I there?"

This didn't seem like the right time to tell her something upsetting.

"I expect I'll have some answers for you soon," Grant said. "But first I have to go to Bow Street to meet with Sir Ross. After that, I'll fetch some clothes from your town house."

As Grant strode through the narrow hallway that led to Cannon's office, he nearly collided with two other Bow Street officers, George Flagstad and Neil Henry Keyes. Flagstad was in a good mood, revealing that he'd just been given the lucrative assignment of visiting the Bank of England while quarterly dividends were being paid.

Keyes, by contrast, was quiet and reserved. He was a stocky but well-exercised man, who invariably took great pains with his appearance. His clothes were expensive and superbly tailored, and his prematurely white hair was always perfectly cut and styled.

"Morgan," Keyes said, "I heard you were sent to investigate a bloat found at the watermen's stairs last week."

"I did." Grant gave him a wry glance. "My good coat was ruined when I had to pick up the wet corpse and—"

"Please," Flagstad said, "spare us the details. It's too early."

"Has the case been closed?" Keyes asked.

"Not yet," Grant said. "Why?"

"I'm offering help, if needed. Unlike you, I have extra time to fill. But of course, I haven't had the benefit of all your publicity."

Grant winced inwardly at the jab.

Bow Street officers had always been allowed to take on private work if someone offered to hire them for special tasks. It could be as simple as delivering a warrant or summons, or more complex, such as locating a missing person or serving as a bodyguard. The price was whatever both parties had agreed upon, but gratuities and rewards were often added. For Grant, the success of the Morgan of Bow Street books had multiplied his annual income several times over.

Most of the Bow Street officers had taken the situation in stride. Now and then they subjected Grant to a bit of friendly mockery, such as debating loudly in front of him whether his jaw was shaped more like a lantern or a spittoon. Or one of them would pretend to stare dreamily into his eyes and marvel, "Have a look at these piercing orbs, will you?—they really *are* like emeralds." And the others would chime in with: "I'd say they're more like a dew-kissed meadow at dawn," or "Green as a majestic tree frog, they are."

But there had been no joking from Keyes, who

found the situation difficult to bear. He would have loved the celebrity, not to mention the financial rewards, and felt they should rightfully have been his.

When Grant had first started at Bow Street, Keyes had been the one to show him the ropes, and had been generous with his time and advice. They'd developed a solid friendship, even gone out drinking together. The friendship had cooled over the past five years, however, and now Grant felt uncomfortable around him.

"I'll take the case, if you like," Keyes offered. "I need the work, and it wouldn't do for our celebrated Mr. Morgan to be seen investigating a dead whore."

Grant gave him an alert glance. "Why do you think the victim was a prostitute?"

"Probability. Most Thames steps are built adjacent to public houses or brothels."

With a brief smile, Grant said, "There's not much to investigate, I'm afraid. The corpse wasn't in a talkative mood."

He continued to the chief magistrate's office, where Cannon welcomed him in and bid him to close the door. After Grant explained the latest developments regarding Vivien Duvall, the usually taciturn magistrate made no effort to hide his astonishment. "You're sure she's not putting on an act?"

"Very. For what it's worth, Linley is of the same opinion."

Cannon reached for the lidded coffeepot on his desk and poured mugs of the bitter brew for himself and Grant.

Grant tasted the steaming beverage, which was strong enough to remove paint, and shuddered slightly. "Has it ever occurred to you to add milk and sugar?" he asked.

The magistrate gave a brief shake of his head. "More efficient to drink it black." He took a swallow and set down his mug, his thoughts returning to Vivien. "Poor woman," he said. "I can't imagine what she's feeling." He made a temple of his fingers as he continued absently. "Although we're formed by experiences, it's our memories of them that guide every thought and action. Without those memories, you would still be a version of yourself . . . but that would be a far cry from the person you spent years becoming."

Troubled, Grant remained silent. Only to himself could he admit that he was reluctant for Vivien to return to the way she had been. Would her gentleness simply vanish? Would she start to treat him with contempt again?

After a meditative silence, Cannon said, "You have this woman at an utter disadvantage, Morgan. I expect you to behave honorably."

Tempted to tell the magistrate to mind his own damned business, Grant stood and set his empty mug on the side table. "I don't need a lecture," he said. "Nor do I deserve it. You know me well enough to be sure I wouldn't harm Miss Duvall in any way. But if you want my word, you have it."

"It's not that I doubt your character," Cannon assured him. "I know you to be a man of honor. But I'm also aware of how difficult it is to resist temptation."

Grant blinked in surprise. "You are?"

"To be precise, I'm aware of how difficult it is for *other* men to resist temptation. You're residing with a woman who is vulnerable: physically, mentally, and emotionally. But until Miss Duvall regains her memory, no act of venereal enjoyment between the two of you could be viewed as consensual. No matter what she may say to the contrary."

Grant looked at him blankly. "Is that what you call it? An act of— My God, no wonder you've been celibate for so long."

"Morgan, did you hear what I—"

"Yes, sir. I'll keep my hands off her." Despite his annoyance, Grant had to duck his head to hide a grin. "Venereal enjoyment," he muttered, and a snicker escaped before he could stop it.

"What the devil is so amusing?" the magistrate demanded.

"Nothing."

"When you've finished tittering like a bridesmaid at the wedding banquet, I have some information to relay."

Sobering quickly, Grant lifted his head. "Does

it have to do with the foot patrol reports? Did they see anything on the night Miss Duvall was attacked?"

"Nothing. Not one sign of anything untoward. No disturbances or arguments, no cries of distress. An exceptionally quiet night, it seems. As for her kin—no luck on that account, either. Not a soul has come forward to make inquiries or report her missing. So far the clerk has found no record of previous residences, nor does Miss Duvall seem to belong to any religious or social organizations. It's as if she appeared out of thin air."

"I'm going to interview Lord Gerard after I leave here," Grant said, "and see what information I can pry out of him."

"In that vein . . . yesterday I called on Lord Sherbourne's mistress, Harriette Porter."

"He must have liked that," Grant said dryly.

Cannon gave him a reproving glance. "Sherbourne knows that as a gentleman, I always treat a woman with courtesy and respect, regardless of her situation. I asked Miss Porter if she knew anything about Miss Duvall's current whereabouts. She had some relevant information to offer."

"She and Miss Duvall are friends?"

"Not precisely. According to Miss Porter, it's a personal rule of Miss Duvall's not to have female friends. However, they chanced to meet at a milliner's shop approximately a fortnight ago, and Miss Duvall mentioned that she had ended her arrangement with Lord Gerard. She added that she was considering a return to Paris, where the *demimonde* is far more accepted than it is here, and courtesans are treated like royalty. However, she also hinted at the possibility of remaining in England, as she'd received a marriage proposal from some unnamed suitor. She hadn't yet decided whether to accept."

Grant regarded him with surprised interest. "He probably wasn't wellborn," he said. "A man from the upper class wouldn't marry a woman from the *demimonde* . . . would he?"

"It's been known to happen," Cannon said. "Although such marriages rarely find acceptance in society. After a woman's reputation has been ruined, she has little chance of a fairy-tale ending."

"I'll try to find out more about the mystery suitor when I interview Lord Gerard."

"Call on him earlier in the day rather than later," Cannon suggested.

"Why?"

"He drinks."

"Let me guess," Grant said dryly. "Lord Gerard is a spoiled aristocratic scion waiting to inherit his family's title. To avoid ennui, he spends most of his time as an utter louche, pursuing women, gambling, and drinking himself insensible. His life is an endless succession of dinners, dances, trips abroad, hunting parties in the country, and pleasure-seeking in town."

"That description is probably close to the mark," Cannon said. "I'm not acquainted with the man personally, but from what I've heard, he's not given to violence. He's more like a spoiled child, prone to tantrums and complaining. It seems he's known for often quoting his favorite proverb."

"Which is?"

"A quiet baby gets no milk."

"God." Grant rubbed his face. Cannon had just described the kind of man he most despised. "There's much to look forward to, it seems."

After leaving Bow Street, Grant went to call on Lord Gerard at his house in Mayfair. He ascended the steps of the classically styled manor with its towering columns, and knocked at one of the double doors. Soon it opened to reveal a butler's dour face.

"Your business, sir?"

"Please inform Lord Gerard that Mr. Morgan is here to see him."

Grant saw the instant of recognition on the butler's face, and a faint wariness threaded through the man's tone. "His lordship is not at home, sir. If you would care to leave your calling card, I'll see that he—"

"I don't leave cards," Grant said flatly. "And this isn't a social call. Tell Gerard I need to speak with him, or I'll be forced to search the house until I find him."

"Yes, sir." Glowering discreetly, the butler left him at the doorstep. Just before the door closed, Grant shouldered his way inside. He surveyed the entrance hall, lined with gleaming marble columns and statuary.

In a few minutes, the butler returned and showed him upstairs to a private receiving room—a lavish room, the walls covered in white woodwork and octagonal panels of red-and-gold damask.

Lord Gerard was lounging on an upholstered settee, wearing an embroidered velvet dressing gown. A half-filled glass dangled carelessly from his lax fingers. He was florid and disheveled, a man who was in his early thirties, but appeared much older after years of self-indulgence and cynicism.

The image of Vivien with this man, servicing him, pleasuring him, passed before Grant in a disquieting flash.

"Make yourself comfortable," Gerard said. "Morgan, is it? Will you have some Armagnac?"

"Thank you, no." Grant sat in a wing chair with ball-and-claw feet.

"Why are you so damned determined to speak with me?"

"I have a few questions relating to a police investigation. I don't expect it will take long."

"It had better not." Gerard stared at him with growing interest. "Are you by chance the Morgan who—"

"Yes," Grant said tersely.

"You were in that book—*Tale of the Botanist's Betrayal*—"

"Yes."

"*Capital.* The chaps at my club will be all agog when I tell them you came for a visit. Personally, I think you're a beef-head. I always solve the mystery by the end of the first chapter, and it takes you the whole book."

Grant smiled thinly. "I've long suspected, my lord, that a man at your level of intelligence is exactly what the publisher aims for."

Gerard looked pleased. "How may I help you, Morgan?"

"I'd like to know your whereabouts last Thursday around eight o'clock in the evening."

"That's an easy one. Thursdays I'm always at my club, Craven's. At eight o'clock I have drinks before dinner."

"There are people who will verify your presence there?"

"Many."

"When did you leave the club?"

"I was there all night." Gerard's lips curved with a self-satisfied smile. "I had a run of luck at the hazard tables and took a flier with one—no, two—of the house wenches. An excellent evening all around."

"What is the nature of your relationship with Miss Vivien Duvall?"

Gerard's smile vanished. He sat up and leaned

forward. "This is about Vivien, then? What happened? Is she in some kind of trouble? Bloody Christ, I hope it's nasty and unholy expensive, whatever it is. Tell her I won't lift a finger to help, even if she comes crawling."

"Your relationship with her?" Grant repeated.

Gerard finished his Armagnac in a gulp. "For almost two years I paid her bills and bought a long-term lease for her town house. I gave her jewelry, a carriage, anything she desired. All for the exclusive right to bed her. At least, it was supposed to be exclusive. She did whatever she pleased, the she-demon."

"What do you know of her family?"

"She never mentioned any relations."

"Did she ever tell you where she was born, or where she lived as a child?"

"If she did, I can't recall."

"Is Duvall an assumed name?"

Gerard looked perplexed. "Hmm. Never thought to ask. No idea."

"Does she have any particular enemies? Rivals?"

"She's disliked, envied, by many. But I wouldn't name anyone as a particular threat. I say, these are odd questions. Why—"

"When was the last time you saw her?"

"It was at her town house, perhaps a month ago. She ended our arrangement and said she was shutting up the house for the foreseeable future."

"And your reaction?"

"We argued, naturally. I told her it was *my* right, not hers, to say when it should end, and she laughed in my face! As I felt sure she wouldn't leave me without first securing another arrangement, I demanded the name of my replacement. She was quite smug, and said she was considering a marriage proposal from some mysterious suitor." He snorted with bitter amusement. "What rot. Women like Vivien aren't meant for marriage and motherhood. Her body's not meant for children—it's a place of business."

Grant focused blindly on the carpet pattern, trying to clear away the murderous red cloud from his vision. When he was able, he asked in a controlled voice, "Do you have any idea who the suitor was?"

"If he exists at all, he's either a senile old fool or a callow boy."

"Were there any people who might have witnessed the argument?"

"No, only servants. A cookmaid and a footman."

"Their names?"

"I couldn't tell you. If servants are any good at all, one never notices them. Ideally, they're extra-helpful furniture."

"Did you ever strike or throttle Miss Duvall during a dispute?"

"Never. I'm a gentleman, after all. Vivien may be a maddening creature, but I wouldn't want to hurt her."

"What was Miss Duvall's financial situation at the time she parted from you?"

"I believe she's stored away some funds in French banks. And she has a modest annuity. Not enough to survive indefinitely."

"Was she in debt?"

"No, Vivien's afraid of debt. She never even plays cards or dice. Will you kindly tell me what this is all about?"

"At the moment, my lord, there's no information I can share. I may return later with additional questions." Grant stood in preparation to leave.

"If there's an opportunity, Morgan . . . tell Vivien I would take her back. All would be forgiven and forgotten."

"Yes, my lord."

And as Grant departed, he thought with a touch of dark humor, *Believe me, Gerard . . . all is definitely forgotten.*

Chapter Four

Vivien's town house at Trelawney Crescent was set in a pristine white arc of three-story residences fronted with neat little balconies. With its private communal gardens and proximity to shops, the elegant address must have cost a pretty penny.

The interior was dim and musty. Grant drew back curtains and opened windows to admit a rush of fresh air. He wandered through the circuit of first-floor rooms, which had been decorated with light French carpeting and gilded furniture. The walls had been painted in pale shades of pink, green, or blue. There was some middling artwork, but not a book in sight, only a stack of a half dozen old periodicals.

He went up to the second floor, which was ghostly quiet, with most of the furniture covered in white sheets. It was clean and dry inside, the stale air scented of tea leaves, which were used to clean carpets. After opening windows in the main bedroom, Grant turned and stepped back with a start as he was confronted by a life-sized portrait over the bed.

Vivien had been painted in the nude, reclining on a chaise lounge strewn with white sheets, her flesh glowing and voluptuous. The artist had painted her hair so vividly red, it contained hints of purple flame. There was a flushed, replete look on her face, her eyes heavy-lidded.

Swallowing hard, Grant dragged his gaze from the painting. He wandered to a triple-door wardrobe, opened it, and found a considerable amount of clothing. Dresses of brocade, velvet, and gauze, each garment neatly folded and wrapped in silk paper. In the middle section of the wardrobe, shelves contained cloaks, pelisses, shawls, nightgowns, dressing gowns, and wrappers.

He approached a Louis XV dressing table and opened the drawers, searching methodically through a jumble of brushes, jars, ribbons, hairpins. After discovering a false bottom in one of the drawers, he pried it up and found a small book bound in red leather. A diary?

Grant opened the book and leafed slowly through the pages. In small, neat script, Vivien had recorded names, descriptions of sexual activities, times, dates, accounts of private conversations, and what appeared to be extortion payments. A long sigh escaped him.

"Ah, hell, Vivien," he muttered.

It wasn't necessarily a surprise. But blackmail seemed so incongruous with the woman who was staying at his house, he didn't know what the devil to think. Was it possible that memory loss could entirely alter someone's character?

He proceeded to search the rest of the town house, then found a leather trunk and filled it with clothes and shoes from the wardrobe. With some difficulty, Grant went out to the street and managed to find a hackney carriage large enough to accommodate the trunk.

When he arrived home, Mrs. Buttons greeted him at the door. She took his coat and folded it over her arm, shivering at the blast of wintry wind that had accompanied Grant into the house. "Will you want something to eat, sir?"

"No, thank you." Grant set down the trunk and glanced in the direction of the staircase. "How is Miss Duvall?"

"Improved, I'd say. Sore, but a nice soak in the bath seemed to help."

"Good." Grant paused. "What do you make of her?"

"Sir?"

"In general. Her character and disposition."

Mrs. Buttons led him from the entrance hall to the nearby receiving room. They crossed the threshold and stopped to converse in low tones.

"Had you never told me about her disreputable occupation, Mr. Morgan, I should never have guessed it. She doesn't seem at all worldly. As a matter of fact, she's quite modest. Anxious not to cause trouble. We caught her trying to tidy the room, to spare Miriam from having to do it."

"As if she weren't accustomed to having servants," Grant said.

"No, indeed. Whatever kind of family she came from, it wasn't highborn. An upper-class girl, no matter how well-mannered, wouldn't give a thought to the cookmaid's work." The housekeeper paused. "I would also venture to say she's been well educated. And there's her clothing. It wasn't easy to tell, of course, with all of it in such filthy condition. But the garments were made of worsted wool and cotton. No silk or velvet, not a scrap of expensive lace."

Absorbing the observations, Grant nodded. "Thank you, Mrs. Buttons." He hefted the trunk and braced it on one shoulder. "I brought some clothing from Miss Duvall's town house."

"That's good news, sir. We dressed her in Miriam's spare nightgown, but we had no proper clothes for when she's able to leave the bed."

"I'll carry this up to the bedroom. Unless she's

sleeping?" Grant experienced a pang of nerves he hadn't felt since boyhood. What the devil was wrong with him?

The housekeeper smiled slightly. "Go on up, sir. I think she may be waiting for you."

Filled with anticipation, Grant carried the trunk upstairs. The door to his bedroom was ajar, but he paused and knocked at the jamb.

"Come in," he heard Vivien say.

She was curled up in an armchair by the hearth, her bare feet drawn up and to the side, an open book in her lap. Golden firelight illuminated her face as she glanced up at him. She was dressed in a high-necked white nightgown with a blue cashmere lap robe draped over her waist and thighs.

Her eyes widened as she saw the trunk in his hand. "Is that mine?"

Grant smiled and carefully set the trunk near the chair. "All yours."

She went to examine it eagerly, unlatching it and lifting the lid.

Too late, Grant remembered he'd stowed the red leather book in the trunk. Damning himself, he moved to distract her, taking a shawl wrapped in paper silk and handing it to her. "I thought this would be useful," he said.

Vivien gave a little exclamation and opened the soft wool shawl, admiring the embroidery along the border.

As she moved to hold the garment closer to the lamplight, Grant fished the book from the trunk and slipped it into his pocket. The maneuver was quick, but Vivien saw it from the periphery of her vision.

"What's that?" she asked, turning toward him.

Bollocks, he thought, and gave her a blank look. "Nothing. Did you notice that I packed shoes as well? They're in a layer on the bottom."

"What did you just put in your pocket?" Vivien persisted, tilting her head a little as she looked at him.

Thrice-damned fiery bollocks, he thought, but kept his expression pleasant. "A book."

"You found books in my house?"

"Just one."

A little frown knitted her forehead. "There was only one book in *my entire house*?"

"There were some periodicals as well." Grant tensed as she stood and approached him.

"May I see it?"

He tried for a decisive tone. "You have more than enough to keep you occupied for now. Once you've sorted through all your belongings—"

"Give it to me." Vivien held out her hand, staring at him steadily. "If it's my book, I have a right to know what's in it."

Grant shook his head. "It can wait until later."

"Does it have to do with a financial matter?" she asked. "Is it an account book?"

"In a manner of speaking." Grant took a step back as she came closer. "It's nothing earth-shattering," he said, "just something you may not like. And I don't want you to become upset and have a collapse. Therefore, we're going to wait until—"

"Obviously it contains some unpleasant revelation," she said. "If I don't find out what it is, I'll be so tortured by my own imagination that I'll collapse anyway. Let me have it."

Grant made the highly disturbing discovery that he couldn't refuse her. Just what she'd done to make this so, he couldn't fathom. Scowling, he pulled the book from his pocket and gave it to her.

Vivien went to the chair and sat. Cautiously she opened the volume and discovered pages of lists, dates, names . . . and descriptions of sexual acts that caused her to turn scarlet. He heard her breathing stop.

"I'm a prostitute?" she eventually asked, sounding numb.

"Courtesan."

"There's no difference."

"There is, actually." Grant paused awkwardly. "It's more of an upper-class arrangement. Courtesans are skilled at conversation, and entertaining, and—"

"Don't try to sugarcoat it. I let men use my body for their own convenience. *Many* men. Who didn't care about me at all." Vivien stopped turning pages. "These are all things I've done?" she asked faintly, looking ill.

She looked so brittle, as if one touch would cause her to shatter. Grant tensed every muscle against the desire to go to her and offer comfort. But that might not be what she wanted.

"I'm a prostitute," she said again, as if trying to make herself believe it.

"Courtesan." Recalling what Cannon had said, Grant ventured, "It's a consensual and legal arrangement."

"Women consent to a great many things that harm us."

She was as still as some delicate winged creature suspended in amber. Her face was unreadable, gaze turned inward.

Grant went to her and sank to his haunches in front of the chair, settling his hands on the upholstered arms. "Vivien," he murmured. "I'm sorry."

To his relief, she leaned forward and lowered her head to his shoulder, and let out a tremulous sigh. "None of it's your fault."

Gently he caressed her shining red hair and pressed his lips to her head. "What are you feeling?" he asked quietly. "I can't tell."

"Shame," came her muffled voice. "Sadness. Anger. I want to know what choices I made to arrive at this place."

"It may not have been entirely voluntary. Life often sets people on a path without giving them a choice." Grant eased her away enough to look into her troubled face. He decided to take another tack. "People sleep together for reasons other than love. Sometimes it can be impersonal, and there's nothing wrong with—"

"No," Vivien said, surprising him with her intensity. "Even if the sexual act is done without love or caring, it's always personal. It literally can't be anything other than personal. But bringing a payment into it makes the act one-sided. It says, 'The only thing that matters is my satisfaction. Your needs aren't important. You're a receptacle.'" Her face crumpled, and she bit her lip, and a few tears slid out.

"I'm not sure it's always done in that spirit—" Grant began, but shut his mouth promptly as she gave him a dangerous look. In a moment, he said, "If you want to live differently from now on, you can."

She looked down at the book again, her restless brain trying to make sense of everything, trying to fit puzzle pieces together. "This is why," she said.

"Why what?"

"Why I was attacked. I was trying to blackmail someone, and they wanted to murder me for it."

"That's a theory."

"It's the obvious answer."

"The most obvious answer isn't always the right one." Gently Grant pried the book from her hands. "Let me have this. Please. I don't want you to read any more of it tonight."

"I don't want you to read it, either. Your opinion of me will lower with every turn of the page."

Grant looked into her glimmering blue eyes, and a wave of tenderness came over him, like nothing he'd ever felt before. "My opinion is that you're a good woman. An intelligent, charming, genuinely nice woman."

Vivien took in a long breath and let it out slowly. To Grant's relief, her tears had stopped. "Thank you," she said. "But the woman who wrote those things wasn't nice."

"Let's not jump to conclusions about anyone's character based on what they do in bedrooms. Nice people do things in bedrooms."

"I didn't mean *those* things, I meant the black-mail payments. I suppose you'll have to talk to the men whose names are listed in my book." Vivien leaned her head back against the chair and closed her eyes. "How mortifying."

Grant frowned as he tucked the red leather book into his pocket. "I knew you wouldn't like finding out about it. But I was hoping when you did, you might be able to take it on the chin and carry on. Because it's really not—"

"Take it on the chin?" Vivien's eyes opened.

"Sorry," Grant said hastily. "I don't claim to understand women. What I was trying to say—"

"No one can understand *all* women. You can

only understand women one at a time," Vivien said. At his perplexed look, she explained, "You have to think of us as unique individuals. As if we were actual people. You'd never claim men were all alike, would you?"

"No, we are," he said. "There's hardly any variation among us. We're quite simplistic. It's the beauty of being male."

That surprised a reluctant laugh from her.

Seeing the novel Vivien had discarded on the floor earlier, Grant reached down to pick it up. "*Frankenstein*?" he asked, looking at the cover. "I wouldn't have expected you to read this."

"It was in a stack Miriam brought up from the library."

"I hope it doesn't give you nightmares."

"It's a dark story," she conceded, "but more than anything, it's terribly sad." She paused. "My sympathies are with the creature."

"Mine as well," he said. "How much have you read so far?"

"I'm almost halfway through, I think."

"When you're finished, I would enjoy talking with you about it." Regarding her thoughtfully, Grant asked, "Shall I stay and keep you company? Or would you like Mrs. Buttons to come up and help you unpack the trunk?"

Vivien shook her head. "I need some time alone to think."

"Of course." Grant set the book in her lap, intending to rise to his feet, but she surprised him by reaching for his hand. Responding immediately, he closed his hand around hers.

So simple, the clasp of hands. And yet infinite possibilities were born in the small private space between two palms. Reassurance, rescue, protection, promise, fear, or faith. The complex pressure could mean hello, goodbye, thank you, or please. It could open the door to intimacy, an entire seduction woven within the lattice of fingers, the kiss of fingertips, the spark of nerve endings just beneath the skin.

If only Vivien understood that in holding her hand, Grant was holding all of her . . . who she was and had been, and all the hopes and struggles and mistakes she couldn't remember, and all the places the future might take her. He accepted everything about her, without reservation, no matter what.

Everything.

Chapter Five

Reading *Frankenstein* late at night was probably what had caused the bad dreams. Somewhere in Vivien's restless sleep, she was running through a shadowed street, chased by strangers. She came to a bridge and raced across with her lungs heaving, every muscle burning, and reached an embankment wall surmounted by a bronze statue of a river deity. Hiding against the statue, she tried to keep quiet.

To her horror, the massive bronze figure began to move. It twisted to face her, metal arms snaking around her in a merciless embrace.

Crying out in terror, she fought as it clutched

her, turned toward the river . . . and plunged into the black, bitterly cold depths. Its weight pulled her down, the surface receding far above them. She screamed beneath the water, the liquid filling her mouth and throat—

"Vivien, wake up."

She thrashed against the arms around her . . . then saw Grant's taut, anxious face above hers.

Disoriented, Vivien fought to catch her breath, and realized they were both on the carpet. "Wh-why are we on the floor?"

"You fell off the bed," Grant said, his hands running over her limbs. "Are you hurt?"

She hesitated, taking inventory of her aching body. "I don't think so." After a pause, she said, "It was a nightmare. A terrible one."

"Sweetheart." Grant lifted her to the bed and lit a lamp on the table. The placket of his thin linen shirt was open, revealing a powerful chest covered with dark hair. He picked up a clean handkerchief from the table and sat with Vivien, wiping the film of sweat and tears from her face. Gradually the frantic pace of her heart slowed.

"I was drowning," she said, as Grant efficiently straightened the tangled mass of sheets and blankets. "It was so real. I couldn't breathe."

"You're safe now. It was only a dream."

"I'm afraid to sleep."

Grant looked down at her, his hand smoothing her hair. "I'll be right back," he said.

He left the room, and returned in a few minutes with a glass containing a small amount of liquor.

"What's that?" she asked.

"Brandy." Grant handed her the glass and sat beside her, watching as she took sips of smooth fire. "Nightmares are only to be expected after you've come close to death. I know that from experience." He paused, seeming to think back to a distant memory. "Someone once told me it would prevent bad dreams if you set your shoes beside the bed, with the heel of one pointing in the direction of the other's toe, coming and going."

"Did it work?"

"As I recall," he said with a half smile, "it helped."

Vivien took another sip. "You've come close to death more than once, according to the novels about you."

The smile vanished. "Who told you about those?"

"Mrs. Buttons."

Now Grant looked mortified. "Those books are rubbish. You won't find them in my house."

"Your servants collect them."

"The crackbrains," he muttered.

He sounded so disgusted that Vivien couldn't help smiling. "Why don't you like the books? Is it that you're too modest? You don't like being praised for your accomplishments?"

As Grant considered his reply, Vivien saw the genuine frustration in his expression. Her smile faded as she realized the issue of the books bothered him deeply.

"The problem is, they're not my accomplishments," he said. "The books are works of fantasy, about a hero with my name, purported to be me. And now people think I've fought an array of villains that includes clockwork soldiers, a phantom magician, pirates, an evil inventor, and a botanist."

"A botanist?"

"Poison," he said. "The public also seems to believe I routinely jump off buildings and bridges, and survive bombings and bullets, all without a scratch. It puts me in an impossible position. I can't lie and pretend it's real. But if I don't, people are disappointed. I feel like a fraud, and the most exasperating part of it is—" Grant stopped and shook his head. "Forgive me. This is tiresome—"

"Not at all," she exclaimed gently, and patted the edge of the mattress. "Please go on."

Grant sat at the side of the bed as he continued. "I have no damn reason to feel like a fraud. I've apprehended more criminals and solved more cases than anyone in the history of the Bow Street office. I've tripled the records. But the novels have created a version of me that no man could live up to." He raked a hand through his dark hair, disheveling it. "And they're so badly written."

"Oh, dear. The plotting?"

"The dialogue. Stilted and clownish. The hero constantly refers to himself in the third person. Before dashing off to save someone, he'll stop and announce 'Grant Morgan to the rescue' . . . even if no one's bloody there to hear it."

Vivien struggled mightily to hold back a laugh.

"'Grant Morgan never tells a lie' . . . 'Grant Morgan always eats his vegetables' . . ." he continued morosely. "I wish to hell they had made up their own name for the character instead of taking mine."

"But they used yours because they knew it would make the books more successful," Vivien said.

"Exactly."

"Does the publisher ever seek your approval of a story before the book is written?"

Grant gave her a dark glance and shook his head.

"Perhaps you should consult with a lawyer," Vivien suggested.

"Sir Ross made it clear that he doesn't want me to."

Vivien's brows lifted. "Why not?"

"He knows I would stop publication of the books entirely if I could. And that wouldn't be in the interests of the Bow Street office."

"What about *your* interests?" Vivien asked.

His only reply was a half shrug.

He must feel trapped, she thought compassionately. He was being taken advantage of. His accomplishments were being used for someone else's profit.

"I think you should take up the matter with Sir Ross again," she said. "I'm sure he would be very distressed if *he* were robbed of all control over his own name and reputation. As for the public . . . I think part of their enthusiasm for these books is because you're not a nobleman, like the Count of Monte Cristo, or Ivanhoe, or the one in the Waverley novels. You're a common-born man, having exciting adventures and always winning in the end. It gives ordinary people hope, and perhaps a sense of vicarious satisfaction."

"But none of the books are true," Grant said. "They have nothing to do with reality."

"I think that's the point." Vivien took another sip of the brandy and gave him a rueful smile. "I'm not against reality, it's just that there's so much of it. That's why most people need a good story now and then, to give them respite."

Seeing that Grant was listening to her with a faint frown of concentration, she continued, "I think people generally understand you're not *really* fighting phantoms, but they like to imagine you could. And they like what the story represents, which is the real you. I wonder . . . is it possible you could find a way to share their enjoyment of the stories, but also talk to them about your actual experiences? For example, if they say something about the evil botanist, you could reply, 'Yes, wasn't that an exciting chapter? It reminds me of the time I investigated a real case of poisoning . . .'"

Considering that, Grant rubbed his lower jaw. "I could try that. It's treading a fine line, but at least it would give me a way to talk about something true."

"It's like finding out about Father Christmas," she said. "He may not be a real man who comes down the chimney and fills the stockings. But on Christmas Day, there'll still be gifts and a stuffed goose for dinner."

A husky laugh broke from him. "I'm not sure that analogy works. And I hope to hell I'm not the stuffed goose." He reached out and gently touched her cheek with his hand. "But you're a clever woman. You're also the only person who's ever listened to my concerns instead of trivializing them. For that, I could . . ."

He was so handsome, with a lock of heavy dark hair falling over his forehead, that she yielded to temptation before she quite realized what she was doing.

"You could kiss me," she suggested softly, laying her hand against the side of his face. The bristle of his unshaven jaw was scratchy-rough against her soft palm. His breath caught audibly, and then he swallowed hard.

"Vivien—"

She reached behind his head and drew him down until she felt his mouth against hers. His lips were firm and sweet, settling by degrees, until the kiss opened into a soft blaze of sensation. She felt him tremble with the effort to be gentle, his powerful arms braced on either side of her. He searched her slowly, tasting her with the tip of his tongue, and the pleasure of it nearly stole her breath away. The kiss broke into other kisses, gentle, languid, sensuous.

Her head tilted back as his lips slid to her jaw, her throat, finding the soft places where her pulse had begun to throb. She felt his tongue touch her skin, and a sound of helpless desire stirred in her throat.

His breath had roughened, but he was so careful, so tender, skimming his way back up her neck and taking her lips again. One of his hands slid into her hair, long fingers curving over the back of her head. She arched against him, trying to bring herself closer.

Abruptly he pulled away, panting. "No. This isn't right. *Hell.* If I try to kiss you again, promise you'll slap my face."

"I would never promise that," she said. "I might hurt you."

Grant picked up one of her small hands and

looked at it with a ragged laugh. "With this?" He crushed a kiss against her palm and gave her a glance of pure molten longing. After leaving the bed, he looked around the room until he found her slippers. Ceremoniously he placed them beside the bed, heel-to-toe. "There," he said. "No more nightmares."

And Vivien fell in love with him right then, at that very moment. Because heroes didn't just fight large battles and perform great feats of daring.

Sometimes a hero was a man who cared about the small things.

The next day, Mrs. Buttons took Vivien downstairs to the library. "Mr. Morgan spared no expense in housing his books properly," she said proudly.

Vivien stopped to turn a slow circle, her wondering gaze taking in the floor-to-ceiling shelves filled with acres of books. Afternoon sun stole through the windows and reflected off hinged glass doors that protected some of the rarer volumes.

With rest and excellent care, she was recovering rapidly. But she was also going a bit mad from inactivity. Grant would be gone for the great part of the day, working on his investigation, and she couldn't stand being cooped up in the bedroom a moment longer.

Dressed in one of the gowns Grant had brought from her town house, a rose silk muslin trimmed with lace, she wandered happily along the bookshelves. She paused to admire a map cabinet embossed with gold letters. "I'm sure this is the most splendid library I've ever seen, even if I don't remember the other ones."

The housekeeper positioned an upholstered armchair by the fire. "I'll leave you to explore, Miss Duvall, while I go about my duties."

"Thank you." Vivien beamed at her. "I expect to be in here for a *very* long time."

And she was. She explored, read, dozed a little in the chair, and awakened when Miriam brought her a tea tray with delicate sandwiches and slices of toasted pound cake. Then it was back to books again.

She found a shelf of poetry and began stacking volumes in her arms. Wordsworth, Burns, Shelley, Keats. But she paused as she saw a row of philosophy books on the adjacent shelf. She put back the poetry and instead pulled out Hume's *Treatise on Human Nature*, Kant's *Critique of Pure Reason*, and Fourier's *Theory of the Four Movements*. And Descartes's *Meditations*, which . . . seemed familiar.

With growing interest, she carried the books to her chair and began to read a few random pages of Descartes.

There is nothing, among the things I once believed to be true, which it is not permissible to doubt . . .

Her heart began to thump. Her mind swam with impressions.

A door had opened in her mind. She was in a cottage, reading these words in the company of someone she loved . . . a man who had made her feel cherished.

"Good afternoon," came Grant's amused voice in the silence. "What have you found that's so interesting?"

Chapter Six

❧

Vivien whirled to see Grant enter the room. She hurried forward, almost stumbling in her eagerness to share the discovery.

"Grant," she said breathlessly. "I've read this before. I *remember* it! Oh, you can't imagine how it feels to find something familiar—"

"Easy. Careful—" Grant reached out to steady her. "You're sure? What exactly do you remember?"

"I was reading this very book." She showed him the Descartes. "I was in the main room of a cottage—there was a leaky roof, but it was cozy and I was happy—and someone was with me. A man. I can't see his face or recall his voice. But I was fond of him. I remember talking with him, and there were piles of books all around us."

Grant pondered the information, his gaze falling to the book in her hands. "You've read Descartes?"

"Yes. I remember his theory of dualism . . . that spirit and matter are distinct."

Grant half sat, half leaned on the library table, staring at her speculatively. "I wouldn't have expected you to read philosophy."

Vivien frowned. "Because of my profession?"

His mouth twisted. "No, because no one except academics and men of leisure read it. Most people have too many problems to waste time thinking about abstract concepts."

"A waste?" she repeated indignantly. "If that's your opinion, why do you own a book on Cartesian theory?"

Grant looked wry. "Descartes is one of those names mentioned at social occasions by men who like to show off. Since I never had a gentleman's education, I try to learn what I can so I'll be able to understand what they're saying."

Vivien was touched by the vulnerability of his admission. "What do you read for pleasure?"

For answer, Grant went to a bookshelf and pulled out a few well-worn volumes. He brought them to the table, and she looked over them eagerly.

"*Robinson Crusoe*," she said. "I think I've read

that one. And *Gulliver's Travels*." She paused at the copy of *Tom Jones*. "I don't think I know this one."

"It was written by Henry Fielding—the magistrate who founded the Bow Street Runners."

"Would I like it?"

"You might. It's about the life of an orphan foundling . . . his mysterious identity . . . the obstacles and escapades, a star-crossed love affair . . ." Grant went to the sideboard and found a bottle of good red Burgundy. "Would you like to share some wine with me?"

"*Yes.*"

As Grant uncorked the wine and poured two glasses, Vivien saw a smile playing at his lips.

"What is it?" she asked. "Are you happy because I remembered something?"

"Of course." He glanced at her with warm green eyes. "But I was also thinking . . . a beautiful woman, a fire on the hearth, a bottle of wine, and a roomful of books . . . It might not be every man's idea of heaven, but God knows it's mine."

Much later, when afternoon had ripened into dusk, Vivien snuggled in the upholstered chair with a novel in her lap and watched as Grant leafed through pages. Firelight flickered over his beautiful dark hair, making it gleam. She loved the look of his hands, strong and capable, entirely comfortable holding a book.

He had an unconscious habit of touching his face when he read, sometimes rubbing his chin or tapping his lower lip with a forefinger.

Feeling her gaze on him, he looked up with a questioning glance.

Vivien tried to think of a reason for staring. "What's it like to be so tall?"

A corner of his mouth curled upward. "A constant headache. My head has been acquainted with many a doorframe."

Vivien smiled sympathetically. "You must have been a gangly boy."

"A rackabones," he agreed.

"Were you teased?"

"Endlessly. I was in a fight almost every day at Lady of Pity."

"Is that a school?"

"Orphanage," he said matter-of-factly. "I wasn't always an orphan—my father was a bookseller, a good man, but bad at business. A few bad loans to friends and a year of poor sales landed the entire family in debtor's prison. And of course, once you go in, you never come out. There's no way to earn enough money to buy your freedom." His gaze turned distant. "My parents and sister died there, when disease went through the prison."

"How old were you?" she asked.

"Nine or ten. My brother, Jack, and I survived, and were sent to Lady of Pity. But a year later, I was sent to a workhouse."

"Why?"

"Jack was small for his age, and sensitive by nature. The other boys bullied him, so . . ."

"You defended him," she said.

Grant nodded. "After a particularly brutal fight, it was decided that I posed a danger to the other children. But the workhouse turned out to be a stroke of luck. I was hired out to the Keeches, and they took me in to live with them. They were the saving of me."

"What became of your brother?"

Grant's gaze was distant. He didn't seem to have heard.

Vivien tried again. "Where is he now?"

He looked at her then, and something inside her shrank as she realized the answer was something terrible. Something she didn't necessarily want to hear.

Except she did. It was a bridge that had to be crossed if she were ever to truly know and understand him. She went to his chair and perched on the upholstered arm, looking down at him.

"Please," she said gently, daring to caress the dark locks of his hair. "You already know the worst about me. I'll listen with the same kindness you've shown to me."

Color crept over his face. He cleared his throat, but his voice still came out rusted. "I went back for my brother as soon as I was able. I'd secured a promise of work for him at Billingsgate. The orphanage would let him leave if an adult were willing to speak for him. I was nearly fourteen:

close enough. But when I went to fetch him, they said Jack was gone."

"Had he run away?"

A brief shake of his head. "Smallpox. It had gone through the orphanage. Jack died without me there. Without anyone who loved him."

Words failed her. She regarded him sorrowfully.

"If I'd gone sooner—" Grant began.

"No," she interrupted swiftly. "You know that's not right. It's not fair."

A bleak smile touched his lips. "Vivien. You know as well as anyone that life isn't fair, and most of us fail miserably at it."

"That's not true."

He continued relentlessly. "Life is too short for some people and too long for others, and either way there's no point to it. We never end up with the right person, or if we do, we don't realize it until it's too late. We spend years wasting each other's time and blaming others for our mistakes. If we find happiness, it never lasts because life keeps changing. The truth is that nothing matters, because someday it's all going to end."

"I don't think that's what you really believe, deep down."

He gave her a sardonic glance. "Yes, it is. That's why I said it."

"According to the Stoics," she told him, "actions follow perspective. And your actions aren't those of a man who believes it's all meaningless."

That drew a reluctant smile from him. "I'm not going to debate philosophy with you, Vivien."

"Life is beautiful and painful and harrowing, and it's precious *because* it ends. Because we each decide what meaning to give it. As for happiness . . ."

Grant was staring at her as if riveted.

Vivien smiled into his intent face. "Have you ever looked very hard for something, like a key or a set of spectacles, and realized later that you were staring right at it? There was nothing wrong with your eyes. It was invisible because your mind had already decided it wasn't there. That's happiness—a lost thing we could find if we just looked for it in a different way."

Grant leaned forward to kiss her. A brush of silk, so light, but she was caught off guard by a thrill of sensation, all her nerves coming alive. Her balance wavered, and Grant pulled her into his lap in a sort of controlled collapse. He stared at her parted lips, his gaze intent, and she heard the quickening of his breath.

One of his hands cupped the back of her head, and he brought her mouth to his, slowly, as if he were experimenting with something dangerous. Another stroke of fire, gentle and elusive. She began to tremble. Her heartbeat turned heavy, beating in her ears. Wanting more, she nudged forward, but he eased back, forcing her to accept his restraint, even as her breath quickened with impatience. He kissed her slowly, teasing gently, until she writhed a little in the chair and tried to bring herself closer.

He coaxed her open, the tip of his tongue venturing into the silkiness past her lips. She held on to his shoulders, her fingers tightening against the heavy muscle. Gradually he sealed their lips together and licked deep, and she yielded with a soft sound, her mind dissolving. The world was nothing but firelight and feeling, and a man who kissed as if he were trying to steal the soul from her body. The pleasure of it made her dizzy and desperate. Gasping, she curled her arms around his head and neck and responded feverishly, following when he tried to pull back.

His mouth broke from hers. "Vivien," he said, sounding shaken. He cradled her face in his hands, his lips traveling over her cheeks, chin, the tip of her nose. "It's difficult for me to do this and stop."

She stared at him hazily. "I don't care," she said thickly, and sought his mouth again.

His laugh was muffled against her lips. He indulged her for a few head-spinning moments, then pulled back. "I can't lose control."

"Why not?" Her fingertips quested over his shaven jaw, down to the smoothness of his neck.

"For you." He stole another kiss, a soft, delicious tug at her lips. "For your pleasure." He nuzzled the tender space where her jaw met her ear. "For you to know you're always safe in my arms."

"I do." She twisted to capture his mouth again, but he wouldn't let her.

"Vivien." He buried a laugh in her hair and struggled to breathe. "Be still. Talk to me. No kissing. Let's just . . . talk."

"About what?" She could feel the aroused shape of him beneath her, a thick and amazingly hard ridge. The feel of it made her squirm pleasurably, and he grasped her hips firmly to keep her in place.

"Be still, you minx," came his muffled voice.

She nodded and tried to calm herself, and racked her brain for something to ask. "How did you become a Bow Street Runner?"

Grant took a couple of deep breaths. His grip on her hips eased. "When I was working at Billingsgate market . . . there were always pickpockets and petty thieves. Sometimes there was trouble if a jug-bitten navvy wandered over from the docks. Or a brawl might start at one of the nearby taverns. And it wasn't always easy to find a foot patrol. So when there was a problem, the merchants and stall-keeps would shout for me."

"But you were just a boy. A skinny one." She stroked the side of his face and gently traced the edge of his jaw.

He smiled and tucked a kiss into her palm. "When I reached my teenage years, I started growing in every direction. I was big for my age, and fast. And I could dodge through a crowd without knocking people over. If a pickpocket or thief took off running, I'd catch him and keep him secure until police would come to cart him off. And I was good at putting down fights."

"Did you like doing all that?" Vivien asked, playing with his hair, letting the cropped satiny locks slide through her fingers.

"I did. I liked feeling useful. Needed." His smile deepened as he added, "And I loved any excuse that would take me away from cutting and trimming fish."

"That must be difficult work."

"I learned the skills for it. But I never grew to like it. And the work leaves its scars."

Her fingers stilled in his hair. She looked into his face with concern. "Do you have nightmares about it?"

Grant laughed. "No, I mean literal scars." He showed her his left hand. She winced as she saw the ragged, healed-over scar on his palm. "That's from a fish knife," he said. "And these—" He showed her a sprinkling of white crescents. "Opening oysters," he said. "And this one was when a fish bone pierced—" He broke off as Vivien lowered her head and pressed her lips to the scars. "No—it's—sweetheart, they don't hurt now, they're—" He nudged her head upward and stole a brief, hard kiss from her.

"Talking," he reminded her. "What was I—Oh, yes, the fish market. Eventually someone told Sir Ross, who was the new chief magistrate at Bow Street, about my unofficial thief-taking. He came to Billingsgate himself to meet with me, and one thing led to the next." His entire body tensed as Vivien softly kissed the corner of his mouth. "And this," he said darkly, "is exactly what he told me *not* to do with you."

She drew her head back and looked at him in surprise. "Sir Ross talked to you about this?"

"About not taking advantage of you. About resisting temptation."

"Do I tempt you?"

He looked at her without expression. "Not at all."

Feeling playful, she leaned closer until their lips were nearly touching. "Prove it."

"How?"

"I'll kiss you, and you try not to kiss me back."

An unsteady laugh escaped him. "Vivien . . ."

And for a long time after that, there were no words.

It was a quiet but busy morning at Bow Street headquarters, as Sir Ross Cannon finished editing the latest edition of *The Hue and Cry*. The weekly report was circulated to magistrates everywhere in England, containing details of criminals at large as well as law enforcement news.

Just as Grant reached Cannon's office, the magistrate brushed by him with a copy of the report.

"Take a look at this," Cannon said, pausing just long enough to shove the pages at him. "Check for errors. It's going to the printer in ten minutes."

"Where are you—"

"I'll return momentarily."

Grant took the report into Cannon's office. To his discomfort, Neil Keyes was there as well, perusing a procedural manual he'd taken from a bookshelf.

"Morgan," the older man said absently.

"Keyes," Grant responded, picking up a pencil from the desk.

"I've heard a rumor about you." Keyes slid the procedural manual back into place on the shelf.

"Oh?"

"It's being said that the bloat you were sent to investigate turned out to be a young woman— who's very much alive."

Grant kept his gaze on the report in his hand. "Who told you that?"

"Rather not say. But if I've heard about it, so have others." Keyes paused. "If you need assistance, you have only to ask. I may not be as fleet of foot as I once was, but I still have my uses."

Grant sent him a brief smile before turning his attention back to the report.

Sir Ross returned and headed directly for an earthenware jug of coffee on a table in the corner. After pouring the last tepid splash of the brew into his mug, the magistrate called out, "Mrs.

Dobson, my jug is empty. I need it filled as soon as possible."

A response floated from down the hall. "But your nerves, sir . . ."

"I don't have nerves," Cannon called back testily. "If I did, I wouldn't need coffee." He sat and regarded Grant with narrowed gray eyes. "Why do you look like that?"

"What do you mean?"

"Like a rooster that's been spatchcocked and seared in an iron skillet."

The description was more apt than Cannon could have known. After the time he'd spent with Vivien in the library last night, he'd found it impossible to fall asleep. He'd let her kiss and play with him while he'd sat there, rigid in every muscle, as if strapped to some medieval torture device. For long, scorching minutes she'd experimented with kisses, trying to discover all the ways their mouths could fit together. The sensations had been exquisite, the sweet weight of her pressing on his hard flesh, until finally he'd had to put a stop to it, knowing damn well he should have never let it start in the first place.

Now he felt guilty and exhausted—and ravenous for more.

"I didn't sleep well last night," Grant said in a surly tone.

"Sleep," the magistrate repeated with a dismissive flick of his hand, as if it were an unnecessary indulgence. "How is Miss Duvall?"

"Improving."

"And her memory?"

"A bit of progress, nothing significant yet." Grant took the red appointment book from his pocket and extended it across the desk. "I found this at her town house."

Cannon took the book, opened it, and viewed a few random pages. His only visible reaction to the lurid contents was a quick double-blink. "By God, the woman could teach my men a thing or two about how to write detailed, organized reports."

Grant gave him a mock-innocent glance. "I had no idea that was what you wanted in a report. I'll try to make mine more colorful."

"You've started investigating the names in this book?"

Grant nodded. "None are obvious suspects. Yet."

Cannon closed the volume and handed it back to him. "You were discreet, I hope. My preference is not to destroy a man's reputation and family unnecessarily."

"If they were all that concerned about discretion," Grant said, "they wouldn't have been involved with Miss Duvall in the first place."

"What of Lord Gerard?"

Grant shook his head. "I interviewed him and confirmed his alibi; he was at his club at the time of the attack. He had no information to offer about Vivien's past or her family—apparently it never occurred to him to ask. I've never encountered such massive self-absorption. It was actually impressive."

"And the mysterious suitor?"

"Nothing about that, either. Gerard doubts the suitor even exists." Grant rubbed his jaw slowly. "The woman staying at my house doesn't seem remotely capable of doing anything described in that book, including extortion."

"Until she regains her memory," Cannon replied, "you can't be sure who she is, or what she's capable of."

Someone knocked at the door, and Cannon said curtly, "Yes?"

A clerk ducked his head inside the office. "Sir Ross, the French government wants a response to their requisition—regarding the fugitive—"

"Have they sent the deposition on oath from the magistrate in Paris?"

"No sir, just the warrant. How shall I reply?"

Cannon looked exasperated. "Tell them I'll extend the suspect's remand for another week, but they can't have him until I receive an authenticated deposition."

The clerk vanished, and Cannon groaned quietly. "The French want to extradite an upper-class scoundrel who fled here after doing illegal stockjobbing in Paris," he told Grant.

"Why is that a problem?"

"Because he's a friend of the French ambassador, who's pressuring me to not send him back. And I have to keep company with the ambassador next week, at a ball—" Cannon broke off abruptly, appearing to consider something. "Hmm."

"What?"

"I have an idea that might help to push the case along, despite Miss Duvall's memory loss. If you like it, you can discuss it with her, and see what she makes of it."

Chapter Seven

"A ball?" Vivien stared at Grant as if he'd gone mad.

"I'm only relating what Sir Ross suggested," Grant said evenly. "That doesn't mean I recommend it."

They sat together at the library table, with Grant's chair turned to face hers.

"He proposed that I attend a ball given by this woman, this—"

"Lady Lichfield. A long-standing friend. He's certain she'll include extra names on the guest list if he asks."

"And he thinks I should go there to make a

brazen appearance in public to demonstrate that I'm still alive."

"He didn't say brazen."

"If he wants me to behave the way I used to, we can infer brazen."

Grant inclined his head, reluctantly acknowledging the point.

"I won't even recognize anyone," Vivien said.

"I will. I'll be at your side, giving you names and helping when necessary."

Vivien cringed with dread as she forced herself to ask, "Will the men that I . . . my former . . . will any of them be there?"

"Probably."

She heaved a wretched sigh. "And after I'm dangled out there like a baited frog, whoever tried to kill me before may want to try it again."

"It's a risk," Grant acknowledged quietly. "Which is why I don't like the plan. If it were up to me, I'd say no. But it's your decision. If you want to go through with it, I'll keep you safe." His level gaze held hers. "You'll continue to stay with me here, but we would create the illusion that you've resumed living in your town house. And if the bastard goes there—or sends someone—our officers will be waiting."

"What if I don't want to take that risk?" she asked.

"Then we'll carry on as we have been," Grant replied without hesitation. "I'll continue the investigation, and eventually some new evidence will turn up." He took her hand. "I'll tell Cannon we've decided against the plan."

Vivien hesitated before replying.

It would be a hideous evening, she thought, going out among strangers and pretending she hadn't changed.

But what was the alternative?

It was dawning on her, how untenable her situation was. She didn't belong anywhere, with anyone. She wanted nothing to do with her old life, but she was overwhelmed by the prospect of starting a new one.

Nevertheless, she had to put an end to all this and start to make plans for herself.

It was important not to take advantage of Grant or make his life difficult. She was coming to love him more and more. It wasn't merely gratitude for the way he'd taken care of her. It was attraction, liking, and trust.

There was so much to admire about him, a hardworking man who'd made a success of himself. A man who treated her with respect when so many others would have shown contempt. He didn't deserve the problems that came with her.

"I can't stay with you indefinitely," she said.

"Yes, you can."

She shook her head. "People will find out soon. It will cause trouble for you."

"Not at all."

"A Bow Street officer, living with a fallen woman under his roof—"

"Don't call yourself that."

"Your reputation is too important to risk damaging. I'm sure that's one of the reasons Sir Ross proposed this idea in the first place. People believe in you, they trust you—"

"That's not why he proposed it." Grant gave her a sardonic glance. "This is his usual approach to problem-solving." His hand folded over hers. "There's a saying at Bow Street: Know whether you're an anvil or a hammer. If you're an anvil, be patient. If you're a hammer, strike fast and hard." He played gently with her fingers. "Sir Ross is a hammer. Undoubtedly because of all the damned coffee he drinks."

"And you?" Vivien asked with a faint smile. "Which one are you?"

"Anvil."

She stared reflectively into the nearby hearth. "I'd rather do something to draw out an adversary instead of waiting for him to make the next move. I think in this case, the approach should be 'hammer.'" She gave a little nod, the decision made. "I'd like to visit my house as soon as you're able to take me there. I'll need to find something to wear."

Grant was frowning. "Take more time to think about it," he suggested.

"I don't need to. I remember an opening move

in chess . . . the Légal trap, I think. You start by sacrificing the queen. If your opponent takes it, you can achieve checkmate very quickly with only minor pieces."

"You play chess now," Grant said rather than asked, still frowning.

"Yes." Vivien smiled and pulled her hand from his. "I believe I do."

She left the library, wanting to find out if either Mrs. Buttons or Miriam knew how to arrange a lady's hair for a ball.

"I'm not going to sacrifice the queen," she heard Grant call out irritably after her. "I'm going to protect the blasted queen!"

The next morning, Vivien was pleasantly surprised to discover Grant had hired a private carriage to take her to the town house at Trelawney Crescent. It was a beautiful, black-lacquered vehicle pulled by a pair of matched chestnuts.

"We could have gone in a hackney carriage," she said as Grant settled her into the luxurious interior, the seats upholstered with velvet.

He looked indignant at the suggestion. "You, in a hackney?"

After draping a lap robe over her, he sat in the opposite seat and thumped on the ceiling to signal the driver. The well-sprung carriage rolled and jounced buoyantly over the rough London streets. In what seemed no time at all, they reached an elegant row of white town houses arranged in an arc, and stopped before one with a bronze door.

"That's mine?" Vivien asked hesitantly.

"That's yours," Grant said.

The driver held the horses, while Grant helped Vivien from the carriage. He lowered her to the ground, taking her weight until she gained her footing.

Vivien went into the house with him cautiously, waiting in the entrance hall while he lit lamps and drew back curtains. She went to a gilded console table that had been placed against the wall, with a framed mirror hung above it. There was a little gold tray for calling cards, and a delicate Staffordshire porcelain figurine beside it.

She picked up the figurine to examine it more closely. A gentleman and a lady, conversing while the lady bent over to pick wildflowers. But from the back view, the gentleman had pulled up his companion's skirts and pushed his hand beneath them.

Giving the object a scathing glance, Vivien set it back in place just as Grant returned to the entrance hall. From his expression, it appeared he'd already seen the back of the figurine.

"Charming," she said dourly. "This figurine, set right here *in the entrance hall*, tells me everything I need to know about my house."

"It shows a sense of humor," Grant suggested.

"An appalling lack of taste," she corrected,

and wandered past the circuit of main rooms, glancing through doorways. The town house had been tastefully decorated in a feminine style. There was nothing terribly objectionable about it, but she didn't like it. Perhaps it was the colors, all icy pastels. Or the spindly gilded furniture and shiny white stone flooring. Or the absence of books. It all felt cold and sterile. Lifeless.

"It doesn't look like a house where anyone *does* anything," she said, and stopped at the foot of the curved staircase. "My bedroom is up there?"

"Yes." Grant stayed close behind her as she began the climb to the next floor.

"I can manage the stairs on my own," Vivien told him.

"You might have a dizzy spell. Or trip."

She stopped on the steps and turned to face him. Grant was two steps below her, which brought their faces level. "You're being overprotective," she told him.

"It's my job," he said defensively.

"You don't have to stay at my heels every step of the way."

"I do, actually. It's in the manual."

"There is no manual for the Bow Street Runners," she said.

"It will be in the manual when a manual's written."

Vivien felt a laugh bubbling up, but she restrained it sternly. She turned and continued up the stairs, with Grant right behind her.

They reached the bedroom, where a richly carved poster bed had been set in the center of a carpeted pavilion. "The bed is on a stage," she said, taken aback, before asking sarcastically, "Is this a theater? Did I host meetings of an amateur dramatic club in here?"

Grant had gone to draw back the curtains. "I'll remind you," he said, "there's a very large portrait of you in here."

"But why?" she asked. "I certainly don't need to stare at a painting of myself in my own bedroom. And if someone else were here, presumably they wouldn't—" She fell silent, shocked as daylight poured in and illuminated the painting.

There was her naked body, arranged in a horizontal sprawl.

Vivien's eyes widened as she surveyed the startling expanse of pale skin. Deep curves, hips, breasts, nipples, a hint of intimate red curls between her thighs.

"*Ugh*," she exclaimed, and turned away, coloring deeply. "You should have warned me!"

Grant struck a match and lit the bedroom lamps. "I just told you there was a large portrait of you."

"You didn't say it was obscene."

"It's not obscene if it's art."

"Art is obscene if its only purpose is to incite lust!"

"Oh. Well, this definitely does that."

Gathering he had intended that as a compliment, Vivien gave him a withering glance.

"But it's also artistic," he added quickly. "The composition, and the . . . brushwork, it's . . ." He paused with an apologetic grimace. "Should I take the painting down?"

"Please." She decided to start looking for clothes, and headed to a massive wardrobe with triple doors on the other side of the room.

There was a scraping sound and a creak of the heavy frame as Grant hefted the painting and lowered it carefully.

"I'm giving you advance warning," Grant said as he turned the portrait to face inward and leaned it against the wall, "that if you don't like the painting, you're definitely not going to like what's in the—"

A protesting creak rent the air as Vivien pulled one of the heavy doors open.

"—wardrobe," Grant finished.

Vivien stared in bafflement at a collection of a half dozen oblong ivory and stone objects arranged on one of the shelves. They were of varying thicknesses and heights, many of them housed in glass-fronted boxes.

Phalluses, she realized dazedly.

Or perhaps the correct plural was *phalli*?

She felt herself turn crimson from head to toe.

"Why," she managed to ask, "would I collect statues of male reproductive organs?"

Grant approached her from behind, choosing

his words with obvious care. "They're not statues, exactly. They're more what I would call . . .
devices."

"A device for what?" she asked blankly.

"A lady might use one for her private pleasure. Or to enhance lovers' play with a partner." Seeing her lack of comprehension, he
added uncomfortably, "It's usually inserted . . .
somewhere."

She shook her head slowly. "My bedroom is a
chamber of horrors."

"Vivien, how the hell is it that you can recall
a complex chess gambit but you don't recognize
what those are for?"

"I don't know." Frowning, she reached for an
ivory cylinder and found it surprisingly heavy.
"But I'm sure I've never seen one of these. I
wouldn't begin to know what to do with it."

Now there was a tremor of laughter in his
voice. "I'd offer to show you, but I think you
might hit me with it."

"I wouldn't," she said. "I'm fairly sure it
would give you a concussion." She looked more
closely at the carved ivory in her hands. The detail was remarkable: skin texture, veins, ridges.
"It's obscene but well-crafted," she observed,
turning it in her hands. "What do you call one
of these?"

Grant cleared his throat before answering
brusquely, "Dildo."

"What an awkward word. It sounds like a

card-game penalty. Or a Scottish side dish." She gripped it in both hands and brushed her thumb over the indentation at the tip. "What's the etymology, I wonder?"

He sounded a bit strained. "I'm fairly sure that's *not* the question most people ask the first time they see one."

Absently she rolled the shaft between her palms. "It could have originated from Old Norse, or—"

"Vivien, for God's sake, stop playing with that and put it away."

Surprised by the unfamiliar rough note in his voice, she looked up at him.

Grant looked tense and agitated, and his color was high.

Contritely Vivien set the phallus back in the armoire. "I've embarrassed you," she said. "I'm sorry."

"I'm not embarrassed, I'm— Never mind." He had started to pace back and forth.

"I don't blame you for finding the discussion distasteful."

"It wasn't that."

"Then why are you cross?"

"I'm not cross."

"You're speaking loudly and scowling, and you look as if you want to smash something."

He gave her a speaking glance. "Men are suggestible, Vivien. Do you understand?"

"No."

"Certain sights or words cause . . . reactions.

Uncomfortable reactions that are difficult to control. Especially for a man who's been . . . inactive for some time, and therefore . . . flammable."

"But you haven't been inactive," Vivien said reasonably. "You're quite busy with your job, which—" She caught a glimpse of his body in profile as he stalked around the room like a caged tiger. And she realized what kind of activity he meant. "Oh."

To hide her chagrin, she turned back to the wardrobe. She discovered a compartmented tray containing trinkets, among them a weighted gold ball, little silver clamps, silk rope, gold chains, and something that resembled a curtain ring.

Grant was grumbling to himself while pacing. ". . . I'm turning into Cannon, damn it—the blasted monk of Bow Street. No life, no woman, just work—'Finished your work? Good, let's do some more'—" He broke off and looked alertly in Vivien's direction as he heard a series of tiny metallic chimes.

She had picked up one of the gold balls and was shaking it experimentally near her ear. "It's like a little bell," she said.

"Vivien," he growled, "put that away *now*."

"Are you really *that* flammable?" she asked, although she obeyed promptly. "Even when I'm at the other side of the room?"

"*Yes.*"

Contritely she put it away and closed the door. She went to investigate another section of the wardrobe and found shelves of dresses in every imaginable color. It was a dazzling array of silks, velvets, satins, each folded garment covered with a piece of thin translucent paper to protect fragile trim and beadwork. "So many," she exclaimed. "Why would one person need all of these?" She trailed her hand lightly across the rainbow of fabrics. "What was I wearing when we first met?"

"A mermaid gown. Soft green with gauze. There were sparkles at the top."

"You liked it?"

"Very much."

Vivien hunted through the collection until she found a dress that seemed to match the description. "Was it this one?" She shook out the dress and held it up for his inspection.

"That's it."

Vivien looked at it more closely. It was a beautiful green silk with white tulle sleeves and trim. "Shall I wear it to the ball?"

Grant shook his head, his gaze fastened on the dress. "Perhaps something else." Although his expression was carefully neutral, she could tell the memory of that encounter gave him little pleasure.

A wave of remorse came over her. She dropped the garment heedlessly to the floor and went to him. "Was I hateful to you?" she asked apologetically. "Did I say something dreadful?"

"No," he said. "You only set me back on my

heels, which I deserved. I was arrogant and naïve. At the time, I wouldn't have thought a woman as beautiful as you could have a single problem or difficulty."

"Was my situation all that difficult?" she asked skeptically. "Living as a kept woman?"

"None of us can ever really know what someone else's life is like."

Grant kept catching her off guard, saying things like that. He had an innate sense of fairness. A willingness to reevaluate and change his mind, and own up to his mistakes. And more empathy than even he realized. Vivien had the uncomfortable suspicion that he was a much nicer person than she had ever been.

"No matter who I was then," she told him, "it's not who I am now. And it's definitely not who I intend to be."

Grant's gentle hand came to the side of her face, his thumb grazing the edge of her cheekbone. "I like whoever you are. Past, present, and future."

Vivien smiled and stood on her toes to kiss his cheek. Grant turned his face and caught her mouth with his, the fit between them lush and warm and delicious. He searched gently, deepening the kiss until a moan stirred in her throat. She molded herself against him, quivering at the hard pressure of his aroused flesh, and her insides filled with butterflies.

"Vivien," he said, his voice a shade deeper

than usual, "if I could have a few minutes with you . . . to lie with you in my arms . . . I would treasure that memory to my last hour of life."

She looked up at him uncertainly. "You mean . . . now?"

"Here and now. With no one to notice what we do, or how long it might take."

"I . . ." A nervous laugh escaped her. "I'm not sure what you want."

"Only to give you pleasure. To know the taste and feel of you." He watched her closely, trying to interpret her expression. "I promise I wouldn't lose control. I wouldn't take any more than you decide to give."

"But you're not asking to become lovers," she said, needing to be clear.

Grant shook his head. "Not when I don't know whether you've made a promise to someone else. I can't risk destroying something you value, or giving you any cause for regret." He paused. "But I'll take a few stolen moments. If you will."

"And if I would rather not . . . ?" she asked cautiously. "Would you be angry?"

"Good God, no. How could I? You've already given me more happiness than anyone ever has."

"What?" Vivien asked, genuinely bewildered. "All I've done is lie in your bed for days at a time and ask for things."

"That was an excellent start."

She couldn't hold back a laugh.

"You make me happy without trying," Grant said. "It keeps surprising me. I'm happy when it's time to go home at the end of the day and I remember you're there. Or when we talk for two hours, and I thought it was only fifteen minutes. Or when we start at opposite sides of an argument but somehow bring each other to the middle where no one's right. I think I need that."

A grin curled her lips. She lowered her gaze to the lapels of his coat and smoothed them repeatedly. Feeling bashful and excited and nervous, she said, "I don't remember what to do. I wish I did. It's ridiculous to be a courtesan with no skills in the bedroom. You should ask for a game of chess—at least I might be competent at that."

Grant made a sound of amusement. "If it makes you feel better, lovemaking isn't nearly as complicated as chess." His mouth came to hers with tenderly erotic pressure. As he felt her respond, the kiss turned silken and teasing and endless. His fingertips charted the vulnerable line of her throat, the soft hollow where her pulse turned frantic. He toyed with the trim of her bodice before sliding his hand to the shape of her breast. She quivered as she felt him cup the round weight, his thumb playing over the nipple, until it tightened into a distinct bud beneath the fabric.

He kissed her more deeply, his mouth opening hers, his tongue exploring. She was filled with pleasure, brimming with it, until the sheer weight of sensation made her body list heavily against his.

Gradually he lifted his head, his green eyes bright and heat-drowsed. "Come lie with me," he urged. "You don't have to do anything. Just trust me."

She hesitated before nodding.

He crushed his mouth to hers in a brief, exultant kiss before he felt the need to reassure her once more, "I'll stay in control."

As if he'd ever given her reason to fear on that account.

"I'll stay in control too," she said.

Grant smiled, and gave her a look that made every hair on her body stand on end. "You can try," he said, and carried her to the bed.

It began to feel dreamlike as his mouth took hers over and over, in kisses that were lazy, languid, deep, urgent. He lowered himself to the cradle of her hips, careful not to crush her. It excited her unbearably to have the powerful weight of him braced above her, the hard jut of his erection riding the soft groove between her thighs. He slid forward with rhythmic precision, again and again. Slow, deliberate, endless. Each time it seemed to tighten cords of pleasure inside her, ratcheting a tension that went on without end.

The clothes between them were maddening. She tugged at them wildly, craving the feel of his skin.

Grant murmured for her to be patient, relax, but she writhed beneath him until finally he relented with a muffled laugh. His hand traveled along the fastenings of her bodice until the sides fell apart to reveal her white chemise. Grasping the edge of thin white cambric, he pulled it beneath her breasts, and caught one of the pink tips between his thumb and forefinger. Gently he pinched it into stiffness before bending to draw it into the wet heat of his mouth. She felt the flick of his tongue, the light nibble of his teeth.

He moved to her other breast, lavishing the nipple with wet swirls before sucking it deep and tight. Her vision blurred, lashes fluttering down.

Every movement was slow and deliberate as he made love to her, browsing over her body to find places that made her tremble and squirm.

She heard his low, vibrant murmurs as from a distance. "You're so beautiful here . . . and here . . . this curve . . . and this soft place . . ."

Her breath had started to come in aching sounds, no matter how she tried to keep quiet. His mouth skimmed over hers with flirting kisses before settling in a deep, delicious angle. At the same time, one of his hands drew up the front of her skirts and slid beneath her undergarments. Finding the patch of red curls, he parted them with soft strokes, caressing and smoothing until the tender, intimate flesh was spread open for whatever he wanted.

She was utterly lost now, unable to think or speak. All she could do was lie there gasping, waiting helplessly. He took her pleading moans into his mouth, while his fingers teased with exquisite lightness, playing at the wet entrance of her body. Her inner muscles began to clench and unclench repeatedly as if trying to grasp an elusive fingertip, while her hips rode up against his gentle, tormenting hand. His touch slid to the peak of her sex, tracing it with tiny circles of fire.

Her legs spread, inviting more, straining for relief from the impossible need. But his hand pulled back, and his body lifted, and for a shattering moment she thought he was leaving the bed. His name broke from her trembling lips. She struggled to sit up. He hushed her with a brief, hungering kiss and pressed her back down. Between one breath and the next, she felt him push her thighs wider, and then his mouth was on her in a searing liquid search, his tongue painting her intimately.

Nothing existed outside this room, this bed; there was only this man and the sensuous torture he inflicted without mercy. He tickled and stroked with that restless tongue, until her hips caught a high arch and held, while spasms of pure feeling rolled through her, shattering every nerve and thought and awareness. She stopped breathing—then, with a gasp and sigh, she relaxed into a deep, drowsy trance.

His hands cupped her bottom while he nuzzled

gently, seeming to understand how sensitive she was. Even the slightest touch was excruciating. She twitched and uttered a faint protest as she felt the tip of his tongue tracing the soft petals and hollows. But he persisted until it began to feel so good she didn't want him to stop, and her thighs fell open. He drew more shuddering pleasure from her, wringing it from every nerve, soothing her to peacefulness. As his mouth slid lower, she felt the prickle of his beard against her wet, tender flesh, and the peculiar sensation of his tongue entering her.

Realizing he intended to bring her to another climax, she began to wriggle in earnest. "No . . . please, I can't. *Really.* Grant . . ."

He relented with a quiet laugh and rolled off her, and pulled her against his chest.

After he'd held her for what could have been minutes or hours, Vivien restored her clothing and left the bed. Pleasure had loosened all her joints and bones, leaving her as limp as a damp kitchen rag.

"Where are you going?" came Grant's lazy voice.

She glanced back at him with a shy smile. He was a handsome sight, reclining on his side with his dark hair tousled. "To look at the dresses," she said.

"Come back here."

Vivien shook her head, amused, and continued to the wardrobe.

Before she began to sort through the clothing, however, she noticed a small picture on the wall. It wasn't at all in keeping with the rest of the house. It was a cheerful painting, decidedly amateurish, of an old stone-and-timber country cottage.

Why would she keep a picture like this in her bedroom? Had it been a gift? Had she painted it herself?

The longer she stared at the image, the more familiar it seemed.

Something about her stillness must have communicated itself to Grant. He left the bed and came to stand behind her. One forearm came to slide around her middle, and she leaned back into his sturdy support.

Together they studied the painting.

"I looked at it when I was here before," Grant said. "There are no identifying marks or words on the back."

"The cottage is familiar to me," Vivien said absently. "I think it's a place I visited, or perhaps even lived in."

The little house was set on a graveled lane, with an oak tree and pasture beside it. A fruit tree had been trained in a fan shape across a stone wall bordering the pasture.

"Is that an apple tree?" Vivien wondered aloud.

"It appears so." Grant reached out to touch the stonework of the wall and cottage. "Galleting," he commented. "It's a masonry technique. Small pieces of stone are pushed into the wet mortar between large stones or bricks to create a mosaic effect. You're most likely to see it in the southeast, in villages between the North and South Downs. That limits the search area."

"You're thinking of looking for the house?" she asked dubiously.

"I admit, it would be like trying to find a flea in a coal pit."

"Would it be worth the effort?"

"It's another piece to the puzzle." Grant pressed his lips to her temple. "The puzzle of your mysterious past."

"It's not a puzzle I'm going to like," she said glumly. "I'm sure of it."

He turned her to face him, and smoothed back her hair. "There's a reason no one remembers their entire past—the abridged version is all any of us can tolerate. The rest of it has to be left out for the sake of our sanity." A smile touched his lips as he added softly, "But there are a few moments we never want to forget."

Chapter Eight

✦

Just before they were to leave for the Lichfield ball, Grant tossed back a double brandy and went to wait in the entrance hall for Vivien. He'd seen little of her during the day. For hours, there had been mysterious preparations involving bath and hair and complexion. Mrs. Buttons, Miriam, and Vivien had consulted ladies' periodicals and made plans with a diligence Grant hadn't seen since Sir Ross and a group of district magistrates had met to discuss riot prevention.

After that, Mrs. Buttons had sent the footman, Peter, to the apothecary with a list of unfamiliar items to purchase, including rose water, Denmark wash, Circassian oil, pearl powder, and a preparation with the disturbing name of "Virgin's milk." Later there had been an alarming demand for some of the cartridge paper Grant used for guns, which apparently was needed for the use of curling tongs.

Left to his own devices, Grant had bathed, shaved, and dressed in black breeches, waistcoat and tailcoat, and a crisp white cravat tied in a simple knot. When it came to preparing for a formal occasion, as in so many things, the expectations for men were far lower than for women. Thank God.

Hearing Mrs. Buttons and Miriam chattering, he glanced up and saw them following Vivien to make last-minute adjustments to her gown and hair. She descended the stairs, managing a nervous smile as she saw him.

She was impossibly beautiful in a bronze silk gown with a high waist and a deeply scooped bodice. The fabric gleamed and flowed like liquid metal as she walked.

Her hair had been pinned at the crown of her head with shining red curls dangling around her temples and neck. Grant wanted badly to touch one of the perfect coils, but he knew there would be dire consequences from the other women after all the pains they had taken. Smiling, he glanced at the two servants and nodded in thanks.

"Well done," he said, and they both beamed in satisfaction.

Miriam came forward to wrap something around Vivien's shoulders, a length of bronze silk lined with fur on one side, before stealing away with Mrs. Buttons.

Grant looked back into Vivien's upturned face. Her fine-grained skin had been brushed with pearlescent powder, and her lips were touched with something that made them look rosy and soft.

"You're like something from a dream," he said simply. "Too beautiful to be real. I wish I were a poet—you deserve more than ordinary words."

"Thank you," Vivien said, her admiring gaze sweeping over him. "You look very fine."

"There's nothing to worry about tonight," Grant said. "I'll be there to watch over you. Sir Ross will attend as well, and he's assigned a Runner to surveil the estate grounds. All you need to do is make an appearance to demonstrate that you're alive and well."

"And whoever tried to kill me may decide to give it another try."

"Yes."

She looked wry. "At least there's that to look forward to."

"Do you want to call a halt to this?" Grant asked quietly.

"No, not after everyone's gone to such trouble. And if someone intends to do me harm, I'd rather try to flush him out now. I can't live with the constant anxiety of wondering. Nor can I stay with you forever."

"You could." Grant paused, lost in the intense blue of her eyes. "Forever."

Vivien blinked in bemusement.

Now was not the time, Grant thought, instantly annoyed with himself. His own feelings didn't need to be inserted into the situation. It wouldn't help her to have distractions or new things to worry about. He tried to mask his chagrin with a quick smile.

"The carriage is waiting," he said, and escorted her out.

The Lichfield ball resembled any other: a large London house, a small orchestra in the ballroom, the scent and stuffiness and noise produced by too many bodies crowded into overheated rooms. Grant had been invited to such events as a figure of curiosity, someone to make the evening more entertaining. But the attention he'd received on those occasions was nothing compared to the reaction as he escorted Vivien inside. Everyone in the vicinity, men especially, stared openly.

With her vivid red hair and stunning blue eyes, Vivien was like a bird of paradise among pigeons. Hers was not a subtle beauty. It was emphatic, extravagant, impossible to conceal. But that was no excuse for the way people ogled and stared, beyond the point of rudeness. It was almost a form of punishment. Which, perhaps, was the point.

Ill-mannered bastards, Grant thought, and did some narrow-eyed staring of his own, until a few of the onlookers averted their gazes.

Vivien's face was composed, but Grant felt her fingers bite through his sleeve into his arm.

"We're going to approach Lady Lichfield, who's receiving guests," he said. "She's the dark-haired one in the wine-colored gown. A word of warning: Sir Ross told me that Lady Lichfield's manner is best described as 'big "I" and little "you."'"

"She's a snob?"

"Worse than that. A self-appointed gatekeeper of the upper class. On top of that, there's a particular animosity between aristocratic women and those in the *demimonde*—usually because they're being maintained by the same men. Don't be surprised by anything she might say."

"I won't. I'm only surprised that Sir Ross was able to persuade Lady Lichfield to invite me."

"I suspect it has something to do with the fact that she's a widow who's interested in marrying again, and he's an eligible bachelor."

"Sir Ross isn't married?"

"He's a widower, wellborn, from a family of wealth and influence. He and Lady Lichfield move in the same social circles."

"Are they courting?"

"Thankfully, no. Since the death of his wife,

Cannon's only interest has been in work. It's why he's been nicknamed 'the monk of Bow Street.'"

As they waited in the grand Italianate main hall where Lady Lichfield was receiving guests, Grant heard a flurry of comments around them.

". . . is it really her?"

"Surely not. One of *her* kind, here . . . ?"

"Hasn't been seen . . ."

". . . Gerard's mistress . . ."

Grant glanced down at Vivien's face, which was carefully composed. "Try to look as if you're enjoying the attention," he murmured.

Instantly she forced a smile and sent a few provocative glances around the room.

Eventually Lady Lichfield finished her conversation. She glanced at Grant expectantly.

He brought Vivien forward and bowed. "Lady Lichfield, may I introduce Miss Duvall?"

Lady Lichfield responded with a regal nod as Vivien curtseyed.

"My lady," Vivien said quietly, "thank you for your kindness in inviting me this evening."

"I desire no thanks from you," Lady Lichfield replied evenly. "The invitation was extended only because Sir Ross requested it. Have no illusion that you'll ever be allowed back here again."

"I understand, my lady. I remain grateful nevertheless," Vivien said.

The poised and sincere reply seemed to annoy Lady Lichfield to no end. "Aren't you pretty?"

she said, every syllable etched with acid. "Fresh as a country maid—quite extraordinary in a woman so well-used. I've heard about your notoriety in Paris—"

"My lady," Grant interrupted brusquely, "you have a sharp tongue. Perhaps you should save the roasting and carving for the dinner table."

Lady Lichfield stiffened at the rebuke, and gave him a cold glance. "You're a well-liked and esteemed man, Mr. Morgan, with the potential to marry above yourself. One hopes your future prospects won't be damaged by association with a lightskirt."

Before Grant could reply, Vivien said hastily, "We won't keep you from your other guests, my lady."

She tugged Grant toward the ballroom, and he went with her reluctantly.

"The insufferable bitch," Grant muttered. "I apologize for her rudeness."

"It's not for you to apologize," she assured him. "And I was forewarned."

As they neared the ballroom, Grant saw Sir Ross Cannon conversing in a small group. His gaze met Grant's, and he turned to excuse himself from the discussion before coming forward.

"Sir Ross," Grant said, "allow me to introduce Miss Duvall."

The magistrate gave her a precise bow. "A pleasure."

Vivien curtseyed. "I'm so grateful for your help, Sir Ross. I'm in your debt."

"Not at all," Cannon said gently. "I only regret that you find yourself in an uncomfortable situation this evening."

Vivien shrugged. "The discomfort is outweighed by the potential benefits. That's why I'm thinking of this ball as a visit to the dentist."

Cannon regarded Vivien with the beginnings of one of his rare smiles.

Grant's gaze had swept over the ballroom during the exchange. "I just caught sight of Lord Gerard," he said. "From his slightly unhinged expression, I suspect someone's already told him that Vivien is here."

Vivien inched closer to him. "Which one is he?"

"Standing near the back corner, by the column," Grant said.

"The stocky, red-faced one?" Vivien frowned and averted her gaze before asking with difficulty, "Are there any other men here that I . . . that were mentioned in my book?"

"Lord Wenman," Cannon replied. "Wearing a black coat with gold braid, standing beside the potted palms. And Lord Hatton, the older gentleman talking to the footman."

Vivien took a deep breath and exhaled slowly. "Should I try to speak to each of them?"

"That won't be necessary," Grant replied, wanting to spare her the humiliation of facing her former lovers.

But to his annoyance, Cannon said, "It wouldn't hurt to stir the pot a bit."

"Very well," Vivien said, with the look of someone facing an unpleasant task.

"I'll go with you—" Grant was forced to break off as she brought her fingertips to his lips in a swift touch.

"I know how you hate to hear this," she said gently, "but there are some things better done without you. And I can't talk to anyone with you glaring over my shoulder."

"I wouldn't glare," Grant said defensively.

"You're glaring right now."

"In all fairness," Cannon told Vivien, "he can't help it. It's what his eyes do."

That seemed to amuse Vivien despite her tension. A brief grin crossed her face, before she squared her shoulders. "Allow me some time to maneuver," she told Grant. "I'll find you later."

As Vivien disappeared into the crowd, Cannon said thoughtfully, "I rather like her."

For Sir Ross Cannon, the praise was the equivalent of wild enthusiasm.

Grant set his jaw and said grimly, "I think I'm in love with her."

A long silence ensued as Cannon absorbed the statement. "That's . . ."

"Unprofessional?" Grant supplied when the magistrate seemed unable to think of a word. "Unfortunate? Idiotic?"

"Inconvenient," Cannon said.

"From what I've heard, love usually is inconvenient."

"No. Not 'usually.'" The magistrate paused before saying flatly, "Always."

Drawing attention to herself, Vivien thought, was the point of being here, no matter how uncomfortable it made her. Brazenly she wandered through the crowd, introducing herself to strangers, inserting herself into conversations, flirting indiscriminately, and laughing freely. She knew it was how she used to behave, although she didn't understand how she'd enjoyed it. A flush of embarrassment climbed her face, but she hoped people would attribute it to wine or excitement.

Some gentlemen fled as she approached, whereas others spoke to her readily. Some offered compliments, others made insinuations. And some stared rudely, assessing her body, her breasts, as if she were produce from the market.

The way women looked at her was much worse. She was a threat, someone to be mocked, feared, driven away. It was exhausting to pretend she was enjoying herself while being chastened by so many hostile glances.

Needing respite, she made her way to the side of the ballroom, where a long row of glass-paned doors led outside. The glass was frosted with condensed evening mist. It was so hot in here, so noisy and stifling. Longing for the feel of cool air on her skin, she considered slipping out into the damp, dark night.

Someone else was standing near the doors—a young man barely out of his teens. He was drinking champagne a bit awkwardly, not seeming to know how to hold the tall champagne flute. After glancing at her with a quick, shy smile, he experimented with holding the glass at the base.

Vivien wandered closer to him, and dipped into a curtsey. "Vivien."

"Harry." He bowed, nearly spilling the champagne.

"Are you enjoying the ball, Harry?"

"You mean this gaseous swamp full of vultures picking over rubbish? Who wouldn't?"

Vivien smiled. "It's not *that* terrible."

"It is. You think so too, I can tell."

As she saw him adjust his hold on the glass, Vivien couldn't resist advising, "If you touch the bowl of the flute, it will make the champagne warm. Try holding the stem with your thumb and three fingers."

"Sensible." Harry grasped the stem and drank, and she noticed the glimmering clear stones at his shirt cuffs as his wrist lifted.

"What lovely cuff buttons," she said.

"They're just rock crystal backed with foil. My grandfather said he'll give me diamond ones when I'm older. If I'm a good boy."

Vivien smiled regretfully. "You shouldn't be seen with me, then."

"Are you a bad influence?"

"The worst."

"Oh, goody—stay right here."

"And jeopardize your chance at diamond buttons?"

"To hell with my buttons. I'm bored to pieces, and you're the only interesting person here."

"May I ask why you're at the ball in the first place?"

"I've been compelled by my grandfather. I'm supposed to practice mingling in society, and then I'm to find a suitable girl to marry and beget brats." He paused to down the rest of his champagne. "My older brother was supposed to do all of that, but now I've had to take his place."

It was then that Vivien noticed the black crepe armband on his coat sleeve. A sign of mourning for a loved one. "Oh, dear," she said softly. "I'm so very sorry, Harry."

He gave a brief shake of his head at the condolence. Too painful. "I don't suppose you're available?" he asked.

"For what?"

"To marry."

Vivien shook her head with a disconcerted smile. "I'm a woman of ill repute, common-born, and too old for you, besides. Go find a wonderful girl who loves you."

"The devil you're too old—what's your age?"

"I—" She broke off and looked at him in wondering dismay. She had no idea.

"Never mind, then," Harry said. "You're obviously still young enough to breed. You'll do for me."

Amused, she gave him a glance of mock reproof. Before she could reply, however, she heard a low, harsh voice from nearby.

"Harry."

A tall, lean older man had come to stand a few yards away, glaring at them both. His face was long and angular, cheekbones sharp above deeply hollowed cheeks. "Come here, boy," he grated.

Harry turned to Vivien. "The old codger with the face of an undertaker is my venerable grandfather. I'm being summoned—and will likely be punished for the sin of talking with a beautiful girl who made me happy for two and a half minutes."

"Be kind," she murmured.

"To him?"

"And yourself."

Harry reluctantly went to his stern-faced grandfather, who continued to stare at Vivien.

Vivien was perplexed by the venom in the old man's gaze. It was more than snobbery or disapproval. It seemed . . . personal. It made her want to slink away and find a place to hide.

But just as she decided to go in search of Grant,

she was startled by the sudden appearance of a stocky, ruddy-faced man—Lord Gerard. He took both her hands in a possessive grip and stood too close, breathing sour puffs of wine-scented air into her face. His hands were moist, his eyes bloodshot, his complexion damp and spotty. It required all her patience and will to keep from recoiling.

"My God, Vivien," he said in a strained voice. "I literally thought you were dead. How could you disappear like that? Have you no concern for what you've put me through? I had no way to reach you or assure myself of your well-being."

She thought of the pages and pages she had written about her relationship with this man. The intimacies they had shared. Had she felt any genuine desire for him? How could she not have found it revolting?

"William, poor darling," she exclaimed contritely. "I had no choice, I wasn't able. I've had a dreadful time of it."

"Have you been ill?"

"Not ill, exactly. But not well, either."

"Someone said you'd arrived with Mr. Morgan. Is that true?"

Vivien tried to look coquettish. "Perhaps."

"He came to my home to question me, did you know that? About *you*. Why are you here with him?"

"There's no need to worry, William. He won't

trouble us. In fact, he would do anything to please me."

But Lord Gerard didn't look reassured. In fact, he had begun to stare oddly at her.

"You look different," he said.

She raised her brows and looked at him in mock-alarm. "Different? In what way?"

"Something about you has changed."

"I've been through *ordeals*, darling. You simply have no idea. But I'm the same woman."

"Are you?"

"Of course, silly boy." She lowered her voice conspiratorially. "I'm the one who tied you to my bedpost with the belt of my dressing robe. Remember?"

Although that seemed to ease his mind, a trace of suspicion lingered in his gaze. "Slip away and meet me outside," he said. "I need to speak with you in private."

"Where?"

"The lower gardens. I'll be waiting."

After Lord Gerard had left her, she went to another set of doors at the side of the ballroom, waited for a minute, and inconspicuously slipped out to the covered terrace.

There was a movement in the shadows near a support column. Her heart stopped, and she froze.

"It's me," came Grant's quiet voice.

She let out a breath and went to him. He was so big and steady, so infinitely self-assured, she wanted to throw herself into his arms. Instead, she stood in front of him with her fingers knitting together.

"Lord Gerard wants to meet," she said. "In the lower gardens."

"Stay in view of the house. Don't go past the wrought iron gates, understand?"

"Why not?"

"There's a wooded copse and a pond, and I don't like the looks of it." Grant paused before adding darkly, "And make the conversation short, or I'm coming to fetch you."

Chapter Nine

❧

The slope at the back of the manor had been cut in a succession of three terraces. A wide, angled flight of steps led to the expanse of lower lawn, bordered by carefully clipped yews. It was an old-fashioned garden, perfectly manicured with geometrically shaped flower beds and box-edged paths. At the farthest end of the lower gardens, a set of wrought iron gates was backed by the inky darkness of an oak-and-hazel copse.

Vivien wandered through the lower garden, pausing as she heard Lord Gerard's whisper. "This way." A hand wormed between the scrolls of the gate, a finger waggling at her.

In spite of Grant's admonition, she had no

choice but to go through the gate. Reluctantly she went to Gerard, leaving the iron door open.

Lord Gerard was waiting for her in a blue wash of moonlight, his face as pale and formless as blancmange. He made a sudden move to embrace her, and she drew back at once.

"A tease, as ever," he said with a thick laugh.

"What did you want to talk about?" she asked.

He shook his head, studying her. "You're not the Vivien I remember," he said.

"Of course I am. Don't be silly."

"Where have you been all this time?"

She let a sharp note enter her voice. "I don't want to discuss it, or I may cry, and you know how my eyes swell up."

"Did it have to do with your . . . *ahem* . . . little problem?" At her silence, he prompted, "Your condition. Did you have it remedied?"

Vivien was tongue-tied with astonishment. She tried for a sarcastic tone. "What do you think?"

"Obviously you did. What about your betrothal? Did your prospects fall through? I wasn't sure before who it was, but in light of recent events, I think perhaps he might be . . . gone? Permanently?"

"What business is that of yours?"

"Come back to me. You need a protector."

"I already have one."

"Don't say it's Morgan," Gerard exclaimed. "A common thief-taker?"

"He has his uses. And he amuses me for now."

"He can't afford you."

"He's done well for himself. And he has much to offer."

"He's a bruiser. A plodder. He'll bore you to tears before long."

Vivien turned to face away from him, pretending to pout as she looked up at the house. "The night air is too cold. I'm going back inside."

"Vivien." Gerard approached her from behind and grasped her gloved arms, his hands sliding in a downward caress. "Leave Morgan and come back to me. He can't do for you what I can. You know that."

"Do you expect me to discuss it with you out here?"

"When may I visit you?"

"I'll send a note. But first I'll have to make arrangements. Now . . . let's return to the ballroom separately. You first."

"One kiss before I go," Gerard demanded.

"I couldn't stop at one, darling. Go now."

He sighed heavily and walked away. Vivien rubbed her tense shoulders as she listened to the rustle of his retreating footsteps.

Little problem, she thought. *Condition.* What exactly did he think she'd "remedied"? So far, she thought miserably, everything she learned about her past made her feel worse.

She waited one minute. Two.

Just as she turned toward the house, she

jumped at the sound of the iron gate clanging shut.

Her heart started pounding hard against her ribs as she glanced at the closed metal latch. Had Lord Gerard returned?

"William?" she asked cautiously.

No reply. No one was there.

But she could hear someone circling. Someone was with her in the lower gardens.

A pulse leaped in her throat, wrists, knees. Galvanized with fright, she picked up her skirts and bolted toward the closed gate.

Heavy footsteps crashed through grass and leaves. She yelped as someone grabbed her and tossed her to the ground. The impact stunned her, but she climbed to her feet and tried to run. She was caught again from behind, and she struggled in the darkness, pushing, kicking with her slippered feet, letting out muffled cries.

She heard the metal shriek of the gate as it was flung open. There was a terrifying muted bellow, a man shouting, before she was released so abruptly she went careening.

Just before she fell again, she was scooped up and lifted against a brutally hard surface. A familiar voice broke through her panic. "Vivien."

It was Grant. He was breathing hard, his hold crushing around her. "I have you," he said. He called out curtly to someone running past them. "Through the copse, to the right."

Vivien clung to Grant in bewilderment. There were footsteps and movements everywhere—she couldn't make sense of anything.

Carefully he set her on her feet, and kept her against him. "Do you know who that was?"

"I'm not sure but I—I think—" She lifted her hand, fingers curled tightly around a small, hard object. She'd pulled it from her attacker during the struggle.

Someone carrying a hand lantern came to them. It was Sir Ross, his face taut with concern.

Grant was looking down at her shaking fist. "What is that?" he asked. "Show me."

She opened her hand in the light . . . and a rock crystal glittered in her palm.

"A cuff button," Grant said.

Vivien stared at it, dumbfounded. "It was Harry," she said. Shocked and hurt, she broke into tears. "This was from his sh-shirt cuff. But *why*? There was no reason—" She turned her face against Grant's shoulder and began to sob.

He cuddled her closer. "The boy you were speaking with before you came outside?" she heard him ask, and she nodded. Grant spoke to Sir Ross. "Harry Axler. Lord Lane's grandson."

The magistrate was frowning. "Flagstad was the one in pursuit."

"I could tell," Grant said sourly. "He runs like a landed harbor seal. What's on the other side of the trees?"

"A hill that leads to the main drive."

"Christ. Axler will be long gone in five minutes." Grant began to ease Vivien away from him. "If you'll watch over her, Cannon, I'll catch the little bastard."

"No," the magistrate said evenly, "stay with Miss Duvall. There are very few places Axler can go. I'll see to it that he's found and hauled into the Bow Street strong room for questioning." His voice gentled as he spoke to Vivien. "Miss Duvall, may I have the cuff button?"

She gave it to him. "I didn't say anything to provoke him," she managed to say. "I don't know what made him do this. I didn't behave in a way that would have caused him to—"

"Dear lady," Sir Ross said, his expression filled with concern, "men are equipped with reason and intellect—we're not ravening beasts at the mercy of our own impulses. No matter what you may have said or done, it wasn't your fault. The boy will bear full responsibility for his actions. Set your mind at ease."

"I'll take her home," Grant told Sir Ross. "But when Axler is brought in, I want to question him."

"Absolutely not. I'll handle the boy. You're to go nowhere near him, Morgan."

Grant didn't reply. The muscles of his arms and chest were whipcord taut.

Vivien could feel the thrills of fury running through him. "Please, Grant," she whispered, "take me home."

She felt the change in him then, his muscles loosening slightly, his chest rising and lifting with a controlled breath.

"Anything you want," Grant said, looking down at her. "Anything at all."

Vivien waited with Sir Ross while Grant went to tell the driver to bring the carriage partway down the drive, where they could enter the vehicle relatively unobserved. She was shaken and a bit bruised, but the worst damage had been done to her spirit. Nothing about what had happened made sense. She had shared a brief but pleasant conversation with a young man, had liked him, and then had been assaulted by him for no apparent reason.

Sir Ross was right in saying she wasn't to blame—she knew that. But she couldn't help feeling the fault lay in herself. She felt ruined. Tainted.

"You did well tonight," Grant said quietly as the carriage rolled away from the Lichfield manor. "I know it was difficult, but you set yourself to the task despite what it cost you. There's nothing I admire more than that kind of courage."

Vivien was unable to speak, but she formed the words *thank you*, and wiped at her welling eyes.

Grant pulled a handkerchief from his coat and gave it to her.

Vivien blew her nose and cleared her throat. "I hate the way people look at me," she eventually said. "It's humiliating. It feels as if every man I ever slept with has taken a piece of me."

"No," Grant said firmly. "Look at me, Vivien." He took her face in his hands, looking into her blurred eyes with anguished tenderness. "You're a complete human being—no missing pieces. You belong only to yourself." His thumbs wiped over her wet cheeks. "The house we just left," he continued, "is full of sodding hypocrites who've never worked a day in their lives. To the upper class, a woman is only one of two things: someone to bear their pedigreed children, or someone to satisfy their sexual needs. What you need is a working man."

"I do?"

He nodded. "That's the kind who'll treat you as a partner. He'll love you, fight for you, raise children with you, and keep your bed warm. A working man knows he has to take care of what belongs to him—including his woman."

"Does a working man think his woman belongs to him?"

His voice was very soft. "Just as he belongs to her."

Vivien stared at him, mesmerized and nearly sick with longing.

"What is it?" he asked softly.

She shook her head, her throat too tight to speak.

A gently mocking smile curved his lips. "It's too late to turn coward now. Say it."

"I want all that," she burst out. "I want it with you, and it's impossible."

"It's already yours." His mouth came to hers, fierce and tender, crushing a faint sob into silence, absorbing the salt of her tears. It was a kiss that demanded and offered, ravishing deeply, tasting and exploring until a jostle of the carriage ended it. Grant held her tightly and muffled a quiet groan against her hair. "I love you," he said. "So much it hurts. I never knew my heart could do this."

"You don't even know me."

"I know enough. You're smart, kind, and beautiful, and you love books, and you're someone I want to talk to for the rest of my life. I know I want you in my bed every night. As far as I'm concerned, the rest is all details."

"My past—all the men I—"

"Details." Grant settled back in the carriage seat, taking her with him.

"How can you be so cavalier about it?"

His hand came up to toy with a long red curl that had come loose from her coiffure. "The people who took me in after the workhouse—the Keeches—always used to say, 'We serve a god of second chances.'"

"Are you religious?"

"Not particularly, but if I had to choose a god, that's the one for me." He let out a breath of laughter. "I have an endless supply of second chances for you, Vivien." Turning his head, he pressed his lips against her forehead. "I'm not afraid of your mistakes, if you're not afraid of mine."

"I'm sure mine are worse," she said dolefully.

"We'll compare later."

"There are things you don't know about me," she persisted. "There could be terrible surprises."

"I'm not afraid of those, either." He adjusted her more comfortably in the crook of his arm. "I'm willing to bet, Vivien, that the things I love about you won't change a damn bit."

Chapter Ten

The hour was sufficiently late that Miriam was the only servant waiting up when they returned home. As the cookmaid saw Vivien's disheveled condition, she gave a little exclamation.

"The ball was a success," Grant reassured her in an easy manner. "There was a little mishap near the end, when Miss Duvall slipped on a patch of lawn in the gardens, but thankfully, no one saw."

Vivien gave Miriam a wan smile. "If you'll bring hot water to my room and leave it outside the door, that will be all for tonight."

"Won't you need help with your dress, miss?"

"No, I'll manage. Go have some well-deserved rest."

The cookmaid went to fetch the water, while Grant accompanied Vivien upstairs.

Vivien felt much better after the carriage ride. Still shaken, and nervous, but in the middle of the turmoil, there was a definite feeling of . . . optimism? Hope?

Ever since that night she'd been pulled from the Thames, she had felt as if she were walking through heavy fog, unable to see more than a few inches in any direction. She was tired of questions with no answers, having no connection to anyone or anything, being afraid without being sure what there was to be afraid of.

But it was clear now that she needed to start living again, with or without her memory. And whatever direction her life took, it would have to include this man.

She had loved Grant since the first evening they'd spent in his library, reading and drinking wine and kissing. The sight of all that virility and brawn, sprawled in an armchair with a book in hand, had fixed her heart on him for good. She loved it that he was a seasoned Bow Street Runner, a man's man, with a secret romantic streak. She loved his green eyes, and the little lines at the corners that crinkled when he smiled. She loved his mind, sharp and empathetic and curious. She loved him for things she hadn't even learned about him yet.

They reached the bedroom door, and Grant stopped at the threshold.

"Will you come in?" Vivien asked.

He entered without hesitation, but there was something tense, extra-aware, in his movements.

Neither of them, she realized, was quite sure what was going to happen tonight. It was either going to be nothing or everything. But if it was going to be everything . . . they had to find the right words, together, to make every tumbler in the lock turn.

He went to the bedroom hearth and picked up a slender poker, stirring the fire in the grate. The flare of heat sent a dance of light and shadow over his face. What a beautiful profile he had, the nose straight and strong, the jaw sharply angular.

"Grant," she said thoughtfully, "if there's someone I made promises to . . . someone who cared about me . . . I can't help wondering where he is. Shouldn't he be searching? Shouldn't he have come forward? If it were you, wouldn't you have already gone to the police?"

He replaced the poker in the stand and said flatly, "I'd have torn up half of London by now."

"I don't think he exists. No one's trying to find me. And I'd rather you didn't worry about doing something I might regret. I'll decide what I need." She took a quick, steadying breath before saying, "Which is you. Tonight, and every night."

Grant turned slowly to face her, his expression unreadable.

It felt as if all the oxygen in the room had been replaced by yearning. She was breathing it in, feeling it heat her skin like firelight.

"You've had a shock," he said carefully.

"Yes. It was a nasty reminder that some men aren't to be trusted. But why should I let that keep me apart from someone I do trust?" She took such pleasure in the sight of him standing in front of her, the powerful, rangy build, his watchful stillness. "Don't leave me alone tonight," she said.

He came to her in swift strides, gathering her against him so tightly that her heels left the floor. "You have to be sure," he said, his voice raw and scraped. "I have to be more to you than a port in a storm."

Vivien slid her arms beneath his coat, around his lean midriff. "You're both," she said. "The port *and* the storm. You're darkness and lightning, and most of all you're my safe harbor."

Grant sought her mouth with his, trying hard to be gentle, even as every muscle was charged with the force of what he felt and what he wanted. "Vivien," he said after his mouth lifted, "I'm no coward—a man doesn't last long in my profession if he is. But for the first time in years, I'm terrified. You're going to regain your memory, and you may decide to leave me, and I don't know what will become of me."

Vivien tried to think of how to reassure him. "Whatever I remember," she said slowly, "my feelings for you—what I want with you—won't change."

"You don't know that."

"But I do. I've had the chance to look at my own life as a stranger would, and I could never go back to it. I lived in a town house that wasn't at all a home. I slept with men who didn't even look for me when I disappeared. I don't see any meaning in the way I was living. That's why I'm going to change it—with or without you." She paused, her eyes smarting as she brought herself to admit, "But I would grieve to lose you."

"You won't lose me."

He kissed her again, with deep, dizzying ardor, until her heart was pounding and every part of her thrummed with excitement. It no longer mattered whether this was foolish, wise, too soon, or too late. It was necessary. Inevitable.

The kiss broke into other kisses . . . slow, hot, languid, urgent . . . kisses that spoke without words . . . *I love the intimate parts of you, the private spaces only I can touch, the wondrous softness inside you . . . I love your taste, scent, heat . . . I love your flesh, the rise and pulse and shiver of you wanting me . . .*

After a long time, Grant lifted his head, his breath cutting ragged places in the silence. He went to the door, found the brass hot water can outside the threshold, and brought it to the bedroom washstand. After pouring the steaming water into the pitcher, he invited her to come to him with a slight tilt of his head.

Shyly Vivien went to him, and turned to let him unfasten the back of her dress.

His warm hands settled on her bare shoulders, the gentle touch drawing a quiver from her. His hands moved down the row of buttons, loosening the dress by degrees, until it dropped to the floor in a shimmering circle. She stepped out of the pooling fabric and kicked off her slippers. As she faced him in her chemise, gooseflesh rose on every inch of exposed skin.

Grant sank easily to his haunches in front of her, his fingers sliding up her stocking to the place where her garter cinched her thigh. She looked down at his dark head, her hands fluttering to his broad shoulders as he untied her garters and unrolled the stockings.

"Will you tell me what to do?" she asked bashfully. "I wish I could remember my skills."

He flicked a laughing glance up at her. "We'll have to make do with my skills."

"I want to please you—"

"Shhh . . ." Grant breathed the word against the chemise where it covered her tummy, heat sinking through the fragile layer of muslin to her skin. "Just relax."

She quivered, and her knees lost all their starch.

In a moment he rose to his feet, removed his coat, and rolled up his shirtsleeves, every movement relaxed and deliberate. He reached for a silk sponge, soaked it with hot water, and squeezed it over the washbasin.

Vivien stood as if under a spell, while he bathed her one area at a time. Face, neck, arms, upper back, and chest, each gently cleansed and dried in turn. It held the gravity of ritual . . . the sluice of water in the basin . . . wisps of steam uncurling in the air . . . the dance of light from the hearth.

There was nothing overtly sexual in what Grant was doing, no intent to arouse. But none of the lascivious details in the red leather book were half as seductive as this quiet act of caring for her. She turned weak with arousal and antici- pation, butterflies swirling as the chemise was finally lifted away and discarded.

Grant paused for an instant at the sight of her naked body, his breath stopping.

A blush encompassed her as he knelt again, this time pulling a footstool from beneath the washstand. He grasped her ankle and guided her to prop up a foot. She held on to his shoul- ders for balance, while her lungs strained to accommodate her need for more air. Slowly he washed and rinsed her legs. The sponge moved to the shadowed cove between her thighs, every movement careful and reverent as he bathed her intimately.

"I know you and I have our differences when it comes to artistic judgment," Grant murmured, carefully blotting the damp patch of red hair with the towel, "especially when it involves nudity." He set down the towel and slid one hand behind her hips, while his other hand went to the glinting curls, toying gently with them. "But you, sweet love, are a work of art. There's nothing in the world more beautiful than you."

He pulled her hips closer, his fingers spreading the curls, and his face nuzzled against her. A quiver ran through her as his tongue parted the soft furrow of her sex. He licked again, a longer, deeper stroke, opening her, tracing the intricate pleats and petals. Whimpers came from her throat no matter how she tried to hold them back. His hands came to her bottom, cupping the round fullness to grip her in place as his tongue found the tiny, exquisitely sensitive peak of her clitoris. She froze, half crouched over him, panting and transfixed by the slow circling . . . languid flicking . . . and there was a sort of tickling flutter that drove her mad. Her trembling fingers slid into his hair, trying to pull him against her as she begged silently *oh please faster harder more* but he was ruthless in his patience.

She felt his fingertip stroking the wet entrance to her body, wriggling slightly before he was able to slide the length of his finger inside her. It was uncomfortably tight, her inner muscles working against the intrusion, but the distracting teasing never ceased. His mouth was pulling at her with a full, open kiss, stroking and tugging, building a powerful current of sensation.

Her body began to clench around his finger, over and over, and he followed the rhythm, nudging deeper, deeper, until a great wave of feeling rolled up to her and there was no stopping it. She began to shudder, helpless against the long spasms that wrung pleasure from every inch of her body.

Just as her limbs began to fold, Grant scooped her up easily and carried her to the bed. Before she'd even settled fully onto the mattress, his mouth had found her again. Her legs spread, and she writhed as he licked and soothed every last twitch of sensation into peacefulness. His lips skimmed down to the inside of her thigh where the flesh was soft and plump, and she jerked a little as she felt his teeth in the gentlest of bites.

He stood and unbuttoned his waistcoat while gazing down at her with avid hunger, taking in every detail.

Self-consciously Vivien rolled to her side and lifted a hand to her breast.

A quizzical smile touched his lips. "Are you being shy with me?"

For a moment she thought he was going to mock her. But his voice and touch were tender as he pressed her back down and kissed the space between her breasts. "You can't be shy, you're a goddess, you're so beautiful . . . everywhere . . ."

His hand passed along her front as if he were stroking a stretching cat.

With an unsteady sigh, Grant pushed up from the bed and went to the washstand, stripping off his shirt along the way. Her eyes widened at the stunning sight of his back, long and coursed with deep muscle. Without a trace of modesty, he shed the rest of his clothes and proceeded to wash himself.

His body had been honed and punished and exercised until no trace of softness remained. A heavy dark fleece covered his chest, and there was more hair on his arms, legs, and groin. There were a few faded scars, gilded in the light like veins of gold caught in granite. She wanted to feel all the textures of him, rough and smooth. She wanted to be weighed down by him, holding all that masculine power in her embrace.

When he was clean and dry, Grant returned to the bed with a little flask from the washstand cabinet. One corner of his mouth quirked at her questioning glance. "You're very tight," he murmured, setting the flask on the table beside the bed. "This might help."

She had to ponder his meaning for a few seconds. A scorching blush crept up her face. "I'm sorry—" she began awkwardly.

"No, no . . ." Grant sat beside her and gathered her up against him. "It's natural for a woman who's been without a man for a while." One of his hands eased up and down her naked back. "But it also happens when a woman is nervous. Or reluctant."

"I'm not reluctant. Not in the least."

"I wouldn't blame you, love, if you wanted to wait."

"Stay," she said earnestly.

Grant looked into her eyes, assessing her sincerity. "If you change your mind at any moment, say one word and I'll stop right away. Do you understand?"

"Yes. But I won't want to stop." She kissed him and tried to pull him to the bed with her. It was like trying to topple a brick wall.

Looking amused, Grant arched a brow. "What are you doing?"

"I want you to lie with me." Vivien linked her arms around his neck. "I want you to show me the things nice people do in bed," she whispered.

That drew a low laugh from him. He eased down to the mattress and rolled, taking her with him.

She gasped at the feel of his naked body all along hers, the scratchy-soft chest hair against the tips of her breasts, the searing brand of his aroused flesh. Her hand trembled a little as she dared to reach down and touch the heavy shaft, the silken skin overlaying steely hardness. Fascinated, she drew her fingers along the length of it, vibrant with heat and pulses, down to the velvety weights below.

"You're much handsomer than my statues," she said.

He buried a husky laugh in her hair. "Thank you. I hoped you wouldn't regret leaving your collection at the town house."

She tried to wrap her fingers around him, but they wouldn't touch. "You're also larger," she said, a flush rising in her face.

"Possibly," he said modestly, his eyes twinkling. He bent to kiss the soft hollow of her throat. "But there's no need to worry. All you need, love, is some proper attention."

Five minutes after Grant had started lavishing Vivien with the head-to-toe attention she deserved, he knew that making love to her would be the greatest experience of his life. A half hour after that, he wasn't sure he was going to survive the night at all. People could die from pleasure like this—it could stop the heart from beating.

The taste of her skin, veiled by hints of soap and perfume, was almost maddening. Uneven blushes rose to her skin, and he followed the blossoming pinkness all over her, taking his time. She was so sensitive, so responsive, that even the lightest touch made her tremble and squirm.

When he reached her breasts, he spent long minutes kissing the pale curves, suckling the peaks until they were tightly budded. Her hips had begun to stir beneath him, a tiny rhythmic movement that pushed up against his weight and set him on fire.

To his delight, she was no passive partner, but instead explored him with an eagerness that aroused him wildly. Her soft mouth . . . those small hands wandering artlessly over his back and torso . . . as if she were discovering a man's body for the first time. This was something new, this blend of liking and lust and love, more addicting than any drug the apothecary's art could devise.

Vivien climbed over him, and he rolled to his back obligingly, helping her to straddle him. The feel of her naked skin against his was unholy torture. Some of her hair had slipped from its pins, the locks dangling like strands of fire. He was dying to have her like this—to hold her hips and thrust inside her—

No. Too soon for that. She needed time to become accustomed to him. She needed his patience.

Unaware of his struggle for self-control, she leaned down to kiss him. No one had ever kissed him quite the way she did, feeling his mouth with hers, softly consuming as if he were a delicacy set out for her enjoyment. Teasing lips, catlike tongue, lapping sweetly, taking little tastes of him. Her mouth shaped to his, and her soft hum of pleasure resonated all the way down his spine.

He fumbled to retrieve the flask of almond oil from the bedside table, pushed out the stopper with his thumb, and shook a few drops into his other hand.

Vivien held still, her lashes lowering as she felt him massage the oil between her thighs. The heady fragrance of almonds, rich and bitter-sweet, spread through the air. Grant knew he'd never be able to smell it again without becoming aroused.

Slowly he played with the intricate shape of her, the petals and silky-wet warmth, and let a fingertip enter her. She stiffened a little, her thighs gripping his sides. The oil had made her slick and gleaming, but it still wasn't easy; the inside of her body had clamped against him.

"Relax," Grant whispered, using his other hand to spread the damp red curls and tease all around the little pearl of her clitoris. She trembled as he pressed his finger deeper. "Am I hurting you?" he asked quietly.

Her brows drew together, as if she were deep in concentration, and she shook her head.

She was fever-hot inside, so lush and wet, and he wanted nothing more in life than to be part of her, fused and held until there was no separation between them.

With endless patience, he caressed in her in a delicate, deliberate rhythm, sensing her responses and urging them higher, tenderly, as if he were blowing hot coals into flame. The silence was broken by her stifled whimper, and another, and then she couldn't hold back. Her hips nudged forward against his hands, again and again. Her inner muscles clenched hard around his finger, and he slid it deep, stoking the pleasure, thrusting and teasing without stopping. She arched with a cry, hard spasms rippling through her.

Grant drew the sensations out as long as possible, until she collapsed on his chest with a moan. He cradled her in his free arm while his other hand stayed between her thighs.

She was limp, breathing deeply, relaxed in every limb.

But still so tight inside.

He began to add a second finger, but she wriggled evasively, and he withdrew his hand.

"Let me," he coaxed. "I'll be gentle."

Vivien rolled to her back willingly, and he took her mouth in a hungering kiss before reaching for the oil again. A few more drops to make his fingers slippery, and then he parted her swollen furrow with the gentlest of touches. Eventually she was relaxed and stretched enough that he was able to work two fingers inside. Her hips froze in an arch, as if she couldn't decide whether to welcome the invasion or try to throw him off.

He lowered his head and ran his tongue up to the top of the soft little notch, finding the half-hidden bud, and began to lick steadily until her knees drew up and she made an agonized sound, and climaxed violently.

Unable to wait any longer, he settled between

her thighs, and gently rubbed the head of his shaft into the wet cove of her sex. The air was perfumed with sweet almond and salt and hot skin. He pressed with careful intent, even as tremors of longing ran through him. But there seemed no way to enter without hurting her. Changing the angle, he tried again, without success. He went still, every nerve screaming in protest at the prospect of stopping.

"Sweetheart," he said reluctantly, "tonight is still too soon for you."

"No," she protested, "I want you now."

"I don't think—"

"Come closer to me. Closer." She reached down to the stiff length of him, guiding him into place and wrapping her legs around his hips, and his mind went blank.

Blindly he pushed into the molten heat, feeling the tightness gradually give way, and a savage groan of relief escaped him. He lunged deep, was powerfully gripped and squeezed, and his hips rolled once, twice, before a release broke over him, shocking in its strength, and pleasure exploded and poured all through him.

Vivien awakened to the sight of pale dawn light tiptoeing its way across the floor toward the bed. She felt stiff and sore. It smarted a little between her thighs. The muscles running along the insides of her legs were strained. But the soreness reminded her of the previous night with Grant, and brought a faint smile to her lips. Now she would always know how it felt to have him inside her, being possessed and pleasured inside and out. He'd been so tender, so absorbed in her, so attentive to every need. She dimly recalled him wiping her with a damp cloth, and bringing a cold compress for the hot soreness between her thighs, and holding her while she slept. In fact, she thought he might have even changed the compress for a fresh one later on, which had been very considerate.

But where was he now? Disgruntled, she sat up and winced at a twinge of discomfort.

"Don't move," came Grant's curt voice. It was the same tone a person would use to warn someone who was standing on the edge of a cliff, or perhaps near a large spider. Vivien held obediently still, watching as he walked into the room with a small tray. "Let me help you," he said more quietly, and set the tray on the bedside table.

He arranged a neat stack of pillows behind her and guided her to sit back against them.

Vivien took advantage of his closeness by pressing a kiss to his shaven cheek. "Good morning," she said. "Why are you already dressed and running about?"

He gathered her against his shoulder and crushed a kiss against her hair. "I love you," he murmured.

"I love you too." Her bemused smile dissolved

as he drew back and she saw his expression. Grim, worried, practically haunted.

Something was wrong.

"How are you?" he asked with a concern that seemed somewhat out of proportion to the circumstances.

"Quite well. A bit twingey, that's all."

"I brought another iced compress, and some willow-bark tea."

"Thank you. But really, there's no need to fret over me."

Grant sat on the edge of the mattress and took one of her hands, his thumb grazing the backs of her fingers. "Last night after I made love to you, I brought a cloth to freshen you—"

"Yes, that was very thoughtful—"

"There was blood on it. And a few spots on the sheets during the night."

Oh, dear. A wave of hideous embarrassment rushed over her. "I'm so very sorry. I had no idea when my monthly courses would start. I'll put the sheet in cold water and let it soak—"

"I don't give a damn about the sheets." He lifted her hand to kiss her knuckles and the tender inside of her palm. "It wasn't that kind of blood. You were a virgin. The signs were there all along. I was just too much of a sodding idiot to realize it."

Chapter Eleven

She stared at him in bewilderment, her heat beginning to thud unpleasantly. "No, I couldn't have been. I must have bled for another reason. Your size, and—" She broke off, embarrassed and unnerved.

"There are other possibilities," Grant said quietly. "But I'm sure you were a virgin. It explains your reactions—the blushes and modesty, and why you were so tight, and why you weren't familiar with any of it. You can quote philosophy and play chess, even though you don't remember learning those things. Why, then, would you be a complete innocent when it comes to lovemaking?"

Her eyes prickled with tears. "Was it disappointing?" she asked woefully.

"*What?*" Grant's face changed. "My God . . . sweet darling . . . *no.*" He pulled her against him, his lips moving urgently over her face. "It was the best, most wondrous night of my life. No one's ever given me such bliss. You were so lovely and passionate—" He stopped with a soft groan. "And in return I hurt you, and took something from you."

"No," she exclaimed. "Even if I'd been a virgin last night, which I wasn't, I wanted to do that with you. It wasn't something you took. And I loved every minute."

"Did you?" he asked warily.

Realizing he needed reassurance just as she did, Vivien said earnestly, "Of course I did. It was the best night of my life as well."

He looked at her sardonically. "Since you've lost your memory, that's not saying much."

They were interrupted by a tap at the closed door.

"Sir?" came the cookmaid's muffled voice. "Dr. Linley has arrived. Should I send him up?"

Grant gave Vivien an apologetic glance. "I was about to tell you that I sent for Linley this morning, and asked him to stop by before he started his daily rounds."

"For what? Not for a few spots of blood, surely."

"First, I want to make certain I didn't injure

you. Second, I want his opinion on whether you might be someone other than Vivien Duvall."

She shook her head in bewilderment. "But who else could I be? I don't like my past, but if I don't have that, I have nothing. I would be a nameless someone with no life at all."

"You have me. And you have a past, like everyone else. We just don't know what it is yet."

She was increasingly unsettled. "It's a far-fetched idea. Are you pursuing this because you wish I weren't a prostitute?"

To her satisfaction, that annoyed him enough to cause him to leave the bed. "Let's put it this way," he said irritably. "Boxers don't have straight noses. Sewing-women don't have good eyesight. And prostitutes don't have hymens. That's why I'm pursuing this."

"Sir?" came the cookmaid's voice from behind the door again.

"Yes, Miriam," he said brusquely. "I'll go down and meet him."

"I'd rather you didn't bring him up here," Vivien said.

Grant gave her an obdurate glance. "He's going to have to examine you."

The situation was beyond mortifying.

"Do you want to know how I imagined we'd spend this morning?" she asked. "I thought we would probably cuddle in bed, then have breakfast together and read the newspapers. Instead it seems I'll be treated to a doctor with a speculum." She climbed out of bed, wincing a little, and reached for the robe he'd draped at the foot of the bed.

Grant watched her with instant concern. "Do you need help?"

"You've helped enough," she said, turning away from him.

Grant headed downstairs and found Jacob Linley waiting impatiently in the entrance hall.

Before Grant had even reached the bottom step, Linley said, "This visit will have to be brief, as there's an outbreak of typhus at Hammersmith Parish, I have many calls to make, and I'm nearly at wits' end. Why am I here, exactly?"

"Wasn't that clear in the message I sent?"

"As a matter of fact, Morgan, very little was clear about your message. I've had more coherent letters from the local asylum. There was something about Miss Duvall needing to be seen, and a request to bring her file, which I have with me. What do you need?"

Jacob Linley was never this testy. Grant looked more closely at the doctor, who was unfailingly polished, urbane, and even-tempered. At the moment, however, he looked like hell. There were deep circles under his eyes, his golden hair was in disarray, and his coat was badly creased.

"I need you to examine Miss Duvall," Grant said.

"For what reason?"

"I slept with her last night."

Linley sighed and reached up to knead the back of his own neck. "Given the circumstances, do you think it was a good idea to lie with her?"

"It's never a good idea," Grant muttered. "But if I let that stop me, I'd be as chaste as Sir Ross."

The doctor let out a snort of genuine amusement, and then regarded Grant more soberly. "Why do you want me to examine her? Is she in discomfort?"

"Yes." Grant lowered his voice to a vehement whisper. "I made her *bleed*, Linley."

The doctor's gaze turned alert. "How much blood?"

"There were spots on the sheet."

"Spots." Linley relaxed, sighed, and said something under his breath that sounded suspiciously like *God give me patience*.

"Any blood of hers is too much blood," Grant said defensively.

One of Linley's tawny brows arched. "When did you become squeamish about blood? The first time we met, you were carrying a bag of body parts into the coroner's office."

"This has nothing to do with being squeamish. And for both personal *and* professional reasons, I need to know why she bled."

"Morgan, I'll examine Miss Duvall if she so desires. But I want you to understand that occasional spotting after intercourse is not out of the ordinary. She may not have been sufficiently lubricated, or—"

"She was," Grant said indignantly. "I made sure she was!"

"—it's likely you pushed against her cervix, which is delicate and bleeds easily."

After cringing visibly at the word *cervix*, which sounded mysterious, painful, and medically significant, Grant said, "That wasn't the problem. She was a virgin."

Thrown off guard, the doctor paused before replying, "You mean at one time in her life?"

"No, I mean she was a virgin last night."

The doctor stared at him without expression. "Have you lost your mind?" he asked abruptly. "Or is this some spectacularly bad prank?"

"Neither. Listen to me—it was all unfamiliar to her. She knew nothing about lovemaking. Even if she can't remember her past partners or what she did with them, she would still have *some* idea of what to do, wouldn't she? She wouldn't behave like a rank novice."

Linley replied carefully. "Miss Duvall is a lovely and clever woman who's made a lucrative career of catering to the tastes of her male companions. It's possible she thought it would please you if she played the innocent."

"I'd find it flattering as hell to think someone would go to such trouble on my account. But she wasn't playacting."

"How do you know?"

"Have you ever tried to shove a cricket bat through a keyhole?" Grant demanded.

"I can assure you categorically," Linley said with weary impatience, "that Vivien Duvall has not been a virgin for some time."

"I agree," Grant said promptly.

The doctor stared at him without blinking. Then understanding dawned. "Good God, you *have* lost your mind. You think that poor girl upstairs could be someone else entirely? Some unrelated look-alike?"

"Not necessarily unrelated. But definitely a look-alike."

"This is someone's *life*, Morgan. You could hurt her with this nonsense."

"My only desire is to help her," Grant said in annoyance. "Which is why I sent for you. Will you go up there and do your blasted job?"

Linley gave him a cool glance, picked up his doctor's case, and trotted up the stairs. Grant bounded up after him, and waited as Linley knocked on the closed door.

Vivien came to open it. She was wearing a white nightgown trimmed with lace at the throat, and a blue velvet dressing robe with gilt buttons. Her glowing red hair was brushed and pinned in a neat coil at the nape of her neck. She looked vulnerable and irresistibly pretty. It sent a knifelike pain through his heart to see that she was moving with care as she curtseyed to Linley.

"Good morning, doctor."

Linley bowed in return. "Miss Duvall." He gave her the smile that women seemed to love—relaxed, empathetic, encouraging.

Seeing the way Vivien's face changed, as if she'd found herself in the presence of a long-familiar friend, made Grant feel inexplicably surly.

"I won't examine you, if you don't wish it," Linley said quietly. "But I would very much like to chat for a few minutes, and find out how you are. May I?"

"Please come in," she said, opening the door wider.

Grant began to follow Linley across the threshold but was forced to pause as they both turned to look at him.

Clearly he was not wanted.

"I'll need to see my patient in private, old fellow," Linley told him.

Although Grant longed to point out that it was *his* bedroom, he responded with a brief nod. "She needs medicine for pain," he said.

The doctor glanced at Vivien in concern. "You're in pain?"

"*Severe*," Grant emphasized.

"I'm mildly uncomfortable," Vivien protested.

But Grant was determined that she shouldn't have to suffer after spending the night with him. "She needs an anodyne, and some laudanum. Smelling salts wouldn't hurt. And a poultice. And—"

"How about a whiskey?" Linley asked.

"Is that all you're going to recommend after what she's been through?" Grant asked in outrage.

"I meant for you," Linley said, ushering him from the room. "Go have a nip if it will settle your nerves. This won't take long."

But it did. It took a damned long time. Grant paced back and forth in the hallway for hours, or possibly forty-five minutes, while the muffled sounds of conversation came from the room. It sounded as if Vivien were talking volubly—not crying, thank God, but eagerly unburdening herself to Linley.

At one point, Linley rang the servants' bell, and sent the footman, Peter, for a can of hot water. Grant was somewhat relieved, knowing it meant Vivien had agreed to the examination. If he'd accidentally injured her—God, *please* not the cervix, whatever that was—Linley would help her. And with any luck, Linley would provide information that would shed light on Vivien's identity.

After the hot water was delivered to the room, it was far quieter. Murmurs were followed by extended silences. Grant stopped pacing and stood with his back set against the wall, his arms folded. He wondered if Harry Axler had been found and brought to Bow Street. If not, he would go and retrieve the whelp himself. Axler's grip had left bruises on Vivien's arms. Every time he saw them, Grant was filled with a murderous fury he'd never known before. Before all was said and done, he would make it clear to Axler that from now on, any man who wanted his hands to stay attached to his wrists had better never lay a fucking finger on Vivien. *My woman*, he thought. *My lover, my partner, my entire existence.* In the interest of appearing civilized, it wasn't the kind of thing a man could go around saying out loud. But he kept it at the forefront of his mind, savoring it, like a lozenge tucked in the side of his cheek.

The bedroom door unlatched and opened, and Linley glanced out at him. The doctor's expression was difficult to interpret. "Would you care to join us?" he asked calmly.

Grant responded with a wary nod. He entered the room, his gaze arrowing to Vivien, who was sitting on the side of the bed with her slippered feet dangling. There was an odd look on her face, stricken but somehow resigned. As he went to her, he saw that her eyes were glistening. Inwardly alarmed, he reached for a handkerchief in an inside coat pocket and gave it to her.

"Thank you," she whispered, blotting her eyes. He stayed beside her, sliding an arm behind her shoulders, and she leaned against him.

"Morgan," Linley said, sitting in a nearby chair with a medical file on his lap, "Vivien has given me permission to discuss her information with you, so I'm free to answer your questions. First . . . as implausible as it may seem, you appear to have been correct about the issue of her virginity. The spotting came from a torn hymen, the remnants of which were visible during the examination a few minutes ago. That will heal very quickly. If there are further encounters, I suggest you proceed with care and gentleness. A woman's body learns to relax certain muscles as she becomes accustomed to physical intercourse."

The doctor paused for a long moment, his fingers tapping on the file, tracing an invisible pattern on it.

As the silence lengthened, Grant watched him keenly, impatience building until he burst out, "For God's sake, Linley, are you trying to be dramatic? Out with it!"

"I'm considering how best to say it." Linley gave him a warning glance. "I worked hard to earn my medical license, and I'd rather not lose it by breaching doctor-patient confidentiality."

"There are exceptions to confidentiality," Grant said. "Particularly if law enforcement is involved, and a crime has either been committed or may occur. And more importantly"—his voice gentled as he continued—"I'm a friend, Jacob. You know I'll protect your interests, just as I will Vivien's."

"All right, then." Linley's gaze switched to Vivien. "Despite the remarkable physical resemblance, I don't believe you're the same woman I examined at the Trelawney Crescent town house. *That* Vivien was assuredly not a virgin. Furthermore . . ." He looked down at the file as he continued in a professional tone, "As I referenced in my notes, there were other distinguishing physical details."

"Such as?" Grant asked.

"For example, a few healed-over fissures around . . . a certain area. Such scars can't be removed, and certainly wouldn't disappear."

"Scarring from what?" Grant asked. "Buggery?"

The doctor looked wry. "You've never been one to mince words. Yes, small lacerations can occur if the activity is done without adequate preparation."

"Just so we're clear," Grant said, "*this* Vivien doesn't have scarring."

"She does not."

Vivien didn't look at either of them, only kept her gaze fixed on one of the bedroom windows. Realizing she was having to endure a conversation with two men about the most intimate parts of her body, Grant murmured, "I'm sorry." Briefly he touched her hand with his. "I know this isn't pleasant." He began to withdraw his hand, but she caught at it, her fingers entwining with his.

"In addition," Linley said, "my patient at Trelawney Crescent was with child."

Grant looked at him sharply. "Are you sure? Is there a chance you could have been mistaken?"

"Possibly. It was too soon to diagnose the

condition accurately from a bimanual examination. But when a patient has a sufficient number of symptoms—cessation of menstruation, nausea, changes in breast tissue, et cetera, a doctor makes what's called a presumptive diagnosis. There's a chance it was a false pregnancy, but such cases are relatively rare, and usually happen to women who have an overwhelming desire to conceive. Miss Duvall was emphatic that she didn't want a child."

"Damn it, Linley, you should have told me before!" Unable to remain still, Grant let go of Vivien and began to pace around the room. He scrubbed his fingers distractedly through his short hair. "Someone tried to kill her—didn't it occur to you that the pregnancy might have something to do with it?"

The doctor sent him a cool glance. "Do you know what would happen to my practice if it became known that I divulged a patient's private information without her consent? More than a few of my patients are obliged to keep the circumstances of their pregnancies secret for one reason or another. And Miss Duvall was emphatic that no one was to know about her condition."

"I think Lord Gerard was the father," Vivien surprised them both by saying quietly. "Or would have been."

Grant stopped in his tracks.

Before he could ask anything, she continued,

"When I met with him last night, he asked if I'd remedied a certain 'little problem.' He also seemed to think that my marital prospects had fallen through, and that my would-be suitor was permanently gone." Looking sheepish, she added, "I was going to tell you, but we were both . . . distracted."

Dr. Linley exhibited a sudden intense interest in his notes.

Grant stared at him stonily. "You examined Vivien the night she was pulled from the Thames—and you didn't notice *then* that she was a virgin?"

The doctor sighed and rubbed the corners of his eyes with thumb and forefinger. "In my concern for saving her life," he said acidly, "I apparently overlooked the massive importance of a millimeter of tissue at the vaginal entrance."

Grant's mouth twisted and he nodded, conceding the point.

"I did a brief pelvic examination," Linley continued, "and observed the womb was no longer enlarged, which meant she'd either had a miscarriage or taken measures to end the pregnancy. But in the absence of any signs of infection or hemorrhage, I saw no need to put her through a more invasive examination with a speculum."

"Doctor Linley," Vivien asked, "you're positive I'm not Vivien Duvall?"

He met her gaze and replied gently, "I'm positive you're not the woman I examined at Trelawney Crescent. And I apologize for assuming, based on circumstantial evidence, that you were."

"It was the simplest explanation," she said.

"It was," the doctor agreed ruefully. "So much for Occam's razor." He smiled and shook his head. "Pardon, that's an old philosophical principle, to the effect that simpler theories are preferable to complicated ones. But just because something is simple doesn't mean it's accurate."

"Now you've done it, Linley," Grant said, amused as he saw the spark of interest in Vivien's eyes. "Don't mention philosophy to her when you're already late for the typhoid pandemic."

"It's still only a typhoid breakout," the doctor told him.

"I know about Occam's razor," Vivien said. "It's not a principle so much as a heuristic, to avoid stacking a problem with unnecessary complications. Except that sometimes a complex problem can only be solved with a complex answer. Someone once told me . . ." She paused, her gaze turning distant and slightly unfocused. "Someone told me that Occam's razor should never be used to end an argument, only to begin the search for truth. I think . . . it may have been my father."

Grant went to her and gently tilted her face up

to his. "Do you remember anything about what he looks like? Anything else he told you?"

Vivien blinked up at him without seeming to see him. Her shoulders had drooped, as if she were overcome with exhaustion and sadness. "My head feels like a hallway of closed doors."

"More doors will open, in time," Grant murmured, and bent to kiss her forehead. "Meanwhile, it wouldn't hurt you to rest. I'm going to see Linley out, and leave for Bow Street to meet with Sir Ross. I'll return by the time you awaken, and then we'll do breakfast and newspapers."

"It will be lunchtime by then."

Grant smiled down at her. "There's a philosophical principle you may not know about." He lowered his mouth close to her ear and whispered, "Breakfast can happen any time of day."

Linley hefted his doctor's case and approached the bed. "Miss Duvall, allow me to say how much I admire your composure. You're an impressive woman. After everything you've gone through, including these latest revelations, most people would fall to pieces."

"Thank you, doctor," Vivien said. "I'm just trying to take it on the chin." And despite her weariness, she looked up at Grant with an impish gleam in her eyes.

As the two men descended the stairs to the ground floor, Linley remarked, "I've never seen you so smitten. But I can certainly understand why you are."

"More than smitten," Grant said. "I've been fricasseed."

The doctor chuckled. "She's an unusual young woman. Remarkably levelheaded, considering the circumstances. And very sweet-natured."

And mine, Grant wanted to say, but managed to keep his mouth shut.

"I have two thoughts to leave with you," Linley continued. "The first has to do with the resemblance between the woman upstairs and Vivien Duvall."

"Too close for coincidence," Grant said.

"Exactly. The probability of two unrelated people looking nearly identical is virtually non-existent. And that's even before you factor in variables of nutrition and environment, which would also influence someone's appearance considerably."

"So they're cousins or sisters."

"I would think so."

They reached the bottom of the stairs, and the footman appeared.

"Peter," Linley said pleasantly, "my coat and hat, please."

"Yes, sir." While the footman left to find the articles, Linley turned to face Grant. "My second thought has to do with this philosophy business. No one teaches philosophy to girls. It's just not done. In fact, more than a few members of my profession would tell you that allowing women to study the nature of existence and reality would damage the female brain and nervous system."

"What rubbish."

"Agreed. But it's instilled a fear among academics that if they teach some esoteric subject to a girl, they may later be accused of harming her. I can't fathom who would have dared instruct Vivien in a subject she couldn't have done anything with in the first place."

"There could have been a male relative or close family friend who was a philosophy scholar or teacher," Grant mused. "Someone who shared his passion for the subject with her." He paused as Peter returned with the coat and hat. "Thank you for calling on us, Linley. I owe you a round at the local swill-hole of your choice."

"The Rag and Bucket, naturally." Linley grinned at him. "Let's meet Friday—if I haven't come down with typhus by then."

Chapter Twelve

As soon as Grant walked into Sir Ross Cannon's office, he said, "The clerk just told me that Harry Axler was brought in early this morning on a warrant."

"Have a seat, Morgan."

Grant took the chair on the opposite side of the desk. "Have you questioned him yet?"

"No."

"Let me talk to him."

"Not when you would try to shake answers out of him like a jar of hair powder."

"When are you going to—" Grant broke off and gritted his teeth as Cannon silenced him with a gesture.

"Mr. Axler is being held without bail," the magistrate said calmly, "as he threatened the arresting officer with a dueling pistol purloined from his grandfather's gun cabinet. We've stirred up a hornet's nest—I've already been contacted by the lord chancellor's office with a request to set the lad free immediately. I'm ignoring it, of course, but I doubt I'll be able to hold him past this evening."

"Then why aren't you questioning him right now?"

"I'm letting Axler cool his heels while I have my morning coffee." Cannon lifted a mug to his lips, seeming to covertly enjoy Grant's silent battle with his temper.

Full, slow breath, Grant thought. *In through the nose, out through the mouth. One-two-three-four, one-two-three—*

"Axler told the arresting officer that his actions toward Miss Duvall were provoked by something his grandfather said about her," Cannon remarked. "God knows what Lord Lane has against her. It's unfortunate she hasn't recovered her memory yet."

"Even when she recovers it, she may not know anything about Lord Lane."

"Explain."

Reluctantly Grant told him everything that had happened after the Lichfield ball, including what had been revealed during Dr. Linley's visit that morning.

Cannon stared at him with icy disapproval, his fingers drumming slowly on his desk. "I distinctly remember telling you in this very office—"

"I know. I know."

"And yet after the traumatic event Miss Duvall suffered at the ball, you took her home and debauched her?"

"I was comforting her," Grant said defensively.

"As far as I'm aware, the act of comforting doesn't usually require penetration."

It cost everything Grant had to meet Cannon's gaze instead of hanging his head like a shamefaced schoolboy. He decided to brazen it out. "I wasn't asking for your approval."

"Good, because you don't have it."

"I only told you because the information is relevant to the case. And while I'm not proud of what happened last night, it did produce some valuable new evidence."

"I would prefer your evidence-gathering not to involve the despoiling of vulnerable women."

Since brazening it out clearly wasn't going to work, Grant resorted to honesty.

"You're right. I should have resisted temptation. But Vivien asked me to stay the night, and I wanted her too much. I couldn't stop myself. What I feel for her isn't just desire, it's *love*. Nothing like this has ever happened to me before, and I don't—"

"Morgan. Morgan. Stop." Cannon looked as uncomfortable as Grant had ever seen him.

He was leaning back in his chair now, his arms crossed over his chest. "There's no need to go into all that. I didn't intend to start a personal discussion."

"Sorry," Grant muttered. "I forgot how much you dislike emotion."

"I wouldn't put it that way," the magistrate said, seeming affronted. "I believe emotions should be handled like champagne."

"To be shared with friends on special occasions?"

"No, to be bottled up and kept safely in the dark."

Although Cannon certainly hadn't meant that as a joke, Grant couldn't hold back a snort of amusement. He ducked down and reached beneath his chair for the small painting he'd brought from Vivien's town house. Cannon had asked to see it after reading the last report.

The magistrate finished his coffee while Grant unwrapped the linen cloth from around the painting and set it in front of him.

"Miss Duvall said this looked familiar?" Cannon asked, staring intently at the canvas.

"Yes, sir." In the silence, Grant ventured, "You see the galleting in the mortar."

"Indeed."

"And the way the apple tree is trained on the wall, with the branches running diagonally."

"Those aren't apples. They're peaches. You

can tell by the shape of the leaves—long ovals instead of round."

Grant gave him a dubious glance. "Peaches grown outside of a hothouse?"

"There aren't many places in England where one can do that. My family estate is in Berkshire, where the climate is too cool, much to my mother's dismay. She loved the look of peach trees fanned out this way. A French method: *en cordon oblique*. More than once, she complained that only a short distance to the south, in Surrey, peach trees would thrive in the open air."

"Surrey," Grant said reflectively. "That's within the area I intend to search."

"It's not far from here," Cannon said absently. "You could start tomorrow." He tapped a gentle fingertip against a pair of silver-gray splotches near the peach tree. "If I were you, I'd first take this painting to a reputable butcher and ask him what breed these are."

"Rocks?" Grant asked, puzzled, looking at the gray blobs of paint.

Cannon smiled at that. "They're chickens. Take it from a former country lad who grew up on a farming estate. And Surrey is known for its prized regional breeds of poultry."

"I don't like the thought of leaving Vivien," Grant said. "Even for a day."

"She'll be perfectly safe. I'll assign officers to watch over your house in shifts while you're gone." Cannon set down the painting, his smile fading. "If the real Vivien Duvall is still missing, we must do everything in our power to find out what's become of her."

"But I want to go with you," Vivien protested later in the afternoon, as she and Grant lay in bed together.

Grant caressed her naked limbs, seeming to luxuriate in the feel of her skin. "It may take several trips to find the cottage. It may not even be in Surrey. And if I do locate it, I don't know what I might find there. I'd prefer you to stay here and be safe and comfortable."

"Where are you going to start looking?" she asked, but he'd already lost the thread of conversation. His hands cupped her breasts as his mouth went from one nipple to the other, licking and kissing.

Grant had given the servants the rest of the day off, and had promptly taken her to bed. He'd spent a long time making love to her with a gentleness that had aroused her to tense, trembling readiness. He loved to tease and kiss her in unexpected places . . . behind her knees or the sensitive arches of her feet, or in the shadowed undercurves of her breasts.

The world outside had vanished. There was only this bed, illuminated in cool gray light . . . and this man, warm and hard and endlessly inventive.

He showed her how to stroke the thick, burning length of him, the rhythms and pressures that would excite him to release. Entranced by the steely, silken texture of his shaft, she kept trying to guide it between her thighs, where she knew it would soothe the restless craving.

He was adamant in his refusal. "Not inside, until you've healed."

"But I want you to make love to me."

"There are other ways."

"But I want this."

"You're too sore."

"Just for five minutes."

"No," Grant said gently, smiling down at her flushed face.

"One minute."

Even more softly, "No." He bent to draw the tip of her breast into the warmth of his mouth.

She wriggled against him, wanting him with increasing desperation, until he finally smoothed some almond oil over her sex and let her straddle his hips. She rubbed herself over him in long back-and-forth glides, panting and moaning with an abandon that would mortify her later. But it felt too good to stop, her hips bucking against the tantalizing heavy ridge as she rode through one peak after another. Finally he pulled her close with a deep, rough sound, and she felt the liquid heat of his release spread against her stomach. A peculiar but erotic feeling . . . another new intimacy.

His muscled arms went around her as she lay on him, and his breathless laugh filtered through her hair where it was damp at the roots. "Ah, you're so naughty," he whispered.

She smiled and nuzzled against his shoulder.

"Dorking," he said after a moment, his lazy palm traveling down to her bottom.

"Is that what we were doing?" she asked.

Grant lightly pinched a plump curve, making her yelp. "I suspect you know Dorking is a market town in Surrey." His hands moved over her in gentle circles. "It's renowned for its fine poultry, apparently. I showed your painting to the butcher on the way home, and he said those silver-gray chickens were unmistakably a Dorking breed. So that's where I'll start searching for the cottage."

"It's not really *my* painting," she said. "It belongs to the real Vivien."

"You could have been the one who painted it," he pointed out. "Do you feel as if you might have an artistic streak?"

"Not at all."

"That would explain why your chickens look like rocks."

She laughed and rolled off him, and left the bed. "Lie still," she said, shivering at the coolness of the room as she went to the washstand. "I'll do the bathing for a change." She poured hot water over a linen cloth, washed herself, and brought a fresh damp cloth to the bed. Grant lay there with a muscular arm half curled behind his head, lazing like a tomcat as she tended to him.

Gentle and precise, she cleaned his groin and stomach, and paused to trace the sinewy ridges of his stomach with a fingertip.

"I hope you intend to marry me," she heard Grant say.

She looked at him with a faint smile, and saw the glow of yearning in his eyes.

"I'll need my real name first," she said.

"I'll find it for you."

"What will you call me until then?" she asked. "I suppose 'Vivien' will have to do."

"I'll call you 'my love,'" he said, and turned his face to hers as she leaned down to kiss him.

It turned out that Dorking was known for more than just its chickens: it also possessed some of the finest quarries in England, producing lime that was sought after by masons and builders from every part of the kingdom. Upon arriving in the picturesque town, Grant went to the offices of a local lime-burner named Dan Ewart, who ran six kilns.

Ewart was a small, wiry man with dry skin and pale hair, and eyes reddened from frequent exposure to the irritating fumes produced as limestone was baked down to ash. He welcomed Grant into the sparely furnished office. "Will you take a glass of beer, friend?" Ewart asked, pulling a dingy gray cloth off a stoneware pitcher.

"Thank you, no, I won't stay long."

Ewart guzzled beer directly from the pitcher and wiped his mouth with his sleeve. "Lime-burning's thirsty work."

"So I've heard." Grant was disconcerted to see a small trickle of blood from one of the man's nostrils. Quickly he reached into his coat, pulled out a handkerchief, and gave it to him.

Ewart looked at it in surprise. "I couldn't use something so fine as this—"

"Have it," Grant said readily. "Consider it my thanks for a few minutes of your time."

"Obliged to you." Ewart blotted his nose. "Lime dust from the kiln," he said ruefully. "Every time you take a whiff, it turns the innards to blood." He sat on his office desk and gestured for Grant to take the chair. "How can I help you, Mr. . . ."

"Morgan. I'm trying to locate a particular cottage in Dorking. It has some distinctive galleting in the stonework. I thought if anyone could help make a list of local masons who might be able to identify it, it would be you."

"That I could," Ewart assured him. "I know every brick and stone worker from here to the South Downs. Do you have a drawing of the cottage?"

"A painting." Grant unwrapped it and handed it to him.

Ewart took the painting by the frame and studied it. "Oh, I know this place."

Grant blinked in surprise. "*This* cottage?" he said, to be clear. "You know where it is?"

It couldn't be this easy. It was never this easy.

"A mile away as the crow flies," Ewart said. "Miss Victoria Devane lives there. She teaches at one of the town's schools and manages the lending library attached to it. Taught two of my little ones last year. They're right fond of her. A gentle way, she has." He shook his head regretfully. "She stopped teaching. Went off to London last month, came back standoffish and ill-disposed. Not like herself, and no one knows why. Her cookmaid, Jane, goes to the Tuesday market, but she's been standoffish too."

"Does anyone else live at the cottage?"

"The father did, until he died a year ago. Fine old fellow, Mr. Devane, for all that he didn't know how to swing a hammer. A scholar, he was."

"What kind of scholar?"

"Couldn't rightly say. He had some fancy highbrow notions—'Ewart,' he'd ask me, 'how do you know that chair really exists?' And if I said, 'Because it's holding my arse off the ground,' he'd say, 'But that's not proof, now is it?'" Ewart shrugged. "To my mind, a man has to trust what his own arse tells him, or else what is he?"

"A philosopher," Grant said with the hint of a wondering smile.

"All questions, never an answer—that was Devane. Could have been why his wife turned wayward and ran off. Left him with two little girls to raise. Twins, with hair the color of furnace-fire."

"You said one of them became a teacher—what about the other?"

"Miss Vivien. A bit of a trapes-about. Liked to keep company with the lads. Folk say she lives in Paris now and is, well . . ." He lowered his voice to a whisper. ". . . an *actress*."

Grant tried to look suitably scandalized. "I'd like to deliver the painting to Miss Devane's cottage, if you'll tell me where to find it."

"Follow the road that way, past the Punch-bowl Inn. You'll come to a gravel lane that leads off the road to the cottage."

Victoria. Grant savored the syllables as he rode to the cottage. Victoria Devane, a scholar's daughter. A teacher who managed a lending library. God knew it all suited her far better than Vivien's identity.

The cottage awaited him at the end of the lane, its mortared facade dusted with rime frost. Bare peach tree branches splayed over the walls in the shape of a peacock's tail.

Grant dismounted, tethered his horse beside a stone shed, and went to the front door. He knocked and waited for a response. There were sounds within the house, the scrapes of chairs being moved, the porcelain rattle of dishes.

Eventually a young cookmaid came to the door. Her face was drawn and uncertain, her dark hair topped with a blue cap. "Help you, sir?"

"I'd like to speak with the lady who lives here," Grant said.

"She's not at home."

"Go fetch her, please," he said gently. "Tell her I'm a friend."

A scornful female voice came from within the cottage. "Like hell you are!"

"I'm here to help," Grant called back to her.

"You can help by leaving before I put a bullet in your chest."

"Vivien, it's Grant Morgan," he said.

A short silence. Then, *Morgan?* The door opened wider, and the real Vivien Duvall appeared, looking baffled and annoyed. "Bugger. What are you doing here?"

Grant's gaze swept over her and paused at the rounded swell of her stomach. She was holding a small flintlock with a four-inch barrel, a lightweight lady's weapon.

"Put that popgun away before you hurt someone," he said irritably. "And let me inside, if you'd like some news about your sister."

Chapter Thirteen

❧

"I wrote to Victoria that I was in trouble," Vivien said as they sat in a pair of ancient armchairs, "and I would be coming to stay in Dorking with her. But I left two or three days later than I'd planned. By the time I arrived, the ninny had already left to search for me in London. And I couldn't very well go looking for her when I was in danger myself. How was I to know she'd do something so stupid?"

"She went out of love and worry," Grant said. "She wouldn't stay here if she thought you needed her."

"How do you know what my sister would do? You're strangers."

"She's been staying at my town house."

"With you?" Vivien began to laugh. "My prim and proper sister?"

Grant was irritated and puzzled by Vivien's reactions, which seemed slightly off-kilter. "I just told you she was attacked and nearly drowned by someone who apparently mistook her for you. Shouldn't you ask after her well-being? Show a little concern?"

"You already said she's recovering."

"I also said she doesn't remember her own blasted name," he snapped.

"That's probably an improvement." Vivien rolled her eyes as she saw his expression. "Oh, spare me the sanctimonious glances. Look around you—*this* is the life Victoria was leading. If it took a spell of amnesia to push her out of Dorking, I say hurrah for it."

"You're not worried that I might have taken advantage of her?"

"I hope you did," she stunned him by saying tartly. "Victoria is far too much of a goody-good. She's always needed someone to kick the pedestal out from beneath her. After Papa died, I tried to convince her to live with me. I asked—no, *begged*— her to let me introduce her to the right gentlemen. We would have made a fortune—a pair of red-haired sisters. Can you imagine what men would have paid to have us both at the same time?"

"No, I can't," Grant said, recoiling at the thought.

"Victoria would have none of it, of course. What a waste. We would have been a sensation in Paris. But she's always been too much like Papa." Vivien made a face. "The two of them would have driven anyone mad. A person can do too much thinking, you know."

"Not something I've ever been accused of," Grant said, and she laughed.

"My poor sister," she said reflectively. "She's spent her life reading books, writing papers about ethics and principles and other useless frou-frou. Teaching local brats. All of it pointless. She could have had the life I've had."

"A life that's had its drawbacks," Grant pointed out, glancing at her rounded belly. "Unless you want the baby, that is."

"No, this is only temporary. After it's born, I'm giving it away."

"Like an old pair of shoes?"

Vivien smiled reluctantly. "You're an ass, Morgan," she said.

"Yes. But I'm an ass who wants to help. Tell me about the trouble you were in."

After the visit to Dorking, Grant rode back to London. He longed to go straight to his town house to see Victoria, but he forced himself to stop first at the Mayfair mansion belonging to Lord Lane.

Although Lane wasn't at home, the butler reluctantly revealed the earl was at Boodle's, the prestigious London gentlemen's club second only to White's. Its membership consisted of the wealthy, powerful, and aristocratic men who traded power among themselves.

The atmosphere at Boodle's, named after the club's original head waiter, was intentionally dull, providing a relaxed retreat from lives that were already relaxed. The patrons occupied heavy upholstered chairs and enjoyed cigars and brandy, while surrounded by paintings of hunting, shooting, and other country pursuits. The only sounds were the occasional rustle of a newspaper, the clinks of crystal glasses, and the murmurs of porters and footmen.

As soon as Grant entered the club, he was approached by a bespectacled manager with an air of great dignity.

"Sir, may I ask your business?"

"I was told I could find Lord Lane here."

"Is his lordship expecting you, Mr. Morgan?"

"No."

"Are you a patron of an affiliated club?"

"No."

The manager looked vaguely apologetic. "I'm afraid you'll have to seek him out some other time, sir. And at some other place. We must respect our members' privacy."

"This is a police matter. I'm Morgan, from the Bow Street office." Grant lowered his voice to a quiet growl. "If you don't tell me what room he's in, I'll be forced to—"

"Morgan of Bow Street?" the manager asked, his eyes widening.

Realizing there was no need to appear threatening, Grant said pleasantly, "At your service."

"Sir, may I remark what an *honor* it is to make your acquaintance. My wife and I—and our three daughters—we read your books in the parlor every night. I've ordered *Mystery of the Cursed Carnival* from the bookseller in advance, to ensure we receive a copy as soon as it's published."

"I'll return here and autograph it for you," Grant offered.

"Would you? I would be most obliged. My girls will be in raptures."

"Grant Morgan never breaks a promise," Grant said, feeling like an idiot.

But the manager's face glowed, and he said quietly, "Detective, I believe Lord Lane may be in the coffee room, down the hallway to the right. If you would handle the matter with discretion, I would be most obliged."

"I'll have a quick chat with the earl and be gone before I'm even noticed."

As Grant entered the coffee room, a few dismissive glances passed over his travel-dusty clothes. He saw Lord Lane sitting alone near the hearth, reading a newspaper. A plate containing biscuits and a spoonful of ripe Stilton had been set on the small table beside him.

At Grant's approach, Lane slowly looked up from the newspaper. Grief, anger, and frustration had scored deep lines in his complexion, giving it the texture of timber exposed to seawater.

"My lord," Grant said quietly. "I'm—"

"I know who you are," Lane murmured, pausing to finish one last paragraph before deigning to set aside the paper. "How dare you approach me in my club?"

"We'll go somewhere else, if you like."

"What I would like, Morgan, is for you to leave at once. Or I'll have you removed."

Grant glanced around the room at the languid patrons and elderly porters. Other than a footman near the corner, there was no one even close to his size. "I don't think you can," he said.

"We'll see about that." Lane snapped his fingers at a porter, who began to approach reluctantly. Grant sent him back to his place with a single gesture.

"Let's talk in a private room," Grant said quietly. "Now, my lord. Or I'll have to take you to Bow Street and put you in the strong room next to your grandson."

The old man shot him a glance of such venom that Grant felt a crawling sensation down his spine. There was something a bit deranged in the man's eyes.

Lane stood and proceeded past the tables to

a hallway, while Grant followed. "You'll regret this," the older man said in a seething undertone.

"I know," Grant said with a touch of weariness. Every man he questioned or arrested used a variation of the same routine threats.

"You have no idea of the extent of my influence," Lane said.

"I know."

"I'll ruin you. You'll lose everything."

"Mm-hmm."

"You're filth. You're—"

"I know. The lowest of the low."

They entered a private parlor. Although there were chairs by the fireplace, both of them remained standing. In the confines of the small room, tension ricocheted back and forth like bullets.

"I'm here to discuss Vivien Duvall," Grant said.

"I refuse to say anything in connection with that malicious slut."

"She's not my favorite, either," Grant replied. "But you have more cause to hate her than most. You blame her for your oldest grandson's suicide."

As he heard the words aloud, the earl reacted as if he'd been slapped across the face. His jaw began to work and tremble with anger.

"She was responsible," Lane said.

Veins were standing out on the older man's throat and forehead. Grant suspected Lane *wanted* to confess to what he'd done, if only to demonstrate his importance. After a lifetime of avoiding the consequences of his actions, Lane believed he was immune to them. Like many of his kind, Lane had been secluded from the problems of the common masses, until he'd come to think of them as a bit less than human. Disposable, even.

"How was she responsible?" Grant asked.

"My grandson Thomas was a high-spirited and troubled lad, especially after the loss of his parents to typhus. An easy mark for gamblers and thieves. However, every young man must sow his wild oats. I knew with time and maturity, Thomas would become steadier. Then the harlot sank her hooks into him. I warned him that she was using him, she would bring him to ruin, she was evil. Thomas wouldn't listen. He was inflamed with her. The red hair . . . the body she loved to flaunt . . . she cast a spell over every man who saw her. Not long ago, she would have been burned at the stake. I would gladly have lit the match."

"But since that's no longer an option," Grant said, "there was little you could do about her."

"On the contrary. When Thomas told me the woman was with child, and he intended to marry her, I decided to separate them. Everyone in London knew the child was Lord Gerard's, but she told Thomas it was his, and he wanted to believe her. The marriage would have made my family a laughingstock. Worse, had the spawn been a boy, he would have inherited my title and entire estate."

"So you bought Thomas an army commission," Grant said, and added sincerely, "Not a bad plan. It would have afforded him some necessary time away from her."

Lane gave a tiny nod, his eyes glittering. "But he had a moment of weakness," he said gruffly. "Wild, stupid boy."

Grant almost felt sorry for the man. "It was a tragic loss. But Miss Duvall wasn't the one who pulled the trigger."

"She might as well have."

"It's not for you to serve as judge, jury, and executioner, my lord. Hiring someone to dispose of her was going a bit too far."

"Nonsense," Lane said curtly. "Had I wanted the whore dead, I would have done it myself."

"Men in your position never do it themselves."

"You have no proof."

"I will when I've caught your hired man."

Lane stared at him with triumphant malice. "But you won't. Vivien Duvall will soon be in her grave, and the man who put her there will have disappeared from England. There's nothing you can do to stop him."

Unnerved, Grant had to remind himself that Victoria was safe at home with a Runner to protect her.

"Why are you so sure I can't?" he asked.

He could see the battle between caution and vengeance in the older man's expression.

Vengeance won out.

With a chilling smile, Lord Lane said, "Because he's one of your own."

Did he mean someone from Bow Street? *Holy hell.* Grant's heart began to pound.

"I could have bought any of you," Lane said. "You Bow Street Runners are the dregs of society. Not a drop of honorable blood among you—"

Grant strode swiftly from the room without looking back.

"She's responsible," he heard Lane shout behind him. "She has to pay!"

Chapter Fourteen

"The Bow Street officer is here, my dear."
Mrs. Buttons stood at the library door. "His
name is Mr. Keyes, and he's a fine man—the
most experienced man Sir Ross has. We've been
left in good hands."

"I'm sure we have." Victoria stood before the
library window, gazing at the storm clouds un-
rolling like a blanket over London. It was darkening fast. Gusts of wind whipped through the
trees and sent a few splats of rain against the
window.

"May I show him in?" the housekeeper asked.

"Of course."

Mr. Keyes was an average-sized man, jovial and a bit dandyish, with fluffy silver hair. He had a nice smile, and twinkling brown eyes. After executing a precise bow, he said warmly, "Miss Duvall, how do you do?"

She smiled and curtseyed. "Quite well, thank you. We all appreciate your protection, Mr. Keyes."

"It's a pleasure and an honor," he assured her.

A boom of thunder rattled the glass wall sconces and the crystals in the entrance hall chandelier.

"It's going to bucket down," Keyes said ruefully.

"Like last month's storm," Mrs. Buttons agreed.

Victoria felt chilled and uneasy, recalling that last month's storm had occurred the night she'd been pulled from the Thames.

"I must inform you both about a change of plan. As I was leaving Bow Street, Sir Ross directed me to bring Miss Duvall to him."

"To the Bow Street police office? This evening?" Mrs. Buttons asked in surprise.

"Immediately," he said.

"This seems rather untoward, Mr. Keyes."

"I would prefer to stay here," Victoria said, her hand creeping to her throat.

"I understand," he replied. "However, Sir Ross received new information in Morgan's absence, and he needs to speak with you."

"What kind of information?" Victoria asked.

"Does it have something to do with his questioning of Mr. Axler?"

"I suspect that's it," Mr. Keyes replied.

The housekeeper was frowning. "Couldn't Sir Ross come here?"

The suggestion seemed to strike Mr. Keyes as nonsensical. "He's an important man, Mrs. Buttons, and occupied with too many pressing problems to dash off like some errand boy." He turned to Victoria. "We're wasting time. Sir Ross is waiting."

Victoria nodded, but a crawling sensation had spread over her, and her heartbeat felt as fast as a hummingbird's wings.

"Mr. Keyes," she managed to say, "may I take the cookmaid with me?"

"That's a fine idea," Mrs. Buttons said promptly.

But Keyes shook his head. "We're not paying a social call. This is official business. Come, let's away before the storm sets in."

Victoria exchanged a worried glance with the housekeeper.

"If Mr. Keyes says you must go," Mrs. Buttons said uncertainly, "I suppose you must."

Victoria glanced at the darkening sky visible through the window. "If you'll excuse me, Mr. Keyes, I'll change my shoes and put on a warm cloak."

"Make haste, please."

"Yes." But she hesitated, staring at him intently. A memory seethed and writhed in her brain. "Sir . . . have we met before?"

"I don't believe so." Mr. Keyes had such a nice smile. Why did it cause a fearful pang in her stomach?

More thunder pealed, and Keyes glanced at the window. Something about his profile, and the way the jut of his chin met the soft folds of his throat, struck a chord of recognition in her brain. Her nerves shrilled in alarm.

She turned and headed upstairs, having to restrain herself from breaking into a run. When she reached the top, she cast a quick glance over her shoulder. Keyes was at the foot of the staircase, watching her.

As soon as Victoria reached her room, she wiped at a trickle of nervous sweat that traveled from her hairline to the edge of her chin. Something wasn't right. Her body knew it, even if her mind didn't. She felt like a mouse trapped in a barrel with a cat.

She didn't want to go anywhere with Mr. Keyes, and she had a terrible suspicion that he didn't intend to take her to Bow Street.

But she did trust Sir Ross. With Grant still away, he was the only man she would feel truly safe with.

Could she manage to find Sir Ross on her own? She blotted her moist forehead with a sleeve. She didn't know the precise location of the Bow Street office, only that it was somewhere on the other side of Covent Garden. But surely it wouldn't be that difficult to find.

With feverish haste, she went to the armoire and found a dark green hooded cloak. After changing her shoes to ankle-high walking boots, she went out to the hallway. Seeing that no one was there, she broke into a rapid walk toward the stairs—not the main ones, but the servants' stairs at the back of the house.

As she descended the steps, a shape materialized at the first-floor landing. Victoria stopped abruptly. It was Miriam, carrying a basket of folded linens.

The cookmaid stopped and regarded her with surprise and confusion. "Miss Duvall? What are you doing here?"

"Don't tell anyone you've seen me," Victoria said urgently. "Please. I want Mr. Keyes to think I'm still in my room."

The cookmaid's gaze questioned her sanity. "Where could you be going? Miss, if anything happens to you, and I didn't tell anyone I saw you leave, I could lose my position. I could find myself on the streets!"

"I don't have time to talk, Miriam. I'll return later when Mr. Morgan has returned. In the meantime, please keep quiet. It's life and death to me."

Victoria brushed by the dumbfounded cookmaid and continued down to the basement. She passed the door to the coal vault and the kitchen, and let herself out through the back door.

It was a relief to be outside. The storm had paused, but the air was heavy and electric with the promise of more. She hurried across a service road and ran alongside an enclosed fifty-foot-long garden. When she reached the corner, she skirted around to the back and strode toward Covent Garden. The carriageway rumbled with drays, carriages, and horses. Lamplighters climbed to suspended lamps hung from iron brackets, while street sellers called out their wares.

Overhead, towering black clouds had been whipped up by breezes that dodged in every direction. Raindrops began to hit the ground with the force of pennies. Victoria shivered and pulled her hood lower over her face.

The safety of Sir Ross's office was just on the other side of Covent Garden.

At Mr. Keyes's request, Mrs. Buttons brought wine as they waited for Vivien to come downstairs. With a crystal wineglass in hand, Keyes gazed at the quiet elegance of his surroundings. "Your master's done well for himself."

"Our Mr. Morgan works very hard, sir," the housekeeper replied, feeling vaguely defensive on her employer's behalf.

"Hasn't exactly harmed his career to have those novels written about him."

"Those aren't Mr. Morgan's doing."

"Oh, I'm aware of that. The publisher could have chosen any of the Bow Street officers to feature as their dashing hero. But why him? He has accomplished no more than the rest of us."

Mrs. Buttons supposed his envy was understandable. If an average Londoner was asked to name anyone at the Bow Street police office, Grant Morgan was the first that came to mind, followed by Sir Ross. None of the other Runners, including Keyes, enjoyed anything close to that level of fame.

And Mr. Morgan's proficiency, along with his strapping build and good looks, made him the obvious choice for an adventure hero. She wouldn't point that out, however, knowing it would only annoy Mr. Keyes.

As Mrs. Buttons pondered how to reply, Miriam came to the door, looking distraught.

"Ma'am, I thought I should come to you right away, even though she said not to."

"What is it, Miriam?" Mrs. Buttons asked.

"She left. I couldn't stop her."

Mrs. Buttons stared at her in surprise. "Miss Duvall left the house?"

"How long ago?" Mr. Keyes barked, causing both women to start.

"Five minutes, sir. I passed her on the servants' stairs. I wouldn't tattle, except . . . she's in danger out there, isn't she? Have I done wrong?"

"No, Miriam," the housekeeper soothed, patting the girl's arm. "You did exactly as Mr. Morgan would have wished."

Keyes shocked them by throwing his goblet to the floor and leaving without another word. As he strode from the room, wine spread over the fine hand-knotted carpet in an ugly blood-colored stain.

Cautiously Victoria walked beneath the arches of Covent Garden's covered arcade, where people milled around shops and stalls. Customers and sellers were all busy trying to conclude their business ahead of the storm. She blended into the crowd, letting the flow of shoppers carry her past stalls and carts laden with sacks of shelled peas . . . large tin vessels of milk . . . baskets of new potatoes, apples, cabbages, cauliflower, and beans. The thoroughfare became too crowded for anyone to move, obliging her to pause in front of an herb-and-root stand. Victoria found herself beside a row of glass jars filled with leeches. A little cardboard sign proclaimed: *Imported from Sweden—3d. apiece—BEST*

She wrinkled her nose in revulsion as she stared at the squirmy dark leeches. The creatures were supposed to predict the weather: they rose to the top of the jar when a storm was coming. There was a poem about that, wasn't there? . . . She could almost recall a line about leeches rising . . . risen . . .

Suddenly the verse came to her.

The leech, disturb'd, is newly risen,
Quite to the summit of his prison.

At some point in the past, she had argued with someone about leeches . . .

"Papa, wouldn't it be nicer if I put a cold cloth on your head?"

"That won't help with the migraine, Victoria," came her father's weak voice. "Be a brave girl."

Her sister, Vivien, came into the main room of the cottage, where their father reclined on a sofa. "The brandy I brought from Paris will do far more for your headache than a leeching, Papa."

"My dear, this is the only treatment that helps."

Victoria cringed while plucking one of the leeches from the jar with silver tongs.

"Good heavens, how you carry on," Vivien mocked, watching in amusement. "Just think of it as a garden worm."

"A worm with teeth," Victoria said with a grimace. Gingerly she placed the leech on a wineglass she had covered with a piece of gauze.

"What is that?" Vivien asked, watching in amusement. "Why did you make a little bed for it?"

"I read about this method in a magazine," Victoria said. "You gently tip the glass against the patient's skin . . . like this . . . and the leech will roll onto the right place and bite." But the leech tumbled onto Papa's neck. "Oh, drat, *drat*—" Trying to stifle a little squeal of revulsion, Victoria reached down and scooped the squishy, slimy creature back onto the gauze-covered glass.

She glanced at Vivien, who was convulsing with laughter, and she couldn't help giving in to it as well. She had to set down the wineglass, and they leaned against each other, snorting.

Despite the intense pain of his headache, their father smiled slightly. "What a pair of gigglepots," he said. "The two of you haven't changed since you were five."

"I'm sorry, Papa," Victoria said contritely, struggling to regain control. "Leeches make me nervous."

"Mind over matter," he counseled.

"Yes, Papa."

But just as Victoria began to reach for the wineglass, she heard Vivien say gravely, "Mind over maggot."

Victoria battled another burst of laughter, her shoulders shaking with it. "Vivien," she finally managed to say, "go somewhere else. Anywhere."

"Absolutely not," Vivien gasped, wiping a stray tear from her eye. "I want to see how you manage to stick that thing onto Papa's head."

Steeling herself, Victoria brought the wineglass close to Papa's head and tipped the rim against his temple. The leech rolled across the gauze and rested limply against the waxen skin. But it wouldn't latch on. "Why won't it bite?" she asked in frustration, nudging it back onto the gauze. "Maybe it's not hungry? The book suggested stimulating its appetite with a few drops of beer, but I'm not sure—"

"For the love of mercy," Vivien said in exasperation. "Feeding it beer? Next you'll want to teach it drinking songs and take it to a boxing match. Give the wretched thing to me and move out of the way."

Gratefully Victoria handed her the wineglass.

Instead of trying to apply the leech with the glass, Vivien grasped the slimy creature with her fingers and held it to Papa's temple. "*Bite*, you little fuck-worm!"

The leech obeyed and started sucking.

"Daughter, your language," Papa reproved.

Vivien fished another leech from the jar and applied it to his other temple. That leech bit down as well.

"I fear life in the theater has had an unseemly influence on you," Papa murmured, but he reached out and patted Vivien's hand in thanks.

While he relaxed and closed his eyes to let the leeches do their work, the sisters went into their shared bedroom.

Victoria reached out and hugged her twin. "*Thank you*. I couldn't bring myself to touch it. I don't know how you did."

Vivien laughed softly. "I've had to do far more disgusting things in the service of a lover."

"*Ugh.* Please never, ever tell me what they were." Victoria went to the washstand and used soap and water to remove any trace of slime from her fingers. "You told Papa you're an actress?"

Vivien reached for the soap and began to wash her own hands. "It's not far from the truth. I'll have you know, I've honed some first-rate acting skills in the bedroom: 'Oh, what a beast, how will it ever fit? Poor little me! Would you mind if I bite down on a handkerchief?'"

"Do they believe you?"

"No, but they love it. Flattery can turn a boiled carrot into a rod of steel."

"There's no other life that would suit you better?" Victoria asked, regarding her with concern.

"No, and it would suit you just as well, if you'd give it a chance."

Victoria shook her head. "I want to marry someday."

"No, you don't, or by now you would be the wife of some plodder in Dorking. Come to Paris with me. There's *so much* money to be made. I have my own carriage and horses, and a French chef, and an apartment on the Champs-Élysées. Any of my dressing gowns costs enough to support a family for a year. All you have to do is entertain gentlemen and do a few little things to keep them happy. It's easy. It doesn't even take long."

"You just said it was worse than touching leeches," Victoria said, wrinkling her nose.

Vivien laughed. "One becomes accustomed. And it's better than this. You're wasting your life here."

"Who would look after Papa?" Victoria pointed out gently.

"We'll hire someone. His condition is worsening by the day. Soon he won't even know who's taking care of him."

"I'll know."

Wrenched back to the present, Victoria ducked her head and used her gloved fingers to wipe at the wet corners of her eyes.

I'm Victoria Devane. My sister is Vivien. I live in a cottage in Dorking. I teach at a stone schoolhouse with a green door. My father was a scholar. My mother left us when we were still too young to remember her—

"Tell yer fortune, dearie?" came a cheerful voice. A diminutive, gaudily dressed old woman wearing bangles and bright scarves stood in front of her. "Only tuppence to learn the secrets of ter-morrer."

Dazedly Victoria shook her head and turned away. Her heart gave a painful extra thump as she caught sight of Mr. Keyes in the crowd.

She hurried toward the massive portico of the opera house, where a crowd had gathered to protest a recent rise in prices. After slipping into the swarming throng, she let it carry her to the other side of the opera house, where she sought shelter in the lee of a Doric column. Leaning back against the cold stone, she stood very still, trembling with nerves, while people surged and booed and moved around her.

She remembered Mr. Keyes's inhumanly calm face as he had come into Vivien's town house when Victoria had been there alone. She could still feel his brutal hands on her throat, cutting off her air, as she had begged for her life.

He believed she was Vivien, and he intended to kill her.

Chapter Fifteen

The sky opened up, a deluge pouring over the marketplace, streaming into gutters and down cellar steps. Vendors rapidly stowed baskets of produce into wagons and carts, while porters and buyers left with their purchases. The crowd dispersed, people darting in every direction to seek shelter. Pickpockets took advantage of the pandemonium to harvest watches, coins, and handkerchiefs from unguarded pockets.

Victoria peeked around the column and saw with a shock that Mr. Keyes was walking toward her. It terrified her that he looked so calm, as if it were a foregone conclusion that he would catch her. It was what Bow Street Runners did best—track down human prey.

She bolted, splashing and skidding heedlessly across the road, darting among wagons and coaches. As she reached the footpath, she tried to read the street nameplate, but it was obscured by sheets of rain. A hasty glance over her shoulder revealed that Keyes was at the other side of the street, waiting for an opportunity to cross over.

There was no choice but to run.

Grant burst through the front door of his town house, his face skull-white as he beheld the three servants in the entrance hall. "Where is she?" he asked without preamble.

They looked at him as if he were a madman who'd just run inside from the street, which wasn't that far off the mark.

"Mr. Morgan," the housekeeper exclaimed. "Thank the Lord you're back. I was about to send a note to Bow Street to ask Sir Ross about his request—"

"What the devil are you talking about? Where's Victoria?"

"Victoria?" Mrs. Buttons repeated, looking baffled.

Grant shook his head impatiently. "Vivien. Miss Duvall. Who was assigned to watch over her?"

"Mr. Keyes."

"Where is he?"

"Mr. Keyes left to find her."

"*Left?* She went somewhere alone?"

Miriam replied in a quavering voice. "I saw Miss Duvall on the servants' stairs, heading down to the back entrance. She said not to tell anyone, it was life and death to her. But I thought it would be best to go to Mrs. Buttons."

The blood was pounding in his ears. "Life and death," he repeated. "What gave her that idea?"

"Sir," Mrs. Buttons said, "as soon as Mr. Keyes arrived, he told us there had been a change of plan, and Sir Ross wanted him to bring Miss Duvall to Bow Street."

Grant's stomach went light, as if the floor had dropped from beneath his feet.

"That was a lie," he said. "Cannon wouldn't have done that."

"Miss Duvall didn't want to go away with Mr. Keyes," the housekeeper continued, "but she agreed and went upstairs to change into her walking shoes. And while we waited for her in the library, she slipped out of the house."

She was too cautious to take a risk for no reason. Something had tipped her off about Keyes, or maybe she was following an instinct. Fear and rage cracked his heart open. He felt his soul run out to the end of its tether.

"I watched Miss Duvall from the back door as she left," Miriam said. "She was headed to the market, looked like."

She was going to Bow Street, Grant thought. As far as Victoria knew, it was the only place of safety other than his house. He turned to the footman. "Peter, run directly to Sir Ross's office. Tell him to send out every man available, including the night watch and horse patrol, to find Miss Duvall and Keyes."

"Yes, sir." The footman was gone in a flash.

"Sir—" the housekeeper began, but Grant ignored her and ran outside as if demons were at his heels.

Rain beat down as he headed toward Covent Garden at a breakneck pace, passing the churchyard of St. Paul's, cornering the eastern portico. Had Victoria gone through the market square, or skirted around it through the surrounding alleys? He could hardly rein in his panic at the thought of how much attention a lone woman with a pretty face and red hair would attract in those places.

Christ, he had to find her before Keyes did.

Blinking hard and using both hands to wipe the streaming water from her face, Victoria blundered down a side street. She realized in despair that she must be heading in the wrong direction. She should have reached Bow Street by now. If only she knew the way. If only a few more minutes had passed before Keyes had seen her.

The hem of her rain-soaked skirts tangled around her ankles as she ran along an alley of dilapidated buildings. She went down a set of basement steps and slipped inside the door.

It was a betting shop, the smoke-filled air swirling ochre in the lamplight. Men huddled at a counter lined with tobacco jars and cigar bundles, and studied lists of odds on the back wall. A bookmaker with leather pouches at each hip swaggered back and forth while jotting down bets with a pencil stub.

There was a rank smell everywhere, a rubbishy odor of urine and tobacco. Shrinking into the nearest corner, Victoria yanked her hood down low over her face and waited. She prayed silently that Keyes would pass the betting shop and search elsewhere.

"Look here." A gentleman's cultured voice interrupted her thoughts, and a pair of black Hessian boots approached. "A pretty little bird has found a dry place to perch during the storm."

Biting her lower lip, Victoria steeled herself not to flinch as the man pulled back her hood. A meaty hand reached for a lock of her hair. "Are you looking for an evening's companion?" he asked. "If so, your search is at an end. I'm your man."

Silently damning him for drawing attention to her, Victoria glanced upward. He looked like a gentleman, clean-shaven and well-dressed, wearing a high-collared broadcloth coat.

"A stranger was bothering me in the marketplace," she said in a low voice. "I wanted to avoid him by hiding in here for a few minutes."

He clucked his tongue in false sympathy and slid an arm around her. "Poor birdie. I'll protect you." He reached for the bodice of her chemise and began to pluck at the fastenings, ignoring her outraged gasp. "Easy now—I just want a look at the goods."

Now the full attention of the room was on them. Even the bookmaker had paused to watch.

"I came here to avoid being molested by one man," Victoria said sharply, shoving at his hands and retreating farther into the corner. "I'm not looking for another."

"I'll keep you warm for a night and pay you well," he told her.

"I need someone to help me to Bow Street," she said desperately. "Have you heard of Grant Morgan? I know he would consider it a personal favor if you took me there safely."

Some of the lust seemed to fade from his expression, and he looked at her with new interest. "I've heard of Morgan. What connection do you have with him?"

A hint of relief broke through her agitation. If this man could be persuaded to take her to Bow Street, she would be safe from Keyes. But before she could say another word, someone entered the betting shop.

After one glimpse of the man's gray hat, Victoria gave a muffled exclamation of fright. "It's him," she said shakily.

"The man who was bothering you?" her companion asked.

Victoria nodded, her throat closing as she stared at Keyes. He was breathing rapidly from exertion, his face set. As soon as he saw her, his eyes gleamed with triumph.

"I'm a Bow Street Runner in pursuit of a suspect," Keyes said, coming toward them. "Give her to me."

The betting shop erupted with unease. The bookmaker came out from behind the counter. "I'm running a straight business, I am! What will it take to keep you pigs out o' my lister?"

"I don't give a damn about what you're doing," Keyes said, coming toward Victoria. "Carry on after I leave. All I need is the woman—she's wanted for questioning."

"He's lying," Victoria cried, throwing herself at the man beside her—grabbing at whatever meager protection she could find. "I've done nothing wrong."

"What crime is she accused of?" the man asked, one arm closing around Victoria.

"None of your concern," Keyes replied. "Give her to me and go about your business."

"Do as 'e says," the bookmaker commanded

tersely. "Hand over the little tart if that's all he wants. 'Tis bad for business to 'ave a Runner about the place."

The man sighed and gently began to urge Victoria forward. "It seems we're star-crossed, dove. Go on with him."

"He's going to kill me," she said, clutching at him.

"Kill you?" the man repeated. "Don't be silly. Whatever you've done, it can't be all that bad. Just give the magistrate a pretty smile, and he'll let you off the hook."

"I'm begging you," she said desperately, "help me reach Bow Street. It's not far from here."

Whatever he read in her eyes persuaded him to help her. The arm around her strengthened. "All right," he said. "Seems I'm going to rescue a damsel in distress, this soggy evening." He turned to Keyes with an affable smile. "I'll accompany the girl to Bow Street," he said. "That's where you want her taken, yes? What difference does it make if I bring her there on your behalf?"

Victoria tensed as Keyes approached, pulling something from his coat. "I'll show you what difference it makes." He used a small but weighted cudgel to strike the man on his head, shoulders, and arms. It made sickening sounds, metal thudding into muscle and bone.

She dodged away in the uproar and tried to push through the crowd.

After Keyes had reduced the man to a moaning heap on the ground, he followed Victoria and grabbed her. She cried out as he seized one of her arms and twisted it behind her, forcing her to bend forward.

Angry shouts filled the betting shop, but Keyes's cold voice cut through the cacophony. "If anyone else tries to tangle with me, I'll charge you with interfering with an officer's execution of his duty."

"Get yer arse out o' my lister!" the bookmaker snapped, and crouched over the injured man on the floor.

Keyes propelled Victoria out of the shop.

"They're all witnesses," she cried. "They'll all say you were the one who took me."

"I'll be long gone before an investigation has begun."

"Why are you doing this?" She gave a pained cry as he twisted her arm harder and pushed her up the steps to the street.

"Quiet, or I'll crack your noggin."

They turned a corner and proceeded along an alley to an abandoned factory building. The roof was partially collapsed, the walls slumping dangerously as if the structure would give way to gravity at any moment.

Victoria screamed and dug in her heels as Keyes dragged her through a yawning gap where there had once been a door. Hot pain exploded on the side of her head, and she stumbled against him, her mind buzzing. While she stood in a daze, he jerked her hands behind her back and snapped handcuffs around her wrists. After tugging off his cravat, he used it to gag her.

Despite her efforts to resist, Keyes shoved her toward a set of rotting stairs and hauled her upward with one of his hands gripped painfully tight in her hair.

They reached the second floor, which was littered with rodent droppings and debris. The sooty walls glistened with rain trailing in from the broken roof.

After dragging Victoria to a corner, Keyes pushed her to the floor, and she fell back in a heap.

Crouching over her, he began to jerk at the fastenings of his breeches. "I should end this right now," he said. "But first I want a taste of what Morgan had."

Victoria rolled over and rose to her knees, but he shoved her back to the floor.

"Stay down or I'll make it worse for you." He began pulling up her skirts, while she kicked at him uselessly. "Women like you are no loss to the world," he muttered. "Parasites. You all want everyone to worship you . . . beg and crawl for your favors . . . you're nothing but a worn-out little purse. Lie still! If you don't fight me, I'll kill you the nice way after, instead of making you suffer."

"Morgan," Flagstad asked, struggling to match Grant's ground-covering strides, "why would Miss Duvall have run off like that? She must have lost her head. Everyone knows Keyes would never harm her. He's a gentleman."

"At the moment, what we know about Keyes is open to question," Grant said brusquely.

"He did nothing out of order. He's searching for Miss Duvall just as we are, to bring her back to safety."

The man's determination to shield his friend made Grant as hostile as a baited bear. Before he could stop himself, he turned and seized Flagstad by his coat lapels. "Stop telling me what kind of man Keyes is—just help me find the bastard."

Flagstad broke his hold and shoved him back. "What the devil is wrong with you? Keyes has been your friend for years!"

Grant ignored him and headed toward the opera house.

"Morgan!" A breathless shout caused Grant to stop and swing around. A constable was running neck or nothing from the north side of the marketplace. "Morgan . . . they sent me to tell you . . ."

Grant reached him in an instant, nearly knocking the young man over. "What is it?"

"Betting shop . . . alley off Tavistock . . ." Gasping frantically, the constable paused and hung his head in the struggle for more air.

"Tell me, damn it," Grant said, grabbing him by the shoulders.

"List-maker claims . . . girl came into the shop . . . asked for help to reach the Bow Street office. A Runner came in and forced her to come away with him."

"Thank God," Flagstad exclaimed in relief, having come up behind them. "Keyes found her."

"How long ago?" Grant asked the young constable.

"Ten minutes, more or less."

Flagstad interrupted eagerly. "They're probably at Bow Street by now. I'll go meet them there."

"You do that," Grant said, and took off at a dead run toward Tavistock Street.

When he reached the betting shop, he found a constable standing at the top of the basement steps with a man wearing a bookmaker's heavy leather pouches.

The bookmaker squinted at him speculatively. "Bloody big'un, you are," he commented. "You must be Morgan. She was asking for you, the girl what came to my place and started the 'ole damned rucktion."

"What happened?" Grant asked.

"Runner came inside to fetch her. She was carrying on, said he was after killing her." The bookmaker shook his head and added with disgust, "Women."

"And there was a fight," the nearby constable prompted him.

"I'd call it a one-sided basting," the bookmaker said sourly. "The Runner knocked the piss out of a customer with a neddy before taking the girl with him."

"In what direction?" Grant asked hoarsely.

"I may know," the bookmaker said diffidently, "or I may not."

The young constable seized him impatiently, giving him a brief shake. "Answer Mr. Morgan's question!"

The bookmaker squawked in outrage. "Rough me up again, an' I'll give you what for!"

"Let go of him," Grant told the constable, and stared hard at the bookmaker. "What do you want?"

"I want the stinkin' police to keep yer arses out o' my lister from now on."

"Done."

The constable began to protest. "But Mr. Morgan, we're supposed to—" He broke off as Grant sent him a murderous glance.

The bookmaker dragged forth a small, skinny lad of eleven or twelve. "This is my odd-jobs boy, Willie," he said. "I sent 'im to follow the Runner. Willie, show the man where they gone."

The boy ran off full-pelt with Grant at his heels.

They came to a rattletrap building with gaping holes where windows and doors had once been. Piles of crumbled brick and rotted timber surrounded it. Every visible wall was buckled and slumped as if the entire structure were about to cave in on itself.

"I'd stay clear, if I was you," Willie said. "Ain't a sound stick o' wood in the place."

Before the boy had even finished speaking, Grant crossed the threshold and went inside. Moss had made parts of the floor slick. Wind gusts made the building groan and shudder as if it were a living creature. Rain trickled through the broken roof and down the walls.

A pattern of scuffs and arcs on the floor caught his attention. His gaze went to the stairs. His heart stopped at the sight of freshly splintered wood.

He bounded up the steps, heedless of them cracking and crumbling beneath his weight. As he reached the landing, a crack of lightning cast blue light across the dismantled factory space.

He saw two figures in the corner. Keyes crouching over Victoria, fumbling at her skirts while she twisted beneath him.

Grant lunged toward the man with no thought or intention save murder. Keyes had only a second to look up before he was thrown halfway across the room. Reflexively Keyes rolled and reached for something in his coat, but just as he withdrew a pistol, Grant seized his arm and slammed it against the floor with crushing force. Keyes screamed and struck out with his other fist, striking Grant's jaw. Grant didn't even feel the blow.

"She's only a whore," Keyes shouted.

Grant didn't reply, only hammered until no more words came from the other man's mouth. Gradually Keyes stopped fighting and brought up his arms to defend his face and head.

When the Runner was subdued to a groaning heap, a muffled sound drew Grant's attention. Panting in bursts, he saw Victoria on her side, watching him with streaming eyes, her throat working.

A thread of sanity penetrated his rage. He searched Keyes's pockets and found the key to the handcuffs. He went to her, dropped to his knees at her side, and unlocked the steel manacles. She quivered as they fell away from her wrists.

Grant untied the gag and hauled her into his lap. The feel of her, soft and small and alive, pulsed all through him.

His relief was unspeakable.

"Grant Morgan to the rescue," she said weakly, her teeth chattering.

He couldn't manage a smile, only gripped her against him and kissed her tear-ravaged face.

"I thought I would die," she said.

"No."

"I thought his face would be the last one I ever saw . . ."

"*My* face is the one you're going to see," he said gruffly. "Every morning. Every night."

"I remembered him. Mr. Keyes. He's the one from before."

Grant knew he was holding her too tightly, but he couldn't seem to make his arms loosen. "I'm sorry," he managed to say. "It's my fault. Shouldn't have left you—"

"You couldn't have known. You found me."

"I'm never letting you out of my sight again," he said vehemently.

The building creaked and swayed as the storm continued to rage outside.

Galvanized into action, Grant set Victoria out of his lap and pulled her up with him. "I have to take you out of here."

She twisted to glance at Keyes's prostrate form. "What about him?"

"Don't worry about him," Grant said, and slid a supportive arm around her back. "Can you walk, Victoria?"

"You know my name? How—"

"I'll explain later." Unable to help himself, he bent and possessed her mouth in a hard kiss. "Let's go. Take my hand, I'll help you downstairs."

Carefully he led the way, testing each step before he allowed Victoria to proceed. It seemed an eternity had passed before they finally reached the ground floor and were able to go outside.

Despite the weather, a small crowd had begun

to gather in the alley. A few people exclaimed and cheered as they saw Grant emerge with Victoria.

"Mr. Morgan," someone said, and Grant recognized the horse patrol officer approaching them.

"Captain Brogdan."

"Glad to see the lady has been safely recovered." Brogdan's smile faded as he glanced at the ramshackle building and asked reluctantly, "Is Mr. Keyes up there?"

"Upper floor."

"Alive?"

"He was when I left him," Grant confirmed. "But he'll need assistance coming down."

The captain frowned as he looked over the building. "I hate to send anyone in there. Place looks none too sound." He paused. "What should we do with Mr. Keyes after we've retrieved him?"

"Arrest him on charges of kidnapping, assault, and attempted rape and murder."

Brogdan closed his eyes for a moment. "God help us all." The news of a Bow Street officer's corruption and criminal activity would strike a massive blow to the public's faith in the justice system—which wasn't all that high to begin with. "May hell sweat me if we shouldn't just leave him up there."

"It's tempting," Grant said darkly. "But he'll have to be tried and held publicly accountable."

"It could take years to regain the ground he's

cost us." The captain gestured to another officer, who led a large bay to them. "Mr. Morgan, may I offer the use of my mount? Chester's a fine patrol horse—he'd be honored to convey you and the lady to Bow Street."

After Grant had lifted Victoria into the saddle and swung up behind her, she leaned back into the shelter of his body. She was sore and bruised, but she didn't mind the discomfort, or even the rain. All of it reminded her that she was still alive.

As they rode slowly along the street, she felt Grant's chest lift and subside with a rough sigh. In a few moments, there was another haggard inhale and exhale, as if his body was struggling against the effort to relax.

"It's over now," Victoria said, clinging to the arm that crossed in front of her, pressing it more tightly against herself. "You stopped him."

"What if I'd been too late?"

"It wouldn't have been your fault," she said. "Some things are beyond your control."

Grant shook his head. "For the rest of my life," he said grimly, "everything will depend on the safety of one small, accident-prone woman."

She gave a nonplussed laugh. "Accident-prone? I'll have you know, before I came to London to look for my sister, I led a very quiet life. The greatest challenge I faced was when Billy Lewthwaite brought his pet toad to the schoolhouse and three of my students went home with warts on their hands."

His head bent, and she felt his lips against her temple. "So your memory's come back."

"Some of it. There's so much I want to tell you. Grant, my father was a philosophy scholar!"

"I know."

"You do? How?"

"I found your cottage in Dorking."

A hundred questions came to her lips at once, but all she could manage were a few little splutters.

"Vivien was there," Grant continued. "I spoke with her."

"You—I can't believe—What did she say? Is she well?"

"Quite well, from all appearances. And very much with child."

"I must see her. I need to go to Dorking as soon as possible."

"Of course."

They reached Bow Street, which was busier than Victoria would have expected at such a late hour. "Why is it so crowded?" she asked.

"They run many public services from the office, in addition to policing and court business. Sir Ross has been trying to hire more magistrates and court officers to ease the burden." He sounded grim as he added, "I suspect it will be ten times harder to secure funding now, after what Keyes has done."

They rode past the public entrances and went directly to Sir Ross's private residence. Grant reined in the horse, dismounted, and reached up for Victoria. A boy in his teens emerged from the building to take the horse, and led him to the stable in back.

Grant kept Victoria's hand in his as they went to the front door.

Feeling exhausted, cold, wet, and sore, she said wistfully, "I wish we could go home."

"Soon," he said gently. "I promise."

He knocked at the door, and it was opened by a silver-haired housekeeper. "Mrs. Dobson," he said.

"Dear me," she exclaimed.

"I need to see Cannon now," Grant said. "We have only a few minutes. Miss Duvall . . . that is, Devane . . . has been through an ordeal and requires rest."

The housekeeper regarded Victoria with kindly concern. "Come this way at once." She urged them through the bustling crowd and brought them to Sir Ross's office, a small room with rectangular windows facing the street.

Sir Ross, who was talking to a patrol officer, stopped in midsentence as Grant brought Victoria into the room. "Morgan," he said. "What is this about Keyes?"

"Hired by Lord Lane," Grant said flatly.

Cannon's shoulders slumped a bit. He rubbed his temples with a thumb and forefinger, as if a headache had suddenly descended. His gaze slid over them both, and he spoke to the house-keeper. "Mrs. Dobson, bring tea and blankets."

"Yes, sir." She disappeared at once.

Efficiently Cannon ushered the officer from the room and closed the door.

Grant arranged a couple of chairs in front of the desk and seated Victoria. "This won't take long," he told her.

"No indeed," Cannon said. He surprised her, and perhaps Grant as well, by lowering to his haunches in front of her and taking her cold hands in a warm clasp. His gray eyes surveyed her with concern. "Miss Duvall . . . the fact that you were attacked by one of my men . . . it grieves me more than I can say. I can offer no sufficient redress for what you've suffered . . . but I give you my word that if I may ever be of service, in any capacity, you have only to ask."

"Thank you," Victoria replied, unnerved to have one of London's most powerful men offer her an apology.

Cannon stood and spoke with Grant until Mrs. Dobson had brought the blankets. When Victoria was wrapped in a layer of wool, with a steaming mug of tea clasped in her icy fingers, the magistrate's implacable gaze returned to her. "Miss Duvall . . . please tell me as best you can what happened this evening."

Occasionally fumbling for words, Victoria de-scribed the events that had passed since Grant had left her earlier in the day. The only interruption came when the office door reverberated from a curious scraping motion. Victoria paused and looked around questioningly at the odd noise.

Cannon rose and opened the door. Immediately a large striped cat with no tail sauntered inside the office. After surveying the visitors with a speculative gaze, the cat jumped into Victoria's lap.

She gasped in surprise and handed her tea to Grant as the massive feline settled in a furry heap over her thighs. "A police cat?" she asked. "Does he live here, Sir Ross?"

"*She* does," the magistrate replied. "She wandered in from the street one day. Small and half-starved. We made the mistake of feeding her."

Holding the purring cat in her lap, Victoria finished her explanation and waited quietly while the other two talked briefly. The office was warm, and she felt herself relaxing.

"I need to take her home," Grant said eventually, and nudged the cat from her lap. "I'll return first thing in the morning."

"My carriage will convey you to Bedford Street." Cannon opened the door for them. "Miss Devane, I hope you'll suffer no lasting ill effects from tonight."

"I'll be good as new after some rest," she assured him.

Grant frowned. "I should send for Linley," he said. "He should have a look at you."

"Again?" Victoria protested. "No. I'm tired of being poked and prodded. Please take me home and let me rest."

Grant's expression changed as he looked down at her, and he adjusted the cloak on her shoulders. "Whatever you wish, love."

Mrs. Dobson came to the threshold of Sir Ross's office as they watched the pair leave. When she glanced back at Ross, the housekeeper wore a pleased, slightly bemused expression. "I never thought to see our Mr. Morgan tamed by a slip of a girl," she said. "He's fallen hard, hasn't he?"

"So it would seem. Poor bastard."

An affectionate smile brightened Mrs. Dobson's plump face. "Someday, sir, a woman may yet reduce you to the same state."

"I'll slit my own throat first," he replied calmly. "Mrs. Dobson, bring me a jug of coffee."

The housekeeper looked outraged at the suggestion. "At this hour?"

Sighing, Cannon returned to his desk while she proceeded to lecture him.

Chapter Sixteen

❧

"I expect we'll have another novel out of this," Mrs. Buttons exclaimed after Grant and Victoria had returned home. *"The Case of the Treacherous Traitor."*

Grant shook his head and groaned at the thought.

After surveying their filthy, bedraggled condition, the housekeeper turned to Miriam and Peter. "Both of you, start carrying up hot water from the kitchen."

They obeyed quickly, heading downstairs.

Grant accompanied Victoria up to her bedroom, and stopped at the doorway.

She spoke softly, mindful of being overheard. "Will you come to me after you bathe?"

He shook his head.

Surprised, she drew back a few inches. "You won't?"

"You said you'd had enough of being poked and prodded."

She reached out and slid her arms around his lean waist. "I meant from anyone other than you."

He smiled. "You need to sleep."

"Help me relax first," she coaxed.

A reluctant laugh rumbled in his throat, and slowly his arms came around her. "I have no self-control, sweet love. None at all."

"I wouldn't mind."

"I would. I intend to protect you from everything and everyone. Including myself." He bent and kissed her chastely. "Good night, love."

"I'm very sorry about today, miss," Miriam said later, after she'd helped to wash Victoria's hair. "I should have done as you asked. From now on—"

"It's all forgotten," Victoria told her. "We'll make a new start tomorrow."

"You're very kind, miss. Thank you."

After Victoria dressed in a white nightgown and matching pelisse, she sat by the fire and combed her damp hair. Idly she extended her bare feet to let the heat play over her toes.

Grant had finished bathing by now, she

thought. Undoubtedly he had been right about sleeping in separate beds tonight. They both needed rest.

But sleep seemed like an appalling waste of time when the man she loved was only a room away.

Before she was even conscious of making the decision, she had left her room and gone to his door. Hesitantly she turned the knob and entered the bedroom.

Her eyes widened at the sight of Grant stretched out on the guest bed. He held a book in his hand, reading with a slight frown on his forehead and a moody set to his mouth. His hair was still wet, gleaming like black satin.

The covers had been pulled up to his lap, but it was obvious he was naked. The firelight played over tightly knitted muscle and sinew, and over the dark fleece of hair on his chest.

Grant glanced in her direction, blinked in surprise, and reflexively covered his lap with the open book.

Charmed and amused by the defensive gesture, Victoria wandered farther into the room.

"What are you doing in here?" Grant asked.

"I wanted to see how you were."

"I'm fine."

"Do you usually read naked in bed?" she asked casually.

"Yes. Before I go to sleep. Which is what I was about to do."

"What are you reading?"

"Go back to your room, Victoria."

Ignoring the command, Victoria crept closer and looked at the cover. "Thomas Brown. *Lectures on the Philosophy of the Human Mind*." A smile spread across her face. "You're reading philosophy?"

"If it's important to you, I want to understand more about it."

She looked over his long-limbed form, all that beautifully woven muscle and sinew laid out for her in a masculine buffet. "You shouldn't read in such bad light," she said. "You'll strain your eyes."

"That's not the only thing I'll strain if you don't leave."

"I can't fall asleep."

Grant sat up and swung his legs over the side of the bed, the muscles of his stomach flexing as he kept the book over his lap. "You would in less than a minute, if you went to bed and closed your eyes."

"You're going to need a bigger book," she said, noticing the volume was no longer able to conceal him. "Possibly an encyclopedia."

He laughed reluctantly. "Sweet love . . . in the past few days, you've been manhandled and set upon by entirely too many people."

"You don't want me?"

"I want what's best for you."

"Well, that would be you." Staring into his dilated eyes, Victoria reached for the top button of her pelisse. She fumbled a little as she tried to pull it through the tiny silk loop. It was stuck. She tugged harder and the button popped off entirely, hitting the glass lampshade and bouncing to the carpet. Glancing at Grant sheepishly, she said, "I'm not well-versed in the art of seduction."

In the next moment, the book landed on the floor beside her with a thud. Grant reached for her, lifted her easily, and deposited her on the bed. "I'd say you're doing something right," he said, climbing over her. He gave her enough of his weight that she could feel the hard jut of his erection. "You seduce me every time you enter the room," he said. "With every smile or glance. With the most commonplace word or gesture. You seduce me by breathing." As her fingers returned to the row of buttons, he laid a gentle hand over hers. "What if I just hold you tonight?" he asked.

"Yes. After you make love to me."

"Victoria . . . sweetheart . . . will you trust me to know what's best for you, just for tonight?"

"No. Trust me to know what's best for myself."

She lay beneath him, watching his face as he fought the inner battle of desire versus conscience.

"Damn it," he said softly, and his fingers went to the buttons at the front of her pelisse. Slowly he undressed her, his gaze drinking in every newly revealed inch of skin. He caressed her entire body with his gentle fingers and clever mouth, starting at her toes. By the time he reached her flushed face, she was hot and breathless.

After spreading her thighs, he settled over the cradle of her hips, not entering her, just relishing the sensation of being pressed together front-to-front. His hand cupped her jaw, thumb stroking lightly across her lips until they parted. Lowering his head, he let his mouth shape and play with hers, his tongue stroking in a restless, erotic search.

With a rough gasp, he buried his face in the loose locks of her hair and strove to calm himself. "You feel too good," came his muffled voice. "Ah, I'm in hell."

"Not heaven?" Victoria asked, and pushed out her lower lip in a pout.

His head lifted, his green eyes sparkling as he looked down at her. "There's a good part of hell," he told her.

"There is?"

"Mmm. Second circle." He bent again, and she felt his lips gliding over her neck until he found a sensitive place on the side. "There are large beds . . . everyone's naked . . . well-heated . . .

and there are all kinds of interesting toys to play with . . ."

She giggled and squirmed as he proceeded to describe a variety of items and what uses they might be put to. They kissed lavishly, ardently, rolling slowly across the bed. When they were both too aroused to wait any longer, Grant spread her thighs and began to enter her. She moaned in pleasure at the luscious pressure, hardness easing into softness.

Part of her mind went dark and quiet, all thought extinguished in the pure physical awareness of being possessed by him. He tried not to hurt her by thrusting, only held himself inside while her flesh worked to take him deeper. Sparks danced across her vision, and she jerked and moaned and pushed upward impatiently. One of his hands slid beneath her bottom and kept her fused against him, controlling her movements.

She whimpered in protest, but his mouth covered hers, and he licked at the soft sounds, savoring them.

He began to move in subtle, deep-rooted lunges, keeping himself buried and allowing only an inch or two of motion . . . steady, rhythmic, tireless. Nothing existed except the hard presence of him, holding her open, gently teasing out new surges of wetness and warmth. His hand trailed lightly over her front, fingertips stroking and rolling her nipples. Sensations rippled through her, bringing her closer and closer to the edge.

Grasping her hips in both hands, he adjusted her higher, and a new sensation spread through her, not just from her pelvis but all along her spine. It built and built, radiating everywhere, and all she wanted was to be lost in the feeling forever. He filled her completely, but she tried to take even more of him inside, her body clamping and pulsing helplessly on the thick, swollen shaft. He pumped harder, rocking against the plump rise of her mons until signals darted up to the base of her skull . . . finally, finally releasing heavy shocks of pleasure that were like losing consciousness.

His lips grazed her neck, his breath rushing against her skin. Turning her head, she sought his mouth blindly, and he kissed her, sending his tongue deep. More pleasure, cresting high and hard, her inner muscles gripping him until his rhythm broke.

He made a guttural sound and went still, drawing tight until his frame vibrated like the cord of an archer's bow.

The pleasure didn't stop even then, only swelled and ebbed with each small movement or change of position. He relaxed on his side, still locked inside her, relishing the pulses and shivers of her body.

Hot and exhausted and satiated, Victoria lay in his arms, one thigh resting on his hip.

"This is the best part," he said, his voice low and drowsy. "Holding you until we both fall asleep . . . knowing you'll be here when I awaken."

Chapter Seventeen

Victoria protested with a sleepy sound as she felt Grant leaving the bed. He laughed quietly and returned to kiss her throat gently. The early morning bristle of his jaw drew a pleasant shiver from her.

"I have to leave for Bow Street," he murmured.

"Is it morning already?"

"I'm afraid so." He smoothed the wild cascade of her hair.

"Stay a little longer."

"I can't, love. There's too much to be done today. But I'll return soon." He kissed the soft white skin of her breast. "I plan never to spend more than a few hours away from you."

Victoria stroked his hair and sighed wistfully. "I wish that could be true."

He looked at her closely, his smile fading. "Why can't it?"

She found it difficult to think clearly as his hand came to rest low on her abdomen, his thumb brushing the rim of her navel. "Some things have to end properly before new things can begin."

"You're referring to your former life?"

"It's not really my *former* life. My house is there. My belongings. My students . . . the lending library . . . friends in the chess club . . . I must go back. There are too many things I still can't remember."

"I'll take you for visits."

"I must go home to stay, not visit," she said gently. "I need time to catch up with myself."

"Your home is with me," Grant insisted. But as he read her expression, he groaned and buried his head against her sheet-covered middle. "No. Ah, *damn it*, Victoria, I knew this would happen."

"I'm not leaving you," she said earnestly, stroking his dark head. "I'm just going away for a while."

"Why doesn't that reassure me?" came his muffled voice.

"I promise I'll come back."

"When? Do you have a particular time in mind?"

"Not really . . ."

"Give me a guess."

"Perhaps after Vivien's baby is born."

Grant looked up at her in outrage. "That will take *months*." His head dropped back to her lap. *"Fuck."*

"Grant," she protested, stroking the bunched muscles of his shoulders. "You understand why I need to go back. I'm not fully myself yet. And if I decide to leave the life I've always known, I'll want to visit friends and say goodbye, instead of simply disappearing."

"If you decide?" Grant sat up and stared at her fixedly.

She lifted her shoulders in the hint of an apologetic shrug.

"What about a betrothal before you go?" he asked. "Could we at least have that promise between us, if we're to spend so much time apart?"

Victoria was powerfully tempted to agree, for her own reassurance as well as his.

But something troubled her, an uneasiness that must be addressed. She had no idea what was causing it. All she knew was that she had to figure it out in safe and familiar surroundings, where she could uproot the feeling, lay it bare, and examine it.

"I can't," she said softly. "Before I'm able to make that kind of promise, I need to spend time in my own home and think about everything that's happened." She hesitated. "Would it suffice to know that I love you?"

Grant sat up and regarded her grimly. "Apparently it will have to."

Their gazes held in the silence.

"I'm late for work," he said.

She nodded, a frown pinching between her brows. "I won't keep you."

But he didn't leave the bed. He reached out to the curve of her breast, fondling gently, squeezing the tip between his thumb and forefinger. Her eyes half closed. The sheet was pulled away from her, and he leaned forward, his mouth sealing over the nipple.

She felt two of his fingers settle lightly at the cleft between her thighs, sliding up and down until the tender flesh felt hot and eager. A breathless sound escaped her as his fingertips pushed back the plump hood of her mound and tickled around the swelling bud.

He leaned forward, pushing her back against the pillows.

A sheet was still caught between them. She tugged it away, needing to feel all his skin against hers, and made a little sound of protest as she felt him draw back.

Grant hushed her softly and turned her onto her stomach. Confused, she felt him pull her hips up until she was braced on her elbows and knees. The heat of his shaft rested intimately along the crevice of her bottom as he bent over her. One of his hands flatted on her stomach and slid down between her thighs. Slowly he played with her and spread her open.

His lips brushed against her back, her shoulder, while his teasing fingers stroked through melting wetness and heat. There was the taut head of his shaft, fitting against her entrance, pressing inward. The hard length of him reached new places inside her, and she pushed back rhythmically, gasping at each slow plunge.

Her body closed around him, pulling at the rigid wet length. He fused their hips together and began a tight, deeply satisfying grinding that shot bolts of pleasure through her. As he reached the summit, he fell silent, shuddered hard, then collapsed on his side with her. A purring sigh escaped her lips.

"Well," Grant said a few minutes later, with a trace of satisfaction, "that should give you something to think about."

Despite the extra time spent in bed with Victoria, Grant was only a few minutes late to the Bow Street office. As always, the magistrate's expression was composed, but Grant knew the burden he shouldered was considerable. After Keyes's criminal actions, Bow Street would be under siege from the press, the public, and the government. A hailstorm of shite, as a clerk had glumly described it.

"One of the few advantages we have," Cannon told Grant, "is the goodwill and admiration the public bears for you. Your heroic image may be the only thing that will prevent our funding from being cut in half."

After asking about Victoria's welfare, Cannon told Grant that Keyes was in custody and had made a full confession. He would be charged and tried as quickly as possible in an effort to minimize publicity and controversy. All Cannon needed from Victoria was for her to appear in his chambers before he sat for his second session that day, and give her deposition in front of a clerk.

"Victoria won't have to face Keyes in court, then," Grant said, having already decided he would go to hell and back before allowing her to be in the same room with him.

"No, there's no need to put her through yet another ordeal," Cannon replied. "Her testimony in chambers, as well as Keyes's own confession, will be sufficient to bind him over for trial before the King's Bench."

"And Lord Lane?" Grant asked. "Is he to be arrested this morning? If so, I volunteer for the task."

The magistrate paused in the act of lifting a coffee mug to his lips. "You haven't heard? Lord Lane is dead."

"*What?*"

"He suffered an attack of apoplexy last evening, just after your departure from Boodle's."

On one hand, Grant was glad Lane had finally gone to meet his Maker. On the other hand, he was distinctly sorry the old codger had managed to escape the humiliation of being indicted, tried, and punished. "What good news," he said. "I only wish I'd been able to stay at Boodle's long enough to see it."

Cannon frowned at his callousness. "That comment is beneath you, Morgan."

"It's because of that vengeful old codger that Victoria has been repeatedly attacked and almost killed. It's been devastating for her, no matter how bravely she's handled it. And while she may eventually recover from being brutalized by Keyes last night, I'll never stop being tortured by thoughts of what almost happened."

The magistrate continued to skewer him with a disapproving stare.

Grant cursed beneath his breath and hung his head guiltily. "Hang it, Cannon, I can't be dispassionate like you. Not about this. I'll be noble about everything else, but I can't tolerate any threat to Victoria's safety or happiness. It's a bloody miracle I didn't kill either Lane or Keyes—and that little whelp Harry Axler would do well to sleep with one eye open from now on. I love Victoria so much that—"

"Morgan," Cannon interrupted hastily, "there's no need to go into your personal feelings. I'll overlook your comments in light of the circumstances."

"Thank you."

"From now on, however, it's important to guard against expressing yourself impetuously."

"Why?"

"I've decided to appoint you as assistant police magistrate, to serve alongside me."

Grant stared at him blankly.

"The position automatically confers honorary knighthood," Cannon added.

"Christ." Grant shook his head in amazement. "I'm honored, sir, but . . . I'm not suited for that."

The magistrate regarded him intently. "Why do you say that?"

"My education, to start with. I've never studied Latin or the law."

"You have much to learn," Cannon agreed. "But you're capable of it."

"Isn't there a requirement for you to appoint a lawyer?"

"No. A law degree is preferred but not mandatory. So far there are no limiting qualifications with respect to these appointments. If you'll agree to study law in your spare time, I'll train you as a solicitor."

"But magistrates always come from the upper class. You know I'm a commoner."

"That's what makes you the best choice by far for the position. Bow Street was designed as a poor man's court. People come here knowing they'll have a chance of being heard and helped. Confidence in the courts varies among other districts, but here people believe in the honor of a Bow Street magistrate. Who better to understand and administer to them than one of their own? The public will only live by the law if they believe it to be fair." Cannon paused. "I'm offering you a position of considerable power, not only in matters of policing and criminal justice, but also in distribution of financial relief to the poor. I know you'll conduct yourself honorably. I could find a better-trained man to fill the position—but no one nearly as trustworthy. I would choose the man with character every time."

Grant looked down at his hands and flexed the scraped knuckles. What Cannon had proposed would be far more than a change in occupation, or even income. It would elevate him to a higher position in society—a chance few men ever had. But the challenges that would come with living "above his buttons," as it was called, were impossible to predict.

"You've earned it," Cannon said, seeming to read his thoughts. "Furthermore, you'll have friends at your side to help guide you through it. Count me among them."

Grant smiled at him. "I suppose I'll need a more settled lifestyle if I'm ever to have a wife and family."

"It would spare a wife much worry," Cannon agreed, "not to have her husband risk his life constantly in the course of his daily work. A police magistrate's schedule is demanding, mind you. But it would allow you to come home for dinner, and sleep in your own bed at night."

"I'll accept, then, with thanks," Grant said. "I can't be a Bow Street officer forever. God knows I don't want to find myself lumbering along a footpath one day with a younger officer kicking up dust far ahead of me. And a more respectable occupation might make Miss Devane more inclined to marry me."

"That reminds me . . ." Cannon hunted among the documents on his desk and handed one to Grant.

"What is this?" Grant asked warily.

"A contract. Call it redress. I met with the publisher of the Morgan of Bow Street novels and told him I would pursue a cause of action on your behalf unless you and he could come to an agreement on the use of your name and image. You have the right to stop publication altogether and receive compensatory damages. However, if you sign this contract, allowing him to continue publishing the books, he'll give you approval rights before each new one is published, and pay you a fair percentage of past and future publications. That would include a check for the amount listed on page two."

Grant turned the page and nearly toppled off his chair. "Ten thousand pounds?"

The chief magistrate smiled at his astonishment. "It seems being Grant Morgan is a lucrative business. That check for past due royalties is yours, by the way, whether or not you decide to sign the contract." He tilted his head slightly, his gaze quizzical. "Do you think you could tolerate remaining in the public eye and allowing the book series to continue?"

Grant considered the question and nodded. "I think I can find a way to live with it and not have to lie or feel like a fraud. I might even find ways to do some good with it. May I ask why you decided to talk to the publisher?"

"You have Miss Devane to thank for that." Cannon gave a quiet laugh as he saw Grant's expression. "I spoke with her at the Lichfield ball, just before you and she departed. Despite having just been assaulted by Harry Axler, she retained the presence of mind to speak to me about the adventure novels. She pointed out that if you weren't allowed to control your own name and reputation, it could result in disaster for the entire Bow Street office. For instance, a book could depict you behaving in an ungentlemanly or unheroic manner. She also questioned the legality of the publisher's actions, as well as the ethics of setting the Bow Street office's interests above yours." The chief magistrate paused before admitting reluctantly, "She was correct. And I owe you an apology."

"Accepted," Grant said.

"A man could do far worse," Cannon observed, "than to have an intelligent woman championing his interests and standing up for him. She would make a fine wife, Morgan."

"I know," Grant said, and sighed shortly. "When I proposed, she asked for time to return home to Surrey and gain her bearings before making significant decisions about the future."

"That's wise of her," Cannon said. "The question of marriage is complex for women." At Grant's quizzical glance, he continued, "The law confers absolute authority on a husband. From the vantage of a magistrate, it's not an authority that even the best of men handles well. If I were a woman, I'd want to be very sure of a man before submitting to it. If she's asked for patience, by all means give it."

"I will." Grant hesitated. Cannon was an intensely private man, and had rarely mentioned his late wife, Eleanor, who seemed to have been a pleasant woman with fragile health. Ever since she had died in childbirth four years ago, Cannon had directed all his tremendous energy and will into his work. As far as anyone knew, he kept no mistress, and had no plans to marry again. Which made Grant wonder what kind of marriage it might have been.

"In light of your own experience with marriage," he asked, "you would recommend it?"

"Yes," the magistrate said without hesitation. He paused and appeared to drift into a sweet, long-forgotten memory. "With the right woman . . . it's not half-bad." He collected himself, but the gray eyes remained warmer than Grant had ever seen them. "Good luck, Morgan."

Victoria sat at a stone table in the center of the garden square outside Grant's town house. It was cold and damp outside, but the fresh air helped to clear her mind. There were many decisions to make, not all of them pleasant.

"What are you doing out here?"

A masculine voice penetrated the swirl of her thoughts. Lifting her head, Victoria saw Grant standing there, and her heartbeat quickened. An irrepressible smile curved her lips.

Grant sat in a nearby chair, facing her, and took her hand in his. With the other hand he caressed the cool skin of her cheek, his thumb lightly brushing one of the shadows beneath her eyes. "You should take a nap," he murmured. "We'll have to go to Bow Street for a deposition later this afternoon. I'll make sure it goes as quickly as possible, but it will still be tiring."

Victoria leaned the side of her face into his hand. "Grant, if it's possible . . . I'd like to go to Dorking afterward."

Grant looked surprised and affronted. "Today?"

"I want to see my sister. I want to go home."

He removed his coat and placed it over her shoulders. The silk-lined wool held the warmth and scent of his body, and she snuggled into it with a shiver of comfort.

"Yes," he said reluctantly, "I'll take you there after the deposition. But I don't like the idea of you staying in that cottage with only a young cookmaid and a sister who's with child. It's inviting trouble."

"Nothing ever happens in Dorking. We'll be quite safe."

"If something did happen there, it would happen to you."

Victoria chuckled. "There's no need to worry. Oh, I can't wait to see my house, and familiar people and places . . ."

His dark brows drew together. "Did you have suitors there?" he asked abruptly. "Were you—or *are* you—courting with someone?"

"No." Her lips quirked. "I've never been sought after."

"Why not? What in God's name is the matter with the men of Dorking?"

"For one thing, I was always busy teaching,

and taking care of Papa. For another . . . I'm not to every man's taste."

"Of course you are. A man would have to be mad not to want someone like you."

Her smile turned pensive. "You mustn't idealize me," she said. "I have many flaws. I'm too private and independent by nature. I need quiet time to read and think and write every day. I'm interested in a field of study that hardly anyone likes or understands, and isn't meant for women in the first place. I'm dreadful at small talk, I have no interest in social gossip, and I'm not especially tidy."

"Everything you just said makes you more perfect."

She laughed and reached up to caress his jaw. "Tell me your flaws," she prompted.

"You've been living with me—you already know about them." Grant took her hand and gently rubbed the backs of her knuckles against his cheek, and kissed them. "Victoria . . . I understand that you need to recover from everything that's happened. I'll be patient for as long as necessary. But it won't be easy. And I don't want to become one of the things you'll recover from. I want to stay in here"—he touched her temple with a fingertip—"and here." He touched the center of her chest. "May I write to you?"

"Yes."

"Will you write to me?"

"Yes. You mustn't worry. You're not a passing fancy—you're the man I love."

"If you make me wait too long," he said wryly, "I'll have to go to Dorking to remind you of that."

Chapter Eighteen

In the month since she'd first left for London to search for her sister, Victoria's entire life had changed. Now as she entered the cottage where she'd lived all her life, the sense of relief was powerful and immediate. She gazed at her familiar surroundings in wonder, and felt her sister's hand touch hers. She turned up her palm, and their hands clasped and held. They hadn't done that since childhood. It was a nice feeling.

"Home," Victoria said simply. A place where memories were tucked in every nook and corner. All the pieces to complete the puzzle of herself were here.

The oak shelves in the kitchen, laden with stacks of dishes, pots, and pans. And the cupboard where they put the odd little objects that didn't seem to belong anywhere, such as a tin baby-cup . . . the silver-plated grape scissors they never needed . . . a dented silver herring fork . . . an ancient copper curd sieve.

Here was the sofa where Papa had reclined whenever he'd been able to leave his bed. It was draped with a collection of colorful lap blankets knitted by friends.

There was the bedroom with five beams across the ceiling. And the old wooden headboard she had painted with a pattern of tiny flowers, some of them turning splotchy when she'd accidentally brushed her sleeve across the wet paint.

And books everywhere . . . shelves, boxes, stacks of them.

"Do you remember all of this?" Vivien asked, giving her hand a slight squeeze before letting go.

"I do," Victoria said, turning a circle.

"Well, there's a relief. From what Morgan said, I thought you might have turned into a root vegetable." Vivien put a hand at the small of her own back and made her way to the worn velvet sofa. "I need to sit down."

"What can I do?" Victoria asked with instant concern.

"You can wait on me hand and foot for the next four months."

Victoria smiled, but she was struck by the

difference in her sister's movements, her usual feline grace now tempered with caution.

Self-consciously Vivien rested a hand on the curve of her stomach. "It's dreadful, isn't it? I've been stretched like a sausage casing."

"You look beautiful," Victoria said sincerely.

"It's been an appalling experience so far, and worse every day. I'm a prisoner in my own body. And I have to take the jailkeeper with me everywhere I go."

Victoria blinked, perturbed at hearing a baby referred to as a jailkeeper. "I'm so sorry. From now on I'll be here to help in any way I can." She hesitated before adding, "Perhaps you'll feel differently about the baby after he or she is born."

That comment earned a baleful glance. "You don't really believe that, do you?"

"It's possible."

Vivien sighed and fastened her gaze on one of the cottage windows, and replied with sullen resignation. "Is it also possible, Victoria, that I may be different from you? That I may not have the same feelings? You know I never played pretend-mother with dolls. You know I've never liked children. Why would that change just because I gave birth?"

"I've read that when you see your newborn child for the first time . . ." Victoria's voice faded as she saw the way her sister's jaw was flexing.

"So have I," Vivien said in a lightly acid tone. "Apparently I'll be suffused in the instant ecstasy of motherhood. A baby solves every problem, thank God. It says so in all the ladies' periodicals that instruct us how we should feel. 'In this week's issue, we offer a heartwarming tale about a wicked girl who's been brought low by the consequences of sin—but is saved by the joy of motherhood.'"

"I was only trying to say something positive," Victoria said quietly.

"When someone is drowning, you don't tell them, 'At least we're having fine weather today.'"

"I'm sorry."

Vivien smiled wryly. "Oh, don't. It takes all the fun out of scolding when you apologize so quickly."

Victoria picked up a battered copper kettle and carried it to the pump at the kitchen sink. "Shall we have tea?" she asked, busying herself with filling the kettle.

"Yes. Jane has gone to the baker's, and she'll be back soon with buns and sweets." Vivien took off her slippers and pulled her feet up onto the sofa. "Why didn't Morgan come inside and chat for a few minutes? He practically tossed you from the carriage while it was still rolling."

"After everything that happened, it was easier to part quickly than draw it out."

Grant had helped Victoria from the carriage, taken her luggage to the cottage, and exchanged a few stilted words with Vivien. Then he and Victoria had gone outside to the front door stoop.

They had faced each other in silence, standing at the threshold between her life and his, knowing that by the time they met again, the things they each felt and wanted might be different.

Impossible to say goodbye, knowing what might be lost.

Victoria had swallowed against a terrible ache in her throat, and her vision had hazed with tears.

Grant had reached for her, his hands clasped on either side of her head. His lungs had worked as if he'd just run for miles. "My feelings won't change," he'd said hoarsely.

Victoria had nodded a little within the bracket of his hands, a sob escaping in a faint cough.

"You won't lose me," he'd said. "I'll wait a lifetime."

Their arms had gone around each other, and they'd stood locked together, straining every muscle to press even closer.

And then Grant had let go, and strode to the carriage without looking back.

"Darling," her sister asked, her eyes narrowing suspiciously, "did you and Mr. Morgan form some sort of attachment while you stayed with him?"

Victoria carried the kettle to the hearth and

hung it over the coals on a hinged iron arm. "We may have."

"How would you describe it? A close friendship? Fondness?"

"I've fallen in love with him," Victoria said bluntly.

Vivien appeared stunned. "You and that . . . no. In light of the fact that you were injured and didn't even know your own name, I wouldn't be quick to call it love. It's gratitude masquerading as love."

"It's love," Victoria said, quiet and firm.

"What did it lead to? Kisses? The occasional pat or grope?"

Victoria's color rose as she debated how much to reveal.

"That son of a bitch," Vivien burst out. "He stole your virginity?"

"He stole nothing," Victoria said indignantly, taken aback by her sister's vehemence. "I slept with him because I wanted to and I love him, and I have no regrets, and . . . why are you suddenly so concerned about my honor?"

"I don't give a monkey about your honor," Vivien said. "I'm concerned because you could have made a fortune selling your virginity."

"You're suggesting I should have slept with someone for money?" Victoria was bewildered. "I would never do that!"

"Better than giving your maidenhood away for free."

"You gave yours away for free to Alfie Grinstead in his uncle's hayloft!"

"And it was the costliest mistake I ever made. I might as well have thrown pound notes into a pile the size of a haystack and set fire to it."

"You have no right to be annoyed with me for sharing a bed with the man I love."

"I'm annoyed because you squandered your only chance at a financial windfall."

"I think it's because you don't like Mr. Morgan."

"I neither like nor dislike Morgan—he's not worth thinking about. He's a beef-and-beer plodder who may cut a fine figure in his Sunday coat, but will never be part of the upper class."

"There's an *entire world* of people who aren't in the upper class," Victoria protested. "Honestly, Vivien . . . I've never understood your admiration for aristocratic dandies in silk breeches who have no occupation and expect the rest of us to bow and scrape. Mr. Morgan is a man who's made his own way in the world, and works hard and lives up to his responsibilities. He's entirely deserving of your respect. And he's not a plodder! He's very charming. And smart."

"And a prig."

"A what? You think he . . . no, Vivien, just because he didn't like your naked ballroom decorations doesn't make him a prig."

Vivien arched a brow. "I'm sure he's a master of the bedroom arts," she said sarcastically.

"As a matter of fact, I found him quite pleasing." Victoria tried to conceal her fierce blush by stirring the coals in the hearth and holding her hands out to the radiant heat.

"I'll bet seven stitches to the inch that it lasted two minutes before he rolled over and started snoring."

A quick grin came to Victoria's lips before she could repress it. "You would be wrong." Her gaze remained on the flickering coals as she thought of those sensuous hours in firelight and darkness, the endless attentions he paid her, the slow feasting and stroking and plundering. She already missed him. She was aware of a new kind of craving, an intimate emptiness. As if he'd made a place for himself inside her, and now her body wanted him back.

"Hmm." Vivien stared at her speculatively. "Perhaps he has more imagination than I gave him credit for. That's something, at least. Will he be coming back to see you?"

"Not until I send for him."

"You aren't courting?"

"We're corresponding."

"Letters?" Vivien looked amused.

"He was the one who asked to write!"

"Morgan doesn't seem at all the kind to send love letters. You'll have to let me read one—I'm sure it will be vastly entertaining."

Victoria turned toward her with an impatient huff. "If you would set aside your preconceived notions about him and try to see him as he really . . ." Her voice trailed away, and she regarded her sister with a fixed stare.

"What is it?" her sister asked.

"I wonder, Vivien, whether you and I are seeing *anyone* quite clearly, including ourselves. We've both stepped away from our usual patterns—let's take an honest look at ourselves before going back to what we were doing. As Socrates said, 'Lead not a life unexamined.'"

"I don't see the point."

"To reevaluate our goals," Victoria said.

"I love my goals exactly as they are."

"Do you?" Victoria measured spoonfuls of tea into an old pot with a chipped spout. "So much of life hinges upon chance. A thousand unexpected things pull us off course until we end up somewhere we didn't plan on going. And then we forget it wasn't our original destination." She went to a bookshelf and pulled out several tattered leatherbound volumes. Epicurus . . . Epictetus . . . Socrates . . . Aristotle . . . Locke . . . Descartes. "We're the daughters of a philosopher," she continued, carrying the stack to the table and setting it down with an emphatic thud. "Let's take a thorough look at who we are and what we should do."

"I'm happy with my decisions. I don't need to question them."

"Vivien," she said gently, "you know I adore you. But you're a courtesan, an extortionist, a recent target of attempted murder, and soon to be an unwed mother. It probably wouldn't hurt to question a few of your choices."

In the month that followed, Victoria and Vivien had the luxury of more uninterrupted time together than they'd ever known, even as children. They talked constantly, during teatimes, walks, and household chores, and in the quiet evenings after dinner. The cookmaid, Jane, came to work four days a week, but went home at night to stay with her parents, leaving the sisters to their own devices.

The atmosphere in the cottage became unexpectedly harmonious after the sisters managed to discard their old habit of bickering. The confidences came slowly at first. But somehow they reached a point at which they could say anything without fear, and they found a new ease in being together.

To Victoria's pleasure, a letter from Grant arrived every two or three days. The clang of the letter-carrier's bell never failed to quicken her heart.

According to etiquette books, the ideal courtship letter should be elaborate and carefully composed . . . *"It is with no small trepidation that I undertake the liberty of seeking the inestimable boon of a closer acquaintance with you . . ."*

The letters from Grant, however, were spontaneous and natural, each one a reflection of whatever he happened to be doing at the time.

He wrote about the weighty law books that Sir Ross had given him to read, or about a ring of housebreakers he arrested one night, or about a sad and beautiful ballad he'd heard an Irish girl singing on a street corner. Some of the letters were short and hasty, dashed off in the mornings before he went to Bow Street, or after work. Others were longer and more thoughtful . . . and some were filled with an explicit longing that made Victoria blush from head to toe.

There's too much work to be done, he'd written, *and you're on my mind constantly. I'm trying to limit myself to thinking about you only a hundred times a day. It starts in the morning when I open my eyes and see the pillow where your head used to rest. I've taken to sleeping on the other side of the bed, next to the space that belongs only to you. I stare at the white linen sheet and remember the colors of you . . . blue eyes, golden freckles, red hair, a thousand pink blushes. I miss the feel of your skin turning warm beneath my touch. I miss your hair curling around my fingers. I'm starved for want of you. If you were here, I'd have you on the table and make an eight-course dinner of you—*

"On the *table*?" came her sister's voice from behind her.

Victoria started in surprise and twisted in her chair to discover that Vivien had been reading over her shoulder. "Do you mind?" she asked indignantly. "This is my private correspondence."

But Vivien had already snatched up the letter and hurried away with it like a covetous badger.

"Give that to me," Victoria exclaimed, following her.

"Let me just finish the page—"

"Now!"

Vivien stopped and handed it back to her, laughing. "I underestimated the man—I admit it! He writes a nice letter. High marks for flirtiness. He's still not French, but he'll do."

The next letter had been about a visit to a master carriage builder. It seemed Sir Ross had insisted that Grant needed the convenience of his own carriage. It would take months for the vehicle to be built, and therefore must be ordered right away.

Choosing the vehicle itself was relatively simple, Grant wrote. *When it came to deciding on paint and trim work, however, it all became considerably more complex. I was asked to choose one of a hundred possible colors for the exterior lacquer. I said black, which seemed a safe enough choice.*

But then came a revelation: there's more than one shade of black. Were you aware of this? The carriage builder's assistant set out sample cards of coal, jet, ebony, onyx, slate, licorice, and others I can't recall. It threw me into a state of vehicular indecision from which I still haven't recovered.

I beg your guidance on the following questions: For the carriage floor—oilcloth or carpet? On the doors—

oval windows or rectangular? Curtains—leather or cloth? As for seat upholstery—would you prefer to be seduced on brocade, velvet, or leather? Any advice would be received with wildest gratitude.

"Irresistible," Vivien said with a reluctant grin when Victoria showed the letter to her. "I love it when they play the big hapless male in need of help. Only the smart men do that—a numbskull would die before asking for a woman's opinion."

"How should I reply?" Victoria asked. "I don't know the first thing about private carriages."

Vivien pursed her lips as she considered the question. "Tell him you want the exterior lacquered in the darkest shade of Prussian blue. Have the interior ceiling lined with pleated silk in a light shade . . . champagne, I think. For the floor, French pile carpet in black. The upholstery should be blue plush with leather welting. *No* oval window—order a rectangle with a lined cloth shade and a leather tassel. And be sure to ask for a parcel tray to stow your purchases after you've been out shopping, as well as a built-in umbrella holder."

Victoria looked up warily from the notes she was making. "I wouldn't want to assume the carriage is intended for my use."

"But that's why he's asking. Are you having second thoughts? Is your affection fading?"

"*No.* I miss him dreadfully. But when I think about marrying him and leaving Dorking for good, I feel so uneasy, as if it's all going to go wrong."

"Why?"

"I don't know. I have no reason to feel that way."

Her sister regarded her speculatively. "When you have a feeling for no reason, there's a reason."

Chapter Nineteen

 "I told Thomas if we married, I'd be discreet," Vivien said one evening, reminiscing about Lord Lane's late grandson. They were in the kitchen making Welsh rarebit—her latest craving. At Vivien's insistence, they'd had it for dinner three nights in a row, always sided with fried apples. "But I couldn't be limited to one man forever."

"What did he say?" Victoria scraped a pile of finely chopped cheddar cheese into a bowl.

"He didn't like it, of course, but he accepted it." Vivien poured a few spoonfuls of ale into the bowl, followed by a dab of mustard powder.

"He would have agreed to anything if it meant I would marry him."

"Did you love him?" Victoria asked.

"No, but I was fond of him. Thomas was a dear boy." Vivien stirred the contents of the bowl slowly, while Victoria added a spoonful of melted butter. "I shouldn't have agreed to marry him," she continued, "but he was the heir to his family's title, and would have been filthy rich someday. I had no idea he was so high-strung—or that his grandfather would turn out to be so murder-y." She paused. "I can hardly wait to return to France. The men there are so much easier. They're chivalrous and generous, and so very understanding about things."

Victoria frowned as she arranged slices of toasted bread in a Dutch oven, poured the cheese mixture on top, and covered it with a lid. "Must you go back to Paris?" she asked. She set the Dutch oven in the fireplace and shoveled a few embers and coals onto the lid. Soon the Welsh rarebit would turn into melting golden slabs with crisp edges.

"Oh, yes. *Demimondaines* aren't hidden away there the way we are in England. We take part in public life. We're invited everywhere and have the best of everything. The fashions, the food, the parties—it's all glorious. I should never have come back to England. But I did want to say goodbye to Papa, and then I became involved with Lord Gerard."

"Why do you have to be in the *demimonde* at all?" Victoria returned to the table. "Why not stay here and marry someone?"

"There's no freedom in a respectable life."

"I'm not sure I understand. What kind of freedom do you want?"

"Every kind, but most of all the freedom to leave. There's nothing more important to me."

Victoria stared at her sister intently. "More important than being loved?"

"Love fades. At least when an affair ends, I can start another one with a new man." Vivien held her gaze steadily. "I like having my own money and my own apartment. I spend most of my time doing as I please. I know you don't approve, but it's what I want, and I'm not going to change."

"I haven't said I disapprove."

Vivien regarded her with fond exasperation. "You're radiating disapproval like a muggy little glow-worm. The truth is, I slept with many men for the same reason you never slept with anyone. We each have our way of avoiding connection."

"I don't avoid connection," Victoria protested.

"Then how has it come to pass that you're twenty-five and alone? And a virgin until recently."

"I . . ." Victoria spluttered a little. "I've been busy."

"Of course." Vivien's gently mocking gaze traveled around the quiet cottage. "You've been swamped here in Dorking. So many books to read. So much to ponder about the meaning of everything." In the silence, Vivien picked up a fork, reached over to a dish of soft apples fried in butter, and speared one deftly. She smiled ruefully into Victoria's stunned face. "You're trying to live Papa's life," she said. "It doesn't suit you. I loved him, but there's no denying he was odd, and a bit of a martyr, and afraid of people. It was why he was happy to keep you shut away with him here, in his very small world. At least he had you—whereas you have no one now." She ate the apple slice with a smack of appreciation, and speared another. "The rarebit is probably ready."

Mechanically Victoria went to the fireplace and used a rag to pick up the Dutch oven by the handle. She set it on a hearthstone to cool slightly, while thoughts ricocheted through her head.

There was some truth in what Vivien had said. Maybe a lot of truth. She thought of her father . . . cerebral, kind, but never quite part of the village, never comfortable with going to other peoples' homes or welcoming them into his. Never quite speaking the language of ordinary folk.

"Do you really think he was afraid of people?" she asked.

"Well, afraid of being left by them."

"I'm not that way, I . . . no, wait." Victoria broke off and stared at her sister in amazement. "I think I am," she said in wonder. "I *am* afraid of being left." She'd never understood that about herself until this very moment.

"Of course you are. That's why you want to stay here where it feels safe, and why it seems as if it would all go wrong if you went somewhere else. Darling, this place makes it too easy for you to slip into solitude. You need to live with someone. And that person can't be me, as I'm going back to Paris."

"What about the baby?"

Vivien chewed another bite of apple, taking her time before replying in a matter-of-fact tone. "No, I won't be taking her."

In the silence, Victoria fetched a cup from a shelf and reached for the stoneware bottle of ale they had needed for the Welsh rarebit recipe. She poured some of the beverage for herself and drank a medicinal gulp. Too late, she discovered that even though ale added wonderfully earthy, malty flavors to the rarebit, it was revolting on its own.

Vivien laughed at the face she made. "If you're trying to calm your nerves, you'll have to drink at least ten times that amount."

"If you give the baby away, I think you would come to regret it," Victoria said.

"No, *you* would regret giving it away. I won't."

"Epictetus or Epicurus," Victoria muttered.

"Exactly. You, darling, are a stoic—you do the right thing regardless of the personal cost, and hope happiness will come as a reward. Whereas a hedonist like me will walk right up to happiness and grab it by the bollocks."

"That's oversimplifying," Victoria said. "And wrong. And I'm going to explain why."

"Don't bother. Just tell me—whose life has been more pleasurable and interesting? Yours or mine?"

"Yours—until it resulted in me being strangled and thrown into the Thames! And then nearly murdered in a nasty old factory building."

"I've told you how sorry I am about all that. But it does prove my point: you still ended up suffering far more than I did. In the parade of life, a stoic always follows the horse with a broom and shovel."

"Which would make a hedonist the horse's arse," Victoria said dourly, and her sister snorted with amusement.

"Be careful with this," Victoria cautioned as she gave a pruning knife with a curved blade to Jane. "Make certain every motion goes away from your body. Do you have gardening gloves? Here, take mine."

They were out at the stone wall, pruning the espaliered branches of the peach tree. It was a chilly spring afternoon, but the sky was clear and bright. The air was fresh with the scents of damp juniper and early-blooming lilac, and braced with a touch of smoke from the silver birch logs on the hearth inside.

"Do you want me to tie the new-grown branches to the diagonal wires, miss?" Jane asked.

"Yes, I'll find the ball of string and bring it out." Victoria showed the cookmaid a gnarled gray branch. "This is old wood that's never going to fruit again, so we'll want to remove any branches that look like this."

"Loads of fruiting branches, looks like," Jane remarked. "I expect we'll be making big pots of peach marmalade come August."

Victoria smiled absently, wondering where she would be in August. She went into the house and found Vivien in the kitchen. Her sister was wearing a green high-waisted walking dress and a soft cashmere shawl.

"You're going out?" Victoria asked.

"I thought I'd benefit from a walk in the fresh air."

"I'll come with you, if you'll wait while I wash the breakfast pan."

Vivien cast an appraising glance over her simple cotton dress, white apron, and the loose, long braid hanging over her shoulder. "I don't mind waiting, but you'll have to spruce up a bit and do something with your hair. We can't go into the Punchbowl Inn with you looking like that."

"You said you were going out for fresh air!"

"I will be taking the fresh air on the way to the Punchbowl Inn, and also on the way back.

But in the middle of breathing all that fresh air, I'm going to stop for refreshments and local gossip." Vivien scowled as she saw her expression. "Never mind, I'll go alone."

"No, I'm definitely going with you, or you may come back tipsy."

"The midwife said I could have a few sips of wine now and then."

"Wait for me. I'm going to wash the pan." Victoria took the ball of string from the odds-and-ends cabinet and handed it to Vivien. "Would you take this outside to Jane, please? She needs it for the peach tree."

Her sister heaved a sigh and left the kitchen.

Victoria went to the sink, where she'd left the metal pan to soak. Industriously she scrubbed the residue of cooked eggs with a mixture of soft soap and bicarbonate of soda. As she finished rinsing and drying the pan, Vivien returned to the kitchen.

"A letter from Mr. Morgan was just delivered," Vivien said briskly. "Take off that atrocious apron and dry your hands so you can read it."

"That's odd," Victoria remarked, puzzled. "I didn't hear the letter-carrier's bell."

"You were making too much noise with all your splashing."

"Will you set the letter on the table, please? I'd rather not rush through it—I'll wait until later, so I can read it at my leisure."

"No, read it now. There might be something

interesting in there, and vicarious enjoyment is all I have these days."

Victoria smiled quizzically at her sister's impatience. She dried her hands, took the letter, and sat at the table. The front door opened and closed, and she twisted to see the cookmaid coming inside. "Are you finished with pruning already, Jane?"

"Not yet," the girl replied, "but I wanted a glass of water."

After opening the letter carefully, Victoria glanced up to find both their gazes on her. "Why are you both watching me like that?" she asked with a laugh.

"No one's watching you," Vivien said. "Go on, read."

Victoria shook her head in bemusement and returned her attention to the letter.

My love,

If someone were to ask me how long you've been away, I would tell them it's been exactly one month. But my heart knows the truth: it's been a hundred years.

You're gone, but you're everywhere I look. You're every pair of blue eyes, every flicker of firelight or turn of a page.

It's dawn, and I'm in a devil of a mood. Sleep was impossible last night. I blame Descartes, having read Meditations *before going to bed. Now after tossing and turning*

for hours, I feel as if I've lost a medieval joust.
Armor dented, lance broken, and no sign of the
fair damsel I wanted to fight the world for.

As I sit here facing another endless day
without you, I'm wondering how, exactly, does
one woo a philosopher? How do I sweep your
rational mind off its feet?

Love requires trust, but trusting another
person is the most irrational thing we can do
in this life. People are unreliable, cowardly,
selfish, and worse.

On the other hand, if none of us trusted each
other, there would be no friendship, no family,
no survival. As irrational as trust is, it's the
most rational choice.

Descartes says, "Doubt everything," and
while I know that's how philosophers begin
the search for truth, it's not the best kind of
thinking for everyday life. A philosopher may
look at a chair and doubt its existence. But
sometimes a philosopher just needs to sit in the
chair and eat a sandwich.

As a simpleminded man who's fond of
sandwiches, I rarely, if ever, question reality.
But I delight in women with complicated
minds. I love all the ways your thinking is
different from mine.

And I long for you more than I can bear.

So I have a proposition for you: What if we
take an irrational leap together? Let's accept
each other exactly as we are. We'll enjoy our

differences whenever possible, and overlook them when necessary. Tell me what promises you need from me. I'll keep them faithfully.

I'm asking you to marry me, my soulmate, my partner, my other half. I'm asking you to trust that my devotion to you is as real and steadfast as a mountain. Whether you take it or not, it will be there forever. A million years wouldn't alter it.

Whatever your answer is, I will love you until my last heartbeat.

But I'd rather not have to do it from afar.

> *Yours,*
> *Grant*

P.S. Arrived at the post office too late for this letter to be dispatched in time, so I've taken the liberty of delivering it personally. If you don't feel like talking, a wave at the window would suffice.

Victoria stood, nearly knocking the chair over in her haste. "He's here?" she managed to ask.

A rush of emotion made it nearly impossible to think, or even to see all that well. Everything was shimmering around her. The words were exactly what she had needed, had longed for, without even being aware of it.

She could barely hear Vivien's reply through her thundering pulse—something about Grant having shown up just as she'd gone out to give the string to Jane.

Heedless of the letter that fell from her nerveless fingers, Victoria flew to the door and ran outside.

And there Grant was, big and dark and handsome, standing by the stone wall and the peach tree. As his searching gaze took in her expression, the set of his shoulder relaxed slightly, and his lips curved with one of the slow, dazzling smiles she loved.

"Grant!" She ran to him.

He caught her with a low laugh, lifting her off her feet and turning in a half circle to minimize the impact. "Easy, love. You'll hurt yourself, running up so hard against me."

The familiar scent and feel of him was exhilarating. She clung to him, trembling in every limb as his mouth sought hers. The kiss was rough and raw with excitement, but soon it gentled into something deep and languorous. Slowly she relaxed in his arms, all her senses opening to take him in. When his head lifted, she put her hands to the sides of his face and let out a shaken sigh, realizing this was the first time she'd been able to take a full breath in a month.

"I forgot what kissing you was like," she whispered.

Smiling, Grant rested his forehead briefly against hers. "What else do I need to remind you of?"

He glanced at the front of the cottage, and drew Victoria into the shelter of the wall, where they couldn't be seen from the windows. After removing his wool coat, he wrapped it around her, the silk lining still warm from his body.

"Forgive me for coming here without warning," he said huskily. "I had to see you. I couldn't—"

"Yes," she interrupted, pulling his head down for another kiss. Her tongue touched his, and a hungering sound stirred in his throat.

"Yes to what?" he eventually asked.

"To the letter. To everything."

Grant drew a quick breath. "You're sure? You're not saying it just because I've taken you by surprise?"

"I'm saying it because I want to marry you." Words tumbled out in a reckless torrent. "I've done so much soul-searching, and every time I think about the future, it always leads to you. I need you in so many ways. I think you understand me better than anyone except Vivien. Even though I'm nervous about how different life in London will be, I can't let fear stop me."

Grant looked down at her with tenderness and concern. "I'll make sure you have whatever you need to be happy."

He kissed her again, and she shivered at the delicious feel of it, the cool air scented of a springtime garden . . . the strong masculine arms anchoring her . . . the slow, ravishing kisses that turned her entire body molten.

They heard the sound of the cottage door opening. Victoria pulled away from Grant, peeked around the wall, and saw Vivien leaving with Jane in tow. They were both wearing cloaks and bonnets.

"I'm going on my walk," Vivien announced cheerfully. "Jane's coming with me."

Victoria frowned. "The two of you aren't going to stop at the Punchbowl Inn, I hope."

"We are, miss," Jane said. "But we thought—"

"No, Jane," Vivien told her, "never admit or explain, unless absolutely necessary. Just say 'that's our own business' and look a bit smug."

"But Miss Victoria pays my wages," Jane protested.

"In that case, don't look smug." Vivien pulled Jane along the path with her, and said to Victoria over her shoulder, "We'll be gone for at least an hour."

"Jane," Victoria called after them, "watch over her."

"I will, miss!" the girl called back.

Victoria looked up at Grant ruefully. "It's like asking a kitten to watch over a bull terrier."

He smiled and slid his arm around her as they headed toward the cottage. "Your sister looks well," he said.

"She is. Minnie Curren—the local midwife—

says she's in excellent health. She thinks from the way Vivien's carrying, the baby is probably a girl." She paused. "I hope my sister was nice to you when you arrived."

"Unexpectedly so," he said wryly.

"That's probably because I told her how kind you were to me, when you thought I was her. She was a bit surprised."

"Her opinion of me was that low?"

"Not just of you. I'm afraid her view of men in general is quite cynical."

"After the life she's led, that wouldn't be unexpected."

"But all she wants is to go back to it," Victoria told him. "After the baby's born, she intends to leave for Paris. She's very firm on that point."

"With the baby?"

"Without. She intends to find someone to take her. Or him."

"She may change her mind."

"I don't think she will. We've talked about it for days on end."

Grant frowned thoughtfully. He went to the small paddock, formed by the stone wall on one side and wood rail fencing on the rest of it. The horse he'd ridden from the coaching house was meandering around the enclosure, pausing here and there to nibble at clover and grass.

"Has she asked you to take the baby?" he asked.

"No, and I haven't offered." Victoria watched

as Grant pumped water from the rainwater cistern into a wooden pail and set it inside the paddock for the horse.

Grant turned and set his back to the fence, folding his arms as he regarded her wryly. "What do you want to do?"

Victoria hesitated before replying honestly. "I want to stay with Vivien and care for her until the birth. I'll be there for the baby's first breath of life, and . . . I already feel attached. I think it would be very difficult to know in the back of my mind that the baby was being raised by strangers. On the other hand, it's not fair to ask you to . . . well, to go from being a carefree bachelor to taking on such a burden . . ." Her voice trailed away as she saw the flash of his grin.

"I'm not all *that* carefree," Grant said, and rested his elbows on a fence rail. "I'm used to responsibility." His momentary amusement faded. "That's not what I'm concerned about."

Victoria joined him at the fence.

Grant looked down at her, a stray breeze playing through the locks of his mink-brown hair. "If we take the baby to raise, she'd have to be ours. *Only* ours. Vivien can't reclaim her at some future date, or interfere if she doesn't like the decisions we make."

"She won't," Victoria said. "Vivien doesn't want to think of herself as a mother."

"I understand. But she may feel differently after the baby's born. Some women change their minds. I've seen it happen more than once. She should have the time she needs to choose what's right for herself."

"And . . . if she doesn't change her mind?"

"Then you and the baby and I will be a family," he said simply.

Filled with relief and gratitude, Victoria threw her arms around him, hugging him as tightly as she could.

Grant wrapped her in his embrace, chuckling briefly at her impulsiveness. He smoothed back her hair and stared down at her. "Sweetheart," he murmured, "I'm sure you're aware this will make your relationship with your sister more complex. With all the joy in store, there'll be some pain as well."

"But also love."

"Love most of all." His lips wandered gently over her cheeks and brushed the tip of her nose. Her eyes closed, her face lifting like a Michaelmas daisy following the sun. Everywhere he kissed, she felt her skin come alive. "Let's go inside," he whispered.

Their hands linked as they went into the cottage.

It was remarkable, somehow, to see Grant there in her childhood home. Victoria tried to view it through his eyes: the cheerful jumble of floral pillows, a collection of hand-painted pottery vases, a rainbow of knitted blankets.

Slowly he wandered past the shelves of books, taking note of a horseshoe nailed to the wall and a green pottery plate molded in the pattern of overlapping leaves. He paused at a picture Victoria had made in childhood. Having lacked a canvas, she'd painted a scene of sheep in a meadow directly onto the wall, and framed it with sticks of wood. Although she had later wanted to whitewash over it, her father hadn't let her, claiming it was his favorite picture.

"You painted this," Grant said, touching the scene with a gentle fingertip.

Victoria came to stand beside him. "How can you tell?"

"The sheep look like rocks."

She laughed and pushed at him.

Gathering her close, he stole a kiss from her. "Why don't you show me your bedroom?" he suggested.

The thought of making love with him elicited a throb of response in every soft part of her body. She tilted her head back as his lips slid down her throat, and said breathlessly, "We would have to be quick. They'll be coming back soon."

Grant muffled a laugh against her shoulder. "We've been apart for a month, love. 'Quick' is a foregone conclusion."

"You don't have to worry about my pleasure this time," she said.

He lifted his head, his eyes bright with a gleam of deviltry that brought a flush to the surface of her skin. "You know I'm not the kind to back down from a challenge."

"That was the opposite of a challenge," she protested. "I'm trying to be helpful and—" She broke off with a squeak of surprise as he picked her up with astonishing ease and put her over his shoulder.

"Oh, it was a challenge," she heard him say casually. "Where's the bed?"

For several seconds, Victoria was too consumed with helpless giggles to be able to reply. She could only flail a hand in the direction of the bedroom.

Despite the way he carried her, like a sack of grain from the market, Grant deposited her on the bed with great care. Victoria tried to roll away playfully, but he caught her by the ankle and pulled her toward him.

"There's no escaping me," he said, and sought her smiling mouth with his.

Victoria circled her arms around his neck, returning the kiss passionately. His body was incredibly hard over hers, a mass of dense muscle and coiled power. He gave her some of his weight, settling into the cradle of her hips, and the thick ridge of his erection drew a little gasp from her.

Grant looked down at her with heavy-lidded eyes. "I've missed you," he said, and nudged gently with his hips to demonstrate.

"Tell me what to do," she managed to say.

"Nothing, love." He lowered his head and spoke softly near her ear. "Nothing at all. You're going to lie there and let me undress you. And when every stitch of clothing is gone, you'll have to hold still while I play with you . . . kiss you . . . use my tongue on you. I'm going to fill you until your sweet little body is straining to take every inch of me. And I'll stay deep inside until I feel you shivering and tightening so hard that it makes me come without even moving."

A scalding blush covered her. She was tense in every muscle, trembling with desire, and she was so terribly afraid they would be interrupted. "Just *hurry*."

The provoking man proceeded with maddening deliberateness, removing her clothes as if they had all the time in the world. By the time she was naked, the place between her thighs was pulsing, and mortifyingly wet, and her bare toes had curled as tightly as the wool of a newborn lamb.

But except for removing his shoes, Grant was still fully clothed.

"We don't have enough time," Victoria moaned, fumbling with his waistcoat. She was dying to feel his skin, the flex of tightly knit muscle beneath her hands.

To her indignation, she heard his smothered laugh above her head. "Be still," he said. "You're squirming like a worm in hot ash."

"I want you—I want to feel you—"

Grant hushed her with his lips, and caught her wrists in his hands, bringing them down to her sides. Something about the gentle clasp of those strong hands set off a deep pang of excitement within her. He stared into her wide eyes, perceiving her response, and a faint, knowing smile touched his lips.

"Should I let go of your arms?" he asked, his voice husky.

Slowly she shook her head, wanting to be held down, anchored, just like this.

He kept her wrists pinned against the mattress and kissed his way along her body in meandering paths while she trembled in anticipation. Her sex felt tender and swollen, twitching as his mouth grazed her stomach. Lost in frustration and arousal, she tried to urge him lower, her hips catching a high arch.

His hot breath fanned across her skin as he kissed and nuzzled along the edge of the triangle of red curls. So lazy and gentle, refusing to be rushed. Her heart was pumping, lungs laboring. The urgency climbed until she dug her bare heels into the bedding as if she were trying to crawl away, but he kept her securely in place. It sent the heat even higher, until sweat misted every inch of her skin and turned her hair wet at the roots.

An unrestrained groan escaped her at the first liquid stroke of his tongue. He parted the humid folds of her sex . . . teased with licks and swirls . . . then swept down to penetrate her, hunting for the deepest possible taste. Her head rolled from side to side, her captive wrists straining. His tongue swept up to the tight bud of her clitoris, licking in a steady rhythm. Ecstasy rose in waves, each one stronger than the last, and her knees and shoulders drew upward as if her body were trying to wrap around the sensation. A whimper broke from her, and then she was quiet, occupied with a rush of pure white fire.

Before the shuddering release had faded entirely, Grant had unfastened the front of his breeches. He widened the spread of her thighs and pushed gradually into the wet entrance of her body. His eyes closed, his face set with a frown of concentration as he battled to keep from climaxing immediately.

He began to move in long, steady thrusts. As he leaned down to kiss her breasts, it impelled him even deeper inside. She moaned and trembled, her inner muscles clenching hard on him.

Muttering a curse, Grant wrapped his arms around her, rolled them both, and positioned her to sit astride his hips. She sank down with a gasp, her weight sending him deep into her core. He gripped her hips with his hands and began to push her up and down his rigid shaft, over and over, his gaze devouring the stunning contrast of her naked body against his clothed one. He added a hint of push and pull to the motion, angling her so every forward movement gave her more pleasurable friction.

She grasped the top of the headboard for balance and began to ride him at her own pace, filling herself with the hard length. He let go of her hips and caressed the front of her body, stroking her breasts, playing with her sex. Quivers ran through her until the pleasure became all-consuming, and she arched tightly over him. Grant pushed upward and held, letting out a low groan as he found his own wrenching release.

In the aftermath, she lay limply on his chest while his hand stroked up and down her naked back.

Sighing in contentment, Grant played with a loose lock of her hair. "I can't go another month without seeing you," he said drowsily. "I'll have to start visiting here more often." He paused. "If you have no objection."

"Oh well, if you can't stay away from me . . ."

"I can't."

"Good. Because I don't want to be apart from you, either." Victoria lifted herself away from him, and nearly fell off the bed as her legs gave out.

Grant grabbed her reflexively, and gave her a quizzical glance.

Blushing, she explained, "My legs are wobbly."

"This is a new form of exercise for you," he conceded. "We'll have to do some training."

"When you suggested taking an irrational

leap," she said, descending to the floor with care, "you probably didn't expect me to take it so literally."

Grant picked up her discarded chemise and helped her to put it on. Gathering her against him, he grinned down at her and stole a quick kiss. "As you may recall, sweet love . . . I said we'd do it together."

Chapter Twenty

Three days after the birth of Vivien's daughter, Victoria was awakened at sunrise by the sounds of someone coming into her bedroom. "Vivien?" she asked groggily, squinting through the dimness of the room. "Do you need something?"

"No, all's well. Baby and I are just visiting."

Victoria smiled and drew back the covers. "Come into bed—the morning chill isn't good for either of you."

Her sister climbed into bed and settled the sleeping infant between them.

Yawning, Victoria snuggled the baby into the crook of her arm. "How do you feel today?"

"Healthy as a horse," Vivien said.

"No bleeding or pain . . . ?"

"Just a little soreness. It's indecent, really. Minnie told me she'd never seen anyone have such an easy time of it for the first childbirth."

The midwife had done a first-rate job guiding Vivien through the labor. She had kept Vivien as relaxed and comfortable as possible with a combination of herbal medicines and massage. From the onset of labor to the afterbirth, the entire process had taken only seven hours, from which both mother and child had emerged in excellent condition.

"You were very brave and strong," Victoria said. "I was there with you, and it didn't look all that easy to me."

"It's certainly not an experience I'll ever want to repeat," Vivien said. "My God, I'm glad it's over." She settled deeper into the bedding, resting her head on the pillow next to Victoria's. "You've taken good care of me," she said. "All those nice little meals and poultices, and changing all the bedding and padding. It gave me a glimpse of what having a mother might have been like."

"I'll always be there whenever you or Baby need me." Victoria paused to kiss the infant's downy carrot-colored hair. "You need to choose a name soon—we can't keep calling her Baby."

"She's yours to name."

"Oh, but Vivien, she's—"

"She's your daughter. If you want her."

Victoria was filled with the most confusing mixture of emotions she'd ever known. Joy, longing, sadness, anxiety. "You know I do. I already love her. But I don't want you to make a hasty decision."

"Hasty? I've had the better part of a year to consider it. This is what's best for me, and without question best for her. You'll be a very good mother. A wonderful mother."

"I hope so," Victoria managed to say.

"You will." Daylight crept into the room, gilding Vivien's slender hand as she reached out to the baby's head and stroked her hair lightly. "The surprise in all of this has been Morgan," she continued. "Now that I've become acquainted with him, I think he's not a bad choice for you. He may even turn out to be that rarest of men—one who will value a daughter as much as a son."

Grant had been coming to Dorking every two weeks. It had been gratifying to watch him win over Vivien with patience and good humor, and an apparently limitless tolerance for her irritable moods on difficult days. During those daytime visits, he had done chores around the cottage, such as chopping and stacking wood, repairing the door of the stone shed, and sharpening the kitchen knives. He had even stocked the root cellar with a flitch of smoked bacon, and bins of potatoes and apples. It had been a nice feeling to have a man about the house, taking care of things. Their father, even in the best of health, had never been attentive to practical details.

Victoria frowned as she realized her sister was fully dressed. "Why are you wearing your traveling clothes?"

Propping herself up on an elbow, Vivien said gently, "I'm about to leave."

"What? Today?"

"In a few minutes."

"No, you can't! Minnie said you should rest in bed for at least five to ten days, and it's only been three."

"I'm only going a short distance, from here to my town house. I'll rest there for another day or two while Jane does some packing for me, and then I'm off to France."

"Vivien, this is folly! You could injure your health. There's no need to rush off like this. Why would you plan this and wait until the last minute to tell me? You knew I'd want the chance to say goodbye properly, and talk about things, and—" To Victoria's annoyance, her voice started breaking, and tears came to her eyes. "Don't my feelings matter?"

"I knew you'd insist on a long, drawn-out goodbye, and we'd both turn into watering pots, and I can't." Vivien reached an arm around her, embracing her with the sleeping baby between them. "If there's one person I've ever truly loved in my life, Victoria, it's you. Living apart won't change that. But I have to leave now for my own sake. It's becoming more painful by the day."

"But when will I see you again?" Victoria asked, taking a corner of the sheet to blot her wet eyes.

"Probably not for a long time. Until I'm sure I can hear her call you 'Mama' and not flinch."

"Vivien," she said miserably, "are you—"

"For the love of mercy, *don't* ask me again if I'm sure. It's the right thing to do, but that doesn't mean I'm happy about it. I need you to help me through this last part."

Victoria swallowed hard and nodded.

Her sister tried to sound brisk as she continued. "Now, let's discuss a few practical details. Minnie will visit later this morning with a wet nurse, who'll help with the baby until you're able to find someone in London. After Jane and I leave for France, I'd be obliged to Morgan if he would sell the remainder of my town house lease, and arrange for the furniture to be auctioned—"

"You're taking Jane with you to France?"

"Yes, I've become fond of her. She works hard and has a good head on her shoulders. And she's in raptures at the prospect of living in Paris."

"Will her family approve?"

"No. But she's one of thirteen children—it will take weeks before they even notice she's missing."

"Vivien, she doesn't speak French and she's never been out of Dorking—don't let anything happen to her."

"I'll look after her. In fact, I'll see to it that Jane eventually finds a nice Frenchman to marry. A handsome chef, perhaps, or a doctor." Vivien sat up and looked down at her. "I'll write to you as soon as we're settled in a new place."

It was happening too fast. There were too many things still unsaid, plans yet to be made.

"Will you take a packet ship from Dover?" Victoria asked, sitting up as well.

"No, I'd rather take a coach down to Brighton. I'll cross the Channel in the evening and break-fast at Dieppe."

"Breakfast," Victoria said, seizing on the idea. "I'll find my dressing gown, and put the kettle on to boil. We'll have tea, and I'll fry some bacon—"

"Darling," Vivien said quietly, "Jane's waiting for me. There's a hired carriage outside."

Victoria set her trembling jaw and wiped her eyes with the sleeve of her nightgown. "Vivien, I'm so cross with you for doing it this way."

Her sister leaned over and kissed her cheek. "Give her a pretty name," she said. "A French one might be nice."

Unable to speak, Victoria nodded.

"Stay in bed with the baby while I go," Vivien said. "I'd rather you didn't follow me out and wave goodbye, it's all too maudlin."

Victoria cuddled the infant, a tear falling from her chin into the ruddy wisps of hair. "I love you," she said as her sister reached the threshold.

"I love you too," came Vivien's voice. After a pause, she said, "Both of you."

A minute later, the front door of the cottage opened and closed.

She was gone.

Victoria wept for a minute before managing to bring her emotions under control.

The infant in her arms blinked up at her, waiting placidly for whatever would happen next.

It was only now, at this moment, that Victoria fully understood how much this small being depended on her for everything: comfort, protection, happiness, and survival. It was often said that mothers were supposed to have some kind of mystical knowledge and intuition of their babies' needs. Victoria, however, was going to need a great deal of advice and information. Not myths or old wives' tales, but factual scientific information.

"I'm going to learn everything about how to take care of you," Victoria told her, stroking the baby's little head and kissing her face. "I'm going to raise you to be the bravest, happiest, strongest girl who ever lived. And I'm never going to leave you." She dressed, pinned up her hair, and washed her face. Unfortunately, a good splashing with cold water couldn't entirely remove the puffiness around her eyes or the pink blotches on her face that always lingered after she cried.

After bundling the infant in a soft blanket, she carried her into the main room of the cottage and settled her in a baby basket on the table. She stirred up the hearth fire and hung a kettle of water over it. As her gaze fell on a nearby bookshelf, she saw a history book on medieval French saints and legends, and she went to retrieve it.

"There must be some nice girls' names in here," she told the baby, setting the heavy tome on the table beside her. She began to leaf through it. "Let's see . . . Rosaline . . . Eugènie . . . Colette . . . Maura . . . Austrebertha . . . Genevieve . . ." She paused and looked down at the baby. "That's a pretty one. What do you think? Do you like Genevieve?"

She went to measure tea into a pot, and paused as she heard a knock at the door. "That must be Minnie and the wet nurse," she said aloud. Thank God.

As she went to the door, she squared her shoulders and tried to look calm and confident, instead of thoroughly overwhelmed by the new direction her life had taken.

"Good morning, Minnie—" she began as she opened the door.

But it wasn't the midwife standing there. It

was Grant, his broad-shouldered frame filling up the doorway.

Victoria stared at him in amazement. Her composure shattered. Not just from the surprise of his sudden appearance, right now when she needed him most . . . but also because there was no need to put on a brave face with him. No need to hold anything back. She felt her face crumpling. Before she could even move, he had stepped inside and closed the door.

In the next moment, she was wrapped up in a secure embrace, surrounded by hard muscles and warmth, and it was the best feeling she'd ever known. Here was all the comfort she needed, his hand rubbing over her back, his comforting murmurs soothing her ragged heartbeat.

"Sweetheart . . . darling love . . . Vivien sent word to me yesterday that she was going to leave this morning. I made some arrangements and came as soon as I could."

"She fled as if she were escaping prison," Victoria told him, sniffling. "There was no time to say anything. She wouldn't even stay long enough to have a cup of tea with me."

"I'm so sorry, love. I'm sure it was damn difficult for her to leave you and the baby. But I'm right here, and I definitely want tea, and most of all . . ." Grant drew his head back to look at her, and a smile crept into the corners of his mouth as he asked, ". . . will you introduce me to our daughter?"

The words sent a thrill of delight through her. She took his hand and tugged him toward the table.

"Does she have a name?" he asked.

"I thought perhaps . . . Genevieve? What do you think?"

"It's beautiful." He sounded a bit breathless as he beheld the drowsing baby. "It's perfect for her. My God, look at her. She's beautiful. And so tiny."

Victoria reached into the basket and lifted the infant out.

"I don't want to bother her while she's sleeping," Grant protested.

"She wants to meet her father," Victoria said. "Here, take her—make sure to keep the head supported—"

Carefully she placed the baby into his arms.

Grant looked down at the miniature features with awe. "Hello, Genevieve." He touched one of her hands with a gentle fingertip, and laughed softly. "Do they all start out so small? Her hands are no bigger than shillings."

Standing beside him, Victoria leaned her cheek against the side of his shoulder. "How is it that you're here? Today you were supposed to meet with Sir Ross and the secretary of state for the Home Department."

"Postponed," he said, still staring down at the baby in fascination. "I told Sir Ross I had to fetch my two girls and bring them home."

"He wasn't cross?"

"No, indeed. In fact, he offered his services to marry us in a civil ceremony, if we want him to."

"He has the power to do that?" Victoria asked. "Yes, that would be perfect."

Grant grinned and leaned down to kiss her. "Let's stay here overnight," he suggested, "and you can pack a few things to take back to London on the morrow. We'll send someone later to crate your books and anything else you want. Does that plan meet with your approval?"

She nodded, smiling. "But how are we to go back? By public coach?"

"Public coach?" he repeated, as if the suggestion were outrageous. "Not when we have a brand-new carriage lacquered in Prussian blue to ride home in."

"It's finished? You brought it here?" Victoria flew to the window to see the glossy dark blue vehicle gleaming in the sun. "Oh, it's so lovely!"

"I think we could even fit Genevieve's basket into the parcel tray," Grant said with a laugh. "Here—take her while I go talk to the driver. We'll pay for his lodging at the coaching inn for the night, and have him come back in the morning."

Victoria stayed at the window, watching as he went outside to speak to the driver.

The baby made a few disgruntled peeps, her appetite asserting itself. To Victoria's relief, the midwife and wet nurse appeared at the end of the lane.

"There, there," she soothed the baby. "You'll feel better in just a few minutes, Genevieve." She cuddled the infant, her gaze returning to Grant. He was so handsome, her tall, broad-shouldered man, that it took her breath away. "You're going to love having him as your papa," she murmured close to her daughter's ear. "He's big and brave, and honest. Most people know his name and think of him as a hero, but they don't know how kind he is, or how much he loves books. They know what color his eyes are, but not how they crinkle at the corners just before he smiles. He'll teach you that strong men are also the gentlest . . . and they keep their promises . . . and they're never afraid to apologize. He'll remember your birthday, and he'll know the name of your favorite doll, and he won't tell you no nearly as often as he should. He's a protector of small things. He's not always sure the world is worth saving, but he'll never stop trying. And he'll always do his best to watch over us and keep us safe." She paused and smiled as she saw Grant begin to walk toward them, the sunlight shining on his hair. "But our secret, Genevieve," she whispered, "is that we'll be watching over him too."

Author's Note

Novelist and magistrate Henry Fielding and his half-brother, John, founded the Bow Street Runners, a force of a half-dozen men who became England's first professional detectives. In subsequent decades, the Bow Street Office added foot and horse patrols that are sometimes mistakenly counted as Runners. At any given time, there were never more than a dozen Bow Street Runners total.

The wire hanger as we know it today—shoulder-shaped with a hook at the top—wasn't invented until 1903 by Albert J. Parkhouse, an employee of the Timberlake Wire and Novelty Company. Unfortunately, he came up with it while he was on the clock, so his employer, Mr. Timberlake, secured the patent for himself. Before hangers, most people hung their clothes on pegs or hooks, or folded and stacked them on shelves.

The speculum was used as far back in ancient Greek and Roman times, with improvements being made as time went on. In 1825, the French midwife Marie Anne Boivin invented the two-part "modern" speculum that could be gently adjusted for the needs of each patient. However, credit for inventing the speculum is commonly— and incorrectly—attributed to a controversial male Alabama plantation doctor, J. Marion Sims, in 1867. Women have been written out of history since the days of the stone tablet, so it's up to us to remember and honor the achievements of our long-ago sisters. Thank you for your remarkable work in women's health, Marie Anne Boivin!

In all the historical research I've done, it's possible the weirdest has about leeches. Throughout the 1800s and early 1900s, bloodletting was a common medical treatment for headaches, seizures, pneumonia, infection, and too many diseases and conditions to list. If the procedure wasn't done with a blade or lance, it was accomplished by leeches. Hospitals and average households stored leeches in jars, and used various techniques to apply them. The wine-glass-and-gauze method Victoria used in this book really was described in a ladies' periodical of the time. Nowadays, medical leeches are occasionally used for reattachment operations, skin grafts and reconstructive surgery, to prevent blood clots and improve circulation in areas that need it. Leeches aren't pretty, but they have their uses!

I also had to do some research about strangulation, which is a common feature of domestic violence. It's also a huge danger sign. If your intimate partner ever uses their hands or arm or an object to restrict your breathing in any way, the odds of them eventually killing you go up 750 percent. If there's a gun in the house, the odds go up 1100 percent. Even if you didn't lose consciousness. Even if they left no marks. Even if they're sorry and say they'll never do it again. To put it simply: If they put their hands on your neck even once, they'll probably kill you in the future.

If you've been strangled or choked by a partner, or if you feel like you're in danger, please call the National Domestic Violence Hotline: 800-799-SAFE or 800-799-7233.

As always, dear friends, thank you for your love and support, and for allowing me to share my stories with you.

Love,

Lisa

P.S. For a terrific Welsh Rarebit recipe, visit Kacie Morgan's Welsh food and travel blog named "The Rare Welsh Bit" at therarewelshbit.com

Scroll down to the search bar and type "Best Ever Welsh Rarebit Recipe"

Or the direct address is: therarewelshbit.com/welsh-rarebit-recipe

READ MORE BY
Lisa Kleypas

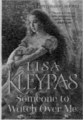

The Ravenals
SERIES

The Wallflowers

SERIES

ALSO